Masha and Alejandro Crossing Borders

a novel

Barbara L. Baer

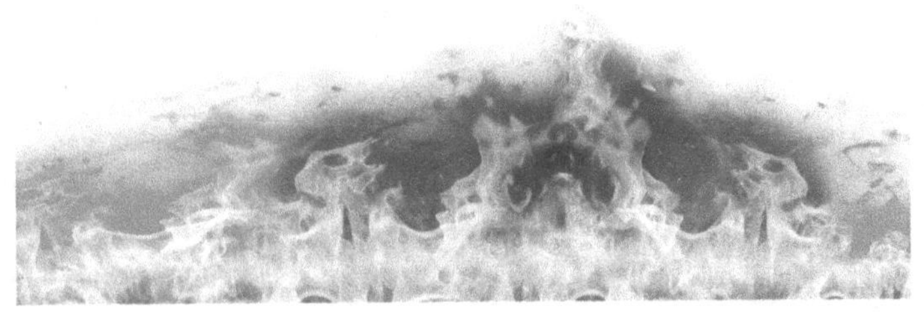

SPUYTEN DUYVIL
New York City

ABOUT OTHER BOOKS BY BARBARA L. BAER

GRISHA THE SCRIVENER

Barbara Baer's amazing novel sheds a unique and yes, a poetic light, on the people who endured the worst of times in Soviet Central Asia, Georgia and "Mother Russia." Barbara has a remarkable ability to delve into the lives and experiences of those so distinct from our own.

Judy Stone, film writer and author *Eye on the World*

THE BALLET LOVER

The Ballet Lover exposes the beauty and cruelty of ballet, the performances, the backstage moments, and the personal drama of the famous dancers Rudolph Nureyev and Natalia Makarova.

Book Glow

THE LAST DEVADASI

A half world away, I was delivered into the streets of India.

Paul Falk, author, reviewer

Barbara Baer managed to portray beautifully all that is beautiful and ugly in the Indian society. I'm a huge fan of novels that deal with social criticism, and I loved how she tackled these social issues. I believe for a book to be good, it needs to explore at least some important themes, and this one certainly does so.

Mina Vucicevic, Reviewer

THE ICE PALACE WALTZ

The Ice Palace Waltz by Barbara L. Baer is a grand getaway, transporting me beyond my world into a fascinating sphere of captivating characters and their travels. As soon as I finished it, I wanted to read again. It's that good.

Marlene Cullan, The Write Spot

To Michael M and L, and to Greg and Galina,
whose transplanted lives inspired this story.

"Am I to leave this Haven of my Rest?"
John Keats, *Hyperion*

"In times of shrinking expectations,…everyone feels like a victim and pushes away outsiders to defend his own corner."
Oscar Handlin

ONE

The phone rang at midnight. Alex scrambled out of bed, careful not to disturb Masha or the kids. The operator asked if Alejandro del Calvo would accept a collect call from San Diego. He was about to refuse when he heard the raspy, "*Hijo mio!*" and a cough.

"Yes, yes, we accept charges. *Estás aqui?* You are here, *Mami?*"

"I am here, in California," she answered in Spanish.

"Where?"

"San Diego, *hijo*. A church. So many lights in the city."

"Are you safe? Is someone with you giving you food? Do you have blankets?"

"Yes, the people are kind. They care for all of us who crossed. They say I need to see a doctor but I don't want to go."

"Please, *Mami*, tell me the name of the church and I'll fly down to get you as soon as I can. We'll take you to a doctor here. I just want you home with us. I am happy, I am so happy, *Mamacita*. It must have been very cold in the desert."

"Better than heat," she coughed.

Alex had to wipe his eyes to see enough to write down the address of the Catholic church where his mother was. "Don't go anywhere, not outside, nowhere until I come."

"I'm going to sleep now, *hijo*. I am so tired," she coughed.

"Tell the people that your son will come to get you tomorrow."

The next day, when Ana Jesus arrived with him in San

Francisco, Alex had to find a wheelchair to get his mother to his car. She was too weak to protest. He saw her arms covered in sores and heard her rasping cough.

"How did you do it, Grandmother?" asked Tomas, Alex and Masha's fifteen year-old son, who sat beside his *abuela* holding her hand.

"I made myself invisible, so small and old, *nieto*, that I imagine they cannot see me. Like your *Papi*, I reached California."

Ana Jesus del Calvo remembered packing whatever food and warm clothes she could into a backpack the day her husband, Guillermo, was dragged off blind-folded by masked cartel men. They'd come back for his oldest son or $500 ransom for them both. "I am a school teacher with five mouths to feed, how do I have that money?" As they walked him out at gunpoint, one masked young man who recognized his teacher whispered, *Lo siento, Maestro.* Alejandro, who was fourteen, heard it all from his hiding place as his mother stood with his two younger brothers, children too young to be recruited at least for now. Ana Jesus knew that if she didn't send her Alejandro north that night, the gangsters would return. "Papi will be back," she assured Alejandro as she bundled up her skinny boy and gave him all the cash she had along with the address of their cousins who worked on a farm in Santa Rosa in Sonoma County.

Now she too had crossed three dangerous borders from El Salvador, across Guatemala, through Mexico into the U.S. She'd seen young women blindfolded and taken from the caravan. She'd helped others when they collapsed on the roadside, all without telling her son that she was making the journey.

The first hours in her son's home in Santa Rosa, Ana Jesus hardly stirred from the couch. Masha, Alex' wife, gently washed her where she lay and smoothed ointments on infected bites. Masha, a nurse, knew her mother-in-law needed antibiotics for her sores and intestinal trouble. The smell of her skin alone signaled infection.

Masha was ready to take Ana Jesus to Sutter Hospital where she worked though there would be a long wait for Covid protocols. Masha tested her and she was negative. But as soon as Masha said they were going to the hospital, Ana Jesus curled herself into a fetal position, looking smaller than ever. "*No, no, hijo, no puedo*," she pleaded.

"*Mamacita*, you're safe with us." Alex held his mother until she unclenched her body. "She says she can't look at another man in uniform." Masha understood enough Spanish, especially medical terms, but she spoke haltingly and let Alex translate.

"We'll take her to the Jewish Health Advocates," Masha said. "They are good people and they ask no questions. Come now, Mama Ana Jesus, you need medicines."

"But we're not Jewish, Masha," Tomas said.

"Makes no difference. Care is free to everyone who cannot go elsewhere."

At the clinic, Masha gave them all masks and told the receptionist that her mother-in-law had just arrived in California and had no insurance. "I'm an R.N. but I can't prescribe and I know she needs medications. I tested and she's negative for the virus," she said. The receptionist's eyes smiled behind her mask as she dialed a number. "We'll see her of course. Is she vaxxed?"

"Her son will ask about vaccinations," Masha replied.

"Good. Here's paperwork, Spanish on the other side." The receptionist turned over the page. "I'll get our provider."

"I'll sit with *Mami* and we'll answer the questions," Alex said.

A short woman almost as wide as she was tall came toward them. She had hennaed hair piled on top of her head, dangly crystal earrings and a mask decorated with sequins so she sparkled. Who is this person ready for Mardi Gras? Masha wondered.

"How are you feeling?" The woman's voice was husky and accented. "I am Dr. Shira." She picked up her stethoscope.

Where do they get these people? Masha felt embarrassed that her medical profession welcomed such a clown-like person. And Russian, on top of it. The Russians dyed their hair the most awful reds, like beets and oranges.

The doctor walked around behind and tapped on Ana Jesus' back.

Ana Jesus couldn't stop coughing.

"Sorry." The doctor placed the stethoscope several places on Ana's back and tapped. "Cough, please once again."

Ana Jesus obliged and again couldn't stop.

"We'll listen to her lungs and heart, most important, then we look all over."

"She's tired. She's had a long journey," Alex said.

"You are Russian?" Masha asked the doctor.

"I was. You come with me," she beckoned Alex and Ana Jesus. "You will wait out there," she pointed Masha to the reception.

Dr. Shira brought mother and son into a small examining room at the end of a narrow hallway. Alone with them, she spoke in halting Spanish. Alex filled in words. "My vocabulary is small," the doctor apologized. "I work on it."

"You're doing great. My mother is relaxed," Alex said.

"Let's listen to the chest again, with skin."

"Skin?"

The doctor laughed. "If you raise Mother's shirt."

Alex helped his mother pull up her blouse and when she did, he saw how thin she was, how the skin wrinkled over her concave navel and her small breasts like dark pockets. Her ribs and chestbone looked fragile under the loose skin. His mother had been a robust woman, thick under her apron, with lovely breasts. He felt tears in his eyes.

Dr. Shira examined the bruises, insect bites and sores, asking only questions where her touch hurt. She left for a minute and returned with a syringe.

Alex held his mother still but the doctor drew blood so carefully that Ana Jesus hardly flinched. "We send these to the lab. Results soon. Mother probably has several kinds of bacteria inside and out but it's her lungs we must worry about."

Dr. Shira opened the cabinet and gave Alex packets. "So you don't have to wait for results. Broad spectrum antibiotics. Keep them in refrigerator. Your wife will know how to give, and for now, I'll make first injection to start."

The doctor knelt before Ana Jesus and touched her shoulder, making no effort to keep down her own skirt over dimpled thighs.

"Will she be all right?" Alex asked. "Would she be better in a hospital?"

The doctor shook her head. "She needs good food and rest after her journey."

Outside, Dr. Shira repeated instructions to Masha and Alex said their doctor didn't think she needed hospitalization.

"I can take care of her," Masha nodded. "I am a nurse at Sutter."

"Yes, good, you will take good care of this dear lady. Does she speak?"

"Yes, of course she speaks," answered Masha with accumulated irritation.

"She's shy about English," Alex said.

"I think she's had much trauma," the doctor said.

Alex shook his head. "She told us no one hurt her but it was a long difficult journey and others were not so fortunate as she was."

"Strong woman. She will be well soon."

Alex thanked Dr. Shira and murmured words of assurance to his mother.

"Please, doctor, what do we pay? My mother has no insurance. I'll pay cash."

"You don't pay. You can donate. Box is there."

"You are so kind, thank you, *muchisimas gracias*. Speaking to my mother in Spanish really helped."

Outside, Masha whispered to Alex, "I didn't like the doctor. She looked foolish."

"What was wrong with her? She seemed capable and kind," he said.

"She didn't look like a doctor and she ignored me."

"But she was good to *Mami* and she gave us medications without charging."

"Maybe," Masha shook her head. "A doctor should give more respect to nurses. I'm not used to being ignored."

TWO

Alex moved Ana Jesus from the couch to the double bed in their room, a choice that rankled Masha as she made up the pull-out in the living room. Their two children, Adrianna and her younger brother, Tomas, hated being squeezed into the one other bedroom. No one had enough privacy in the small house.

Masha honored family and understood Alex's relief reuniting with his mother; at the same time, she resented anyone, her children included, who took away Alex' attentions. The only way she knew to keep from saying words she was thinking—*how can we fit one more person in our small house?*—was to make herself so busy on her days off that they didn't see her expression of dissatisfaction, though Alex felt it.

Their rental was too small for four people, let alone two teenagers waiting for one bathroom, one computer and printer. Even before Ana Jesus' arrival, if Masha and Alex were in the bedroom and wanted to make love, he always felt constrained because the sound carried. They allowed themselves only small whispers of satisfaction.

This couldn't go on much longer or she'd go crazy. If Alex wouldn't act she would. They'd heard rumors that entire blocks were going to be torn down and converted to condos. Alex had seemed unconcerned but Masha added the information to her argument for a move.

Masha searched real estate sites for a larger rental in the neighborhood because they liked the small streets that wove in and out around the Sonoma County Fairgrounds. It was a good neighborhood where Anglo and Hispanic families watched each other's children playing and friends visited. Every summer, Masha grew a small forest of sunflowers, all golden, almost like the Christmas lights spectacles the neighborhood put on in December. She told everyone that sunflowers were Ukraine's flower, the flower of her home country, the golden fields she came from.

Quickly she learned there was nothing to rent with four bedrooms they could afford, not in Sonoma nor neighboring counties, not as far north as Cloverdale, as far east as Livermore, not anything close to their price range. She wouldn't quit.

Masha showed Alex images of homes with a porch and acreage, rivers and forests. He loved them. "That's perfect for us," he pointed to the screen. Then he saw what Masha already knew: these homes were far from Santa Rosa, in counties she'd never heard of, all inland, from the San Joaquin Valley to the Oregon border. "Look, how pretty it is. Three bedrooms, a porch, you can see the river." She showed him numbers, homes to buy from $300,000 on down.

"Too good to be true," he said.

"Why?"

"If it's too good to be true…"

"I'm only asking to take a look. So many trees, so little traffic," she said.

Masha looked up hospitals and saw regional centers in Redding and Shasta with large modern buildings. Maybe fewer sick people, she thought. Masha went to bed and got up exhausted after her long pandemic shifts, with ambulances bringing in sick people wrapped like mummies in stretchers. The more frantic the situation became, with overflows in hallways and so many of their staff getting the virus, Masha never shirked work. "I can take the shift," she volunteered. "You're amazing, You rise to the need," ER doctors told her. Some of the doctors and a few close friends among the nurses knew of Masha's past and what she knew about sickness. Maybe she'd developed an immunity born of hardship that they hadn't known.

THREE

Early spring didn't have the March grassy freshness in the air since so few inches of rain had fallen over the winter. So many days, skies had been blue and cloudless, their beauty ominous forecasters of another dry and dangerous summer, especially for the vast forests of the north, but Masha persisted in her search for properties. One morning, she located a realtor in a small town called Malvina Falls in Trinity County west of Redding; a half-dozen rural properties near woods and rivers had porches and a promise of quiet.

The name of rivers and a zip code were all they knew before Masha and Alex headed north to look. Ana Jesus assured them she was strong enough to take care of herself and that both children would help. Alex and Masha should have a vacation. Masha saw it as time for a tryst with her husband. Alex worried about being away from home and said they wouldn't stay the night.

They made the first part of the drive on back roads, passed the pristine Blue Lakes east of Ukiah, then followed country roads that zig-zagged at right angles through the walnut and almond orchards of Lake County.

"This is beautiful here, Masha, why go further?" Alex asked.

"We'll be to the big highway soon. Not far then. It's an adventure. Trust me."

They passed through valleys where black and white cows, horses and donkeys grazed in the meadows.

"Look, Alex, stripes on that horse. A zebra, two zebras, am I seeing right?"

Alex looked briefly. "During the fires, animals were probably evacuated here."

"I will send a picture or no one will believe a zebra posing just for us." Masha picked up her phone and clicked. "Do they grow sunflowers here?"

"I don't know. This is my first time in Lake County."

"So much space. You can cover all the green with sunflowers and make oil."

Alex nodded and kept driving toward Interstate 5 where the green hills ended and they came though a gap onto six lanes of concrete. Low-lying dense clouds made the flatness even flatter. Clouds hovered in the distance and nowhere else.

"They're over Mt. Shasta," Alex said. "But we're still a long way south."

"Alex, love, look at this, what beauty we are seeing." The perfect cone of Mt. Shasta appeared ahead glowing with snow. She pointed her phone. "I am happy today."

"That means everything to me. I've been worried since my mother arrived that nothing was feeling right with you, *amor*."

"I try to make her welcome. She's a good woman."

"You have been wonderful. I didn't mean that. How do you feel? Your nerves?"

"No more worries about that. Your mother is a real help and I'm so happy she's safe and regaining her health but it's been so crowded in our little house. We haven't been together and you know we need this, Alex."

"I didn't realize how far we'd have to drive to reach this place."

"We'll be there soon." She covered his hand with hers.

"We'll have to start over, everything will be new. I'll leave my work, you'll leave your hospital."

Masha squeezed tightly. "I'm the one who worries, not you. We'll have our own home that belongs to us, I'll plant miles and miles of sunflowers. Hospitals are here."

"Masha, we're not buying a ranch. We're looking for a family home we can afford."

"Where we can do what we like, grow our garden, be young again," Masha said. "In a while, we'll bring your mother and Adrianna and Tomas. Before that, we'll have time to ourselves like we used to. Don't you want that, sweetheart? It's been so long since we were really together."

In the pictures Masha had seen of Main Street, Malvina Falls looked like a sweet small country town, one-story shops lined up as in an old movie, a wide sidewalk with benches, in the distance the steeple of a church. They drove past boarded-up store fronts, shuttered windows, overturned benches, beer cans glinting in the sun. Not a car passed on the street. Masha crossed her fingers until they reached the end of the block where "Trinity Properties," an American flag on its stand at the entrance, stood open.

Edna Robinson, owner and sole agent, looked up at Alex and Masha who were masking. "We're good here, all good, folks." The woman waved away the masks but they kept them on. Mrs. Robinson, tall, wide and lumbering, dressed in plaid shirt and jeans, had a stiff gristle of a braid perched on one shoulder like a parrot.

"I'm ready to go but if you folks want a breather after your drive..."

"We can go," said Masha who'd been hoping for a coffee in "Cup of Java" she'd seen in the pictures online, but the café was closed.

The realtor's big sedan belched smoke from its tailpipe as Mrs. Robinson showed them empty properties in and near town, quoting prices that still seemed too low to believe, a few below $100,000 on lots with wrecks of cars and piles of junk in their yards.

"Just giving you folks a look around. Teasing your imagination. No secret we're in a slump here. I've been saving the best for last, something to make your eyes shine."

She drove them past an uneven row of single story wood-frame houses that became a strip of trailers, then more shacks and rusted vehicles with the frames of large greenhouses, plastic covers flapping. "They look like old west, covered wagons," Masha said quietly in the back seat.

"They're grow-houses," Alex whispered back.

A green and yellow flag with a double XX blew in the breeze that shivered the coiled rattle snake and the words *Don't Tread on Me* written in black. They passed a Confederate flag. "That war was over more than a century ago," Alex said

Mrs. Robinson turned and looked over her glasses at him. "Folks here got their own minds about things, but not to worry. All good and here we go."

At the end of an unmarked packed-dirt lane off the paved road they saw a little brown house with a sagging wrap-around porch. When they came closer, they saw that the front windows were cracked or missing.

Mrs. Robinson turned the key and they walked in.

They all stepped back as if the musty thick air had velocity as well as stink. Masha didn't know if she wanted to enter on a floor covered with bird and mouse droppings in her dream home.

"Uninhabited for long?" Alex took a deep breath

"Folks kept birds inside."

"Looks as if they had a flock in here," he said.

"You'll be getting a fixer-upper with potential in your price range. Misses' wishes."

Alex looked at Masha to confirm the realtor's words. She nodded.

They followed into a dark hallway with bedrooms and bath on either side, the same fetid smells everywhere. At the end of the hall, a door opened onto a creaking deck, fresh air and an expanse of green trees everywhere. They walked further toward a towering stand of oaks that framed the view of a glimmering spring.

"You've had rain lately? We've been so dry," Alex said.

"Not enough. We've had winters with snow but not recently. Next year maybe. Folks say the fishing's good here when we've had more rains."

"Snow!" sighed Masha. "I remember snow. My dad used to fish."

"So did my *Papi*." Alex took Masha's hands.

"You'll make memories here, folks."

They went back in to the living room. Alex uncovered a bulky object under a mouse-hole-chewed blanket in a corner. Mrs. Robinson adjusted her glasses and rubbed dust from the cast iron stove and peered closer. "Hadn't seen one of these warhorses in years. Don't make them anymore. You folks are looking at a classic genuine cast iron collectors' item that heats like a steam engine."

"Why would they leave this?" Alex asked.

"You want to try lifting?" responded the realtor. "You've got the wood back there. Should keep you nice and warm for free."

"Alex, this is called a *pich* in Ukraine. I remember going to a dacha and being so warm. I can see us in rocking chairs toasting our toes."

"There you go. The Missus has imagination." The realtor jiggled the stove pipe and suggested that Alex make sure it was clean or replace it before they start a fire.

"And you've got a fireplace, friends." Mrs. Robinson moved a box and revealed a fireplace. "Doesn't put out the heat but very pretty atmosphere if you like that."

"I like atmosphere and I also like to keep warm," Masha smiled.

"You got both then. Like I wrote you, Missus, this house has potential."

By the end of the day, Alex wrote a $500 check as a good faith deposit on the seller's price of $130,000. He would have liked to know more but Masha was so enthusiastic he didn't want to express doubt. *She doesn't realize we can lose this money when we find a sinking foundation*, he thought.

"We'll be back next weekend and we'll look around one more time," Alex said when Mrs. Robinson pulled up behind their Camry on Main Street.

"That house has good bones," Mrs. Robinson said.

Masha squeezed his hand and kissed him in front of Mrs. Robinson, then reached forward to shake hands with the realtor because everyone must share in the happiness. But before she knew it, the woman disappeared into her door and closed it behind her.

Again, the street was entirely empty, no traffic, no one walking.

"Doesn't she like us?" Masha asked when they were back in their own car.

"I don't know. She's a realtor. If you feel it's right, that's what matters."

"I feel when I'm not liked."

"Are you happy with the house I know I can fix up? Do you like the forest?"

"Yes, I am happy but what does it mean that she doesn't like us?"

"We both still have our accents and I have dark skin. We've changed people's minds wherever we go because we work hard. This house will take a lot of work."

"I hope people aren't all like this woman. I should have said we are from other countries and we're American citizens."

"We're good citizens but you're getting off the reason we're here which is to find a house we can afford. You think even though it doesn't look good, you like it?"

"Yes, I do. I do. We'll go fishing from our own river, like our parents."

"It's only a creek," Alex said.

"I know. I'll plant sunflowers and the creek will seem like a river. Everything you remember from your childhood is bigger." Once Masha had imagined a village where her family had never lived, and a happiness they had never known, the image became a memory replacing the cinder block her parents had had to live in since they'd been expelled from their homeland.

FOUR

Masha had last seen her mother through a curtain of tears.

"You'll be back our healthy girl," Nadya Sergeivna whispered, but Masha clung to her mother. "Why why why?" she cried.

The stewardess for the Aeroflot flight had to pry her loose from her mother and pull her all the way to the boarding gate and up the ladder. Once strapped into place in the perfumed seat, Masha gave up struggling. From then on, she would be alone in the new blue coat and shoes Nadya had bought her with money from America.

In New York, an attendant sat with her until a connecting flight to San Francisco was ready to board. "Don't cry so your eyes are red. It will be good, Masha, you are a big girl, no more tears, be grateful."

Masha, Maria Sergieyevna Kichonok, had been born on a collective farm northeast of Kiev in 1986, two months before the meltdown of the #4 Chernobyl reactor reddened the night sky with its deadly fire. After days of denial about the explosion, the Soviet authorities ordered all inhabitants from their apartments. The buses came one after the other in the smoky hot night. Masha didn't consciously remember this but her mother Nadya never forgot. Even her two-year old brother Maksym retained a memory of the trauma, or so he would say later. Masha's firefighter father, Sergiy, had stayed to battle the blazes. The Russians treated his burns and radiation poisoning in a special Moscow location but Sergiy never recovered enough to work more than sporadically. The family relied on Nadya's teaching and the government subsidies in the relocation towns they were sent to in southern Ukraine before being settled in the Crimea.

As a child, Masha bruised easily and was often sick. A visiting radiation specialist from Livermore Laboratory in California advised Nadya to send her daughter to America but there was no follow up. Masha did well when she could attend secondary school but she missed half the time because of rashes and stomach problems. When Masha turned fourteen, she had not begun her periods. Nadya found the Chernobyl Children's Fund, completed all the forms, and with great difficulty and persistence obtained hospital records and flew with Masha to Moscow where doctors performed tests and told her she qualified for treatment in America.

In San Francisco, an Orthodox priest and his wife met her and drove in the dark for hours without many words. When they reached their parish in Santa Rosa in Sonoma County they fed her milk and bread and showed her to the basement room to sleep.

The Svetlovs were Old Believers, childless and severe. In the basement room Masha had icons and crosses for company. Though the priestess followed the medical protocol, she didn't think the child was ill in her body, but her soul. She wasn't Christian enough. She hung a heavy cross around the girl's neck and made her wear it everywhere.

On Orthodox Christmas, the Svetlovs allowed Masha to call home. She cradled the phone close so the Svetlovs couldn't hear. "Mama, please please, I want to come home. They don't give me enough food, only kasha and sometimes soup." "Nothing is good?" asked Nadya. "Milk and cream. They have cows." "That's good, you will grow strong and well." "But they aren't nice. They're always praying for me, nothing kind. Mama, I have to come home."

Nadya's voice, far away sounding, even more distant because she expressed no emotion—all long distance calls were monitored—"My darling daughter, you have to stay. There is no hope for you here, your father will never be well again and how will we buy a ticket from America? Please, darling, understand and don't make me cry on this blessed day." Masha was going to say she'd run away, but hearing her mother's tears, she knew she couldn't do that. She'd find another way to get home, she vowed to her frayed teddy, *plushovia Miskka*, she still slept with.

In her Santa Rosa high school, Masha heard girls whispering about her clothes, black skirts down to her calves while they wore little ruffles so short sometimes their panties showed. Little by little her English improved and she worked hard in the science classes. She grew taller and more robust from all the milk and butter; her hair that had been a thin pale pony tail now came in thickly with strands of gold in it. Overnight it seemed the Svetlov's milk had made her breasts grow so much that they bought her a bra that compressed the two spheres against her chest. Boys took note. A few girls tried to make friends because boys followed her with their eyes and remarks but she kept to herself. Then the girls called her 'the stuck up Russki'. In her school in Crimea, the refugees from *Chernobyl* had been called 'monster' and 'mutant', so these words meant little to her.

Two days a week, Masha took a bus to the community college in Santa Rosa for English language lessons. She'd become proficient but preferred being away from the Svetlovs. Until she met Alex, she'd been too depressed to openly disobey the church couple's strict rules. Alejandro del Calvo, a recent immigrant from El Salvador, sat down next to her in class one afternoon. He didn't seem able to follow the teacher's instructions in English. She leaned over to help him writing down English words. He didn't smell of soap and scrubbing cleansers the way the Svetlovs did. He smelled of earth and maybe oil in cuticles beneath his short nails.

Masha watched the two Latina girls, twins named Consuela and Cassandra, developed like women, sidle up to Alex. She heard a passing boy whistle and say, "what a rack on those two *chicas*." Alex chatted with the twins in Spanish but soon he returned to her side. Masha hated those girls though Alex always managed to convey, 'I see only you' with his golden-brown eyes.

They continued to communicate through sign language and words they both knew. She learned Alex worked in an auto shop repairing cars and other equipment for cousins who were tenants on a farm south of the city, near the Svetlov's church. He had arrived from El Salvador by crossing borders and evading patrols to reach the cousins who took him in.

In her bare feet, Masha stood three inches taller but the difference never bothered Alex. Her blond beauty glowed before him, her sweetness filled his heart. He never saw her slightly protruding jaw nor a childhood without dentistry. In his eyes, she was perfect. And Masha thought even Alex' acne scars, deep pock marks, gave him a manly look. His quiet self-assurance amazed her because he hardly knew how to speak a complete English sentence when the teacher called on him. He laughed a lot and seemed sure of himself despite his slow language learning.

Masha volunteered to tutor Alex. Together, they found a way to share thoughts as if the mutual attraction gave them their own language. He took a dictionary and constructed a sentence to tell her that his passion was 'making things, fixing things'. She replied that she wanted to help sick people. Soon they were hardly ever apart and Masha, who turned seventeen, felt she was a woman with Alex.

In the little prefab house Alex shared with three other men who worked in the vineyards, he and Masha had a hard time finding privacy; any chance they were alone, they tumbled onto the narrow bed in his room and pressed together with their clothes on. The day he told his roommates he couldn't go out for beers and her guardians were off at a church conference for the weekend, he undressed Masha.

They both shivered with fear and desire. It was cold but they had their own source of heat. He vowed to take gentle care not to frighten her. She didn't seem afraid. How surprised he'd been, then, amazed and overwhelmed as she took off her clothes without hesitation. Her breasts were all the cream he'd ever dreamed of. She lay back on his single cot looking at him. She didn't cry out with pain as men said a woman did the first time though she bled a little and he knew she was a virgin, not that he'd doubted she was pure to be his and no one else's. She wanted him again and they came this time with such waves of pleasure that they screamed together, they laughed and kissed and then, instead of turning away or wanting to sleep, she held him close again until he was ready. This time she cried out with pleasure at a decibel he couldn't match.

When men took a break at the auto shop or the vineyards they talked about women's parts and ended up jacking off behind a building but no one could have foretold that you felt this kind of love and gratitude for a woman. Girls weren't supposed to feel anything like what a guy did, they said, but in weeks that followed, they found a private place whenever they could. She was with him in their desire and release. To see her hair in the moonlight made him almost pray that the angel beside him would not disappear.

Those first months, they shared the world of hurt they carried, homes they had left, mothers who survived in dangerous situations, one father disappeared and the other disabled, siblings they might never see again. They clung together, sometimes heated and slippery from love, sometimes in tears, finding in each other their salvation, their home.

When Masha discovered she was pregnant, they knew they wanted the child of their love to be a legitimate American citizen and made a date to be married in the Resurrection Parrish in Santa Rosa where they went for counseling and assistance.

As she planned the wedding, Alex became aware that

Masha, despite being good at math, had little sense of money. She used a credit card received in the mail to buy a wedding dress with tiny pearls, yards of white tulle, and an intricate veil for the simple ceremony their fellow ESL students attended. When he questioned her spending, she answered without apology, "I pay only 50% price. Mama must see my perfect wedding." Seeing her haloed in her white foam of a dress, Alex forgot her extravagance, though the spread she had catered for the reception had been paid for with another credit card he'd have to pay off with his wages. He worked as a dishwasher in the Lizard Bar managed by his cousin, Ditto. Ditto's older brother, Carlos, owned a repair shop where Alex was so good at body work that he soon dropped out of the language classes.

At eighteen, Masha, glowing with pregnancy and wearing her wedding ring, left the basement room in the Church of the Perpetual Redeemer with nothing more than her old leather suitcase. She left a note to the Svetlovs written in Russian with the address where she would be living in Santa Rosa. She begged them to send her mail from family. In exchange, she promised not to report her move so they could continue receiving subsidies from the Children's Fund.

Finally, Alex saved enough money to rent a double-wide trailer off Moorland Avenue. When their baby girl came into the world with a loud cry and everything perfect, every pink toe and finger where it should be, Masha went crazy, crying with relief from her fear that any child of hers might not be normal. She cried so long and hard that the nurses and Alex became alarmed and took away the baby she was squeezing too tightly. Though her fears lifted by the time they were back in the trailer, Masha wasn't able to feel the joy in Adrianna as Alex did, as if the normal child might be snatched away in the night and she'd wake up to a strange formless creature swaddled in the crib beside her. No matter how often Alex showed her the photographs he took almost every day of their pretty little baby with a ribbon in a stalk of fair hair, she couldn't entirely love perfect Adrianna when she woke up crying with nothing more than wanting her breast.

A year and a half later, Tomas was born after a short labor. Masha's first thought on seeing her baby son was to run from the hospital and hide somewhere. She wanted to start community college but now it would be milk and diapers for another year. Minutes later, Alex was smiling down at her and his son, and she started her crying again. Nurses gave her something to sleep. Before she drifted off, Masha kissed her son, loving him already but making up her mind that one of the first things she'd learn in nursing classes would be how nights of love would not turn into more children.

FIVE

Before their second visit to Malvina Falls, Masha packed household supplies for the kitchen. Alex collected basic tools he'd need, as well as a double futon and blankets to store in a locked unit outside town. When Mrs. Robinson had first pointed out the storage area, a chained Rottweiler had scared Masha into staying in the car. This time, Alex didn't see a dog. He found an open unit and locked up.

As they turned onto their road, Masha pointed out a sign that hadn't been there. *East Staunton* was written by hand in black paint on a piece of board nailed to a stake.

"Did you see that sign before?" Masha asked.

Alex shook his head.

"Funny British sounding name. *Welcome to East Staunton*," she mouthed in the best imitation of an English accent as they pulled into the driveway.

This time, Alex was all business. "We need to inspect what's important in the house, not what we see, old paint and a deck that needs propping up, but inside and under, foundation, beams. We'll see if this place is no bargain but a lemon."

"The house isn't a thing, Alex. It's our home," she said.

"Not yet." He was thinking to himself, *Painting and jacking up the porch are doable if the foundation is good, but if not, she'll have to be realistic about it.*

Inside, Alex scraped back grimy linoleum to a patch of oak floor and imagined it gleaming with natural tones after he stripped it bare. Beams were solid and made a handsome frame for the entrance to the dining room. He didn't like the dark hallway but knocking down walls would be a huge project. In the back, double glass doors would let in more light, and if he built a real deck, they could set up tables and chairs, drink glasses of wine and look out on the stream.

While he probed around inside, Masha explored the untended orchard. Old apple, walnut and pear trees buried in weeds and thick with suckers were beginning to leaf out, and at the end of branches, she saw pink plum flowers. There were still snowbells like little white stars in corners of shade. She made a little prayer and promise to the trees, *I'll take care of you now.*

"Masha," Alex called. "I'm surprised, really. Everything looks solid and well made. Good bones like Mrs. Robinson said. How's the back yard?"

"It's going to be beautiful. Sunflowers everywhere!" Masha felt herself falling even harder for the little house and the neglected orchard. "Come and see."

Alex came out on the back deck smiling. "When we're here next, I'll have a cashier's check for the down payment." Alex was feeling his fingers itch to start work but he looked at his watch. "We can't be too late, it's a long drive."

"Next time we'll stay overnight?" Masha kissed him on the neck.

"Next time."

"But not now?"

"We put everything in the storage, Masha."

"We can get it back and bring it here. Just the futon and coffee pot."

He shook his head. "We'll be leaving Adri to take care of my mother."

"Our daughter is 100% capable of taking care of her. She's almost like a nurse."

Adrianna hadn't fallen behind when Covid closed schools. If anything, she preferred finishing high school without distractions. She herself had never taken part in school social life despite Masha's promptings that she'd missed out on so much because she wasn't American. "You're 100%," Masha told her. "You're such a pretty girl. You could be a cheerleader or the homecoming queen." But Adrianna didn't want anything like that: she would take her GED, skipping her senior year to begin pre-nursing classes at the community college. She didn't even want a prom dress that Masha had saved to buy her.

"It's Tomas," Masha said to Alex.

"Yes, Tomas." During Covid, their son had lost whatever interest he'd had in learning but managed to meet his friends even with the pandemic restrictions. He was drawn to the tatted-up boys, not ms13 but some of them from El Salvador who might turn into gang members. Up to now, Tomas had obeyed his father and not gotten inked but he wanted to. When Alex asked him why, Tomas answered, "I want a tribe, *Papi*, a team I can hang with, who get me."

"I want to bring Tomas here for the summer," Alex said now as they were approaching the interstate and could still see Mt. Shasta to the north. "We'll need his help and I want him out of there." Anything that made Alex think of what could happen to his son, he saw his father, the schoolteacher, Guillermo, forced into a car at gunpoint.

SIX

The third visit to Malvina Falls, Masha and Alex saw two men seated at a counter of "Cup of Java," blurred figures through smudged front windows.

"Sign of life. You want to step in and have a coffee, Masha?"

"I want to walk in the door of our home, our first very own, and make coffee."

"Then here we go, our life savings. You are sure?"

She squeezed his arm. "I am sure." They rang the bell on Trinity Properties, put on their masks and walked in.

Mrs. Robinson didn't get up. "Here early. I hate those things you wear on your face as if we're sick. We breathe the fresh air of freedom up here and putting on bandanas is for robbing a bank." She raised her hands up in mock fear behind her glasses.

"We're used to wearing them for safety. My wife's a nurse and she's taken care of too many people sick with the virus." Alex took Masha's hand.

"In my book, folks hiding their faces are the kind of people who mean you harm and I thank God I'm not indoctrinated by that foreigner Fauci bullshit, excuse my French. You're moving to peace and quiet where folks value the freedoms in our Constitution."

"I'm glad to hear about peace. I've got the check," Alex said.

Mrs. Robinson lit a cigarette, blew two perfect smoke rings and adjusted her braid on her shoulder. Masha looked away to hide a smile: she could almost see a grey parrot about to squawk.

The realtor opened her desk and pulled out keys and a folder. "Here you go. Sellers are wanting a quick escrow." She handed the folder across the table for Alex to read. He moved the papers so Masha could see.

The house had listed at $130,000, a price that wouldn't have bought them a one-room shack in Sonoma County, but to their surprise, Mrs. Robinson said, "I jewed them down five thousand for you. Sellers will take one twenty five, no inspection, no questions asked, sale final. Up here you get your money's worth without government sticking its nose into your business."

"Jewed down, that's like saying..." Alex felt Masha squeezing his shoulder. "I have the cashier's check in the amount you asked for, a percentage of the original price."

Mrs. Robinson inhaled deeply and set the American flag on her desk so it faced them. "You'll use that extra when it comes time to pay the bank each month. You have family members I think you said. Everybody moving up here?"

Alex felt she was asking if they'd be bringing hordes of brown-skinned illegals.

"Our son will move at the end of the school year but our daughter and my mother are staying for the time being in Santa Rosa."

"Our daughter stays with her grandmother, my husband's mother, until we are settled," Masha said.

"Nothing like family. Mine settled here when they could

cut trees where they liked, shoot an owl that kept them awake. We hated that damn owl."

"Owl?" Masha asked.

"Yeah, they find a feather and we can't harvest the trees. That's government."

"One question, Ma'am," Alex cleared his throat. "We saw the school was closed."

"Weaverville and Redding keep theirs open. They got the high schools there."

"I didn't see a library or fire department either, or a sheriff department."

"Government doesn't stop crime, people do. Weaverville and Redding got fire and the law."

Alex could have told the woman that in his experience, criminal gangs would make any beautiful place into a hell. Instead, he asked, "When we start cleaning up the yard and house, is there someone to call to take away the garbage?"

"I can give you Frank's card. He hauls and doesn't charge an arm and a leg. You'll be happy when you pay no taxes for all that stuff you don't ask done for you. We have our eyes open, watching out for government tricks. Leave us to ourselves up here."

Mrs. Robinson slid her glasses down her nose and looked at them with flat dark eyes that had small gold flecks. "I'm all about business because you can see the town needs it. Personally I think kids around here lost their best years smoking the weed, but it was a business and since it's gone legal, folks are just losing money. Some good people are losing their minds over it. Don't quote me on this but be careful what you say."

"We don't gossip or talk politics," Masha said.

"You mean the marijuana growers are losing money?" Alex asked.

"What you do on your own property and behind your doors, and what you sell is not government's beeswax. Yes, Mister, I'm talking about the marijuana going legal. You might as well know you're moving into hard times." Her cheeks had become flushed.

"We'll grow vegetables and sunflowers, they are the national flower of the Ukraine and they make everyone happy to see them," Masha said.

"Sounds peachy." Mrs. Robinson looked at her watch. "I'll deposit your check at five. You've still got a couple hours."

Masha couldn't help herself. "I'll make the fruit trees happy again and next year, we'll bring you apples."

Mrs. Robinson didn't look up from her desk when she said quietly, "The folks whose house you're buying, they fell on hard times. Don't think you're better than them. Like I said, you look around, make sure everything is to your liking. I'll be here and we'll go into escrow. You know the way out."

There was no handshake on the biggest decision Alex and Masha had ever made in the lives. The moment felt strangely smaller than it was.

"Are we in a good place, Alex?" Masha asked when they were outside.

"We're taking our chances, you know that, Masha. We're leaving much behind."

"We are looking ahead."

"Tomas may be the only boy here with brown skin."

Masha squeezed Alex's arm. "Beautiful brown skin."

"Let's go to the storage unit. We can move in a few things to make our home feel right. If we'd told *Mami* we were staying the night, we could drink champagne."

Masha looked longingly at him. "Alex, why can't we drink champagne to celebrate and stay? We'll call."

"I think we should drive back. I thought *Mami* was a bit shaky."

"She's not shaky, she's strong. Adrianna will look after her. She loves your mother." Masha balled her fists and hit the dashboard. "You always choose *them*. My daughter chooses her grandmother."

"Masha what are you saying? Who is 'them'? It's all of us, a family together."

She covered her face with her hands. "It's been so long since we've been alone."

They drove in silence to where green hills surrounded them, the sun shone, animals grazed. And over all, Mt. Shasta spread its crown of fluffy clouds. Masha tried to feel its peace. In the last years, she and Alex had been good partners and parents, hardly ever at odds, but stressful work and Alex' habit of calling her *Mother* made Masha afraid his feelings had changed, that she was more *mother* than wife. When she asked him, "Do you love me still?' he always replied, "I'll always love you." "Like before, when I was younger?" "No one but you and our family, you're my life."

They approached the wire fence where storage units lined up.

Even though the Rottweiler seemed gone again, Masha still hesitated. She was afraid of dogs, even small ones. Tomas had always wanted a dog but she'd refused.

Alex, too, looked around warily. "Something about the yard doesn't look right. Let's find our unit."

On the gravel, beer cans and broken glass glittered. Alex moved ahead. Masha held back as if the dog might suddenly appear, its monster jaws wide and mouth foaming.

Like others in the row, their storage unit had had their locks broken, metal doors left askew and hanging open. Inside their unit, contents had been tossed in heaps, a broken lamp lay on its side, broken cups and dishes.

"Who does this?" Masha sniffed. "Smells bad. Who does this?"

Alex stood staring at the chaos and pulled Masha back into the fresh air. "Whoever wants to, I guess, when it's not guarded. The people the realtor was talking about, mad at someone. They didn't get anything of value here, just made a mess of our things."

"Old dishes. But what an awful thing to do, like they want to hurt us."

"I don't know, Masha."

"And it smells so bad," she said.

"Whoever broke in peed on blankets."

"Like pigs. Bad people were here. Worse than pigs. "

"We can leave everything and go home, I mean home home, Masha. The bank check won't have been cashed."

"We'll lose money we gave to Mrs. Robinson."

"Only the first deposit. We'll get back the certified check."

"Did they steal good tools?"

"I didn't bring good ones, just basics. That's not what I'm thinking about. We'll be on our own here, Masha. I don't think we'll get help if we need it. These folks do what they want, like Mrs. Robinson said. We can start looking again, nearer Santa Rosa."

"But there we can't afford anything. We know that."

Once they were outside the gate and in the car, Masha sighed, "Stuff was stuff. Some people will be good. Even in the worst places some people are good. We've seen worse, isn't that true? What your mother suffered, and my mother. Alex, look there is our white mountain, our queen of snows. How beautiful she is blessing us."

Mt. Shasta, its perfect peak a white cream cone, glowed in the sun.

"I am not a giving-up person," she said.

When they reached East Staunton, the sign lay on its side as if their invitation to go further had been revoked.

They held hands to the front door where Alex lifted Masha off her feet to carry her inside as he'd done when she'd been his bride in a cloud of white tulle.

While Alex walked around measuring windows for new glass, Masha found a rocking chair and sat rocking herself back and forth, trying to calm her mind. In the past, she'd taken anti-depressants when work was too stressful, when she and Alex didn't make love enough. She'd stopped taking them before Ana Jesus had arrived and wondered if she shouldn't renew her prescription. Breathe, she told herself, breathe.

They locked up and started down the main road when a grey pickup with a fender hanging came up so fast from behind it almost ran them over. In his side mirror, Alex looked in the eyes of two bearded men in red ball caps. He saw no place to turn onto a shoulder so kept his foot on the pedal up the hill with the truck on their bumper. On a blind curve just before the crest, thick pines and evergreens on either side, the pickup bumped them, a hanging fender making sparks. Alex couldn't make his old truck go faster so he raised his arms in a sign gesturing he couldn't help being slow but the pickup driver started to pull out to pass when another, larger truck came over the crest heading at both of them. Alex hit the brakes, jerked them right to the side of the road while he held an arm over Masha. For a second, two seconds, it seemed they wouldn't stay on four wheels, then they bounced and settled just as the two men barreled downhill and the driver gave them the finger out the window. "Fuck you, motherfucker," he shouted, and was gone in a trail of dirty exhaust and clanking parts.

Alex turned off the engine. They sat without speaking. Branches rustled overhead as if there'd never been anything but calm this morning. The white mountain hadn't moved. Only his knuckles felt locked onto the steering wheel and Masha was shaking with closed eyes.

"They looked like Barbarians in the comic papers." Masha opened her eyes. "I was really scared, Alex. You saved us."

Alex tried to laugh but his chest hurt where he'd hit the steering wheel.

"Are you all right, not hurt?" she asked.

"I don't think so. Shocked though at the way they didn't even look back."

Masha was trying to breathe normally to minimize the shock. She knew that if they got whiplashed it wouldn't show up for days. "Thanks to you, thinking so fast, you saved us."

"It was close."

"They looked so mean!" She held onto Alex's hand and squeezed. "I'll be fine."

"What the hell!" He pounded the steering wheel. "What the fuck were they doing?"

Masha saw Alex' temple vein throb. His shock quieted hers. She squeezed herself past the steering wheel and pressed her head against his heart. They stayed unmoving for minutes until Masha squeezed back to her seat.

"Look. I got pictures," Masha said. She showed Alex the license plate and beneath the rusted-out bumper sticker with the green flag and its XX.

"We can report them," she said.

"Did you see a highway patrol or law enforcement anywhere in town?"

She shook her head.

"Masha, do we go ahead?"

"None of what happened was personal, do you think?"

"Probably not. All the units looked broken into."

"They're not after us."

"But it's not good to live without rules, without the law."

"We could have been so smashed up."

Alex took her in his arms and held her.

"We'll stay for the night," he said.

"Sleep on the floor. It's OK with me."

"I'll call Adri. Our home belongs to us and no one is going to chase us out."

SEVEN

Tomas bent over picking up and shoveling food packages crawling with earwigs, tin cans and broken glass scattered underfoot, wheel-barrowed one load of junk after another to a dumpster. He kept his hoodie up in the sunshine as he scraped dried dog turds and rocks. They're crazy, he thought of his parents' move into what he called shitsville.

"I want you to imagine how it will be, hijo. The best part is that we don't make so much debt we can never pay off. You were too young to remember but Hector Furtados bought beyond his reach and got trapped in a balloon payment in 2008. Hector was a good man and proud to own but he let himself be tricked into believing what the real estate sharks told him."

"Yea, *Papi*, and you move to nowhere for a yard with turds?" Tomas responded.

"We'll make a good home for your mother, you two children and my mother. We'll all be together. In a few months, we'll transform this for you and the family."

"Why didn't you move onto the uncles' property?" Tomas asked.

"We just didn't." Ditto and Carlos, cousins not uncles, lived with their families outside Santa Rosa city limits on five acres where Alex had arrived worn out and emaciated from his journey north. The cousins tended to the livestock and growing wheat for an old Portuguese farmer who'd owned the land from before the city itself had rules and permits. The Ludvig Avenue property was low and flooded every winter because of the clay that lay in heavy layers on the soil. Ditto and Carlos had dug deep and reached good earth to plant the wheat; they came from generations of farmers in El Salvador and worked hard.

Unlike Alex, the cousins hadn't fled the drug gangs. They came north for opportunity. As tenant workers they saved rent and were enterprising. By the time Alex arrived, they'd started side businesses, a bar and an auto shop. The cousins wanted their cousin to be a full partner in everything but after his marriage to Masha, he resisted their repeated offers to bring the family together.

"There aren't any sidewalks," Tomas complained. "No TV or wifi. My sister won't be able to study without internet. She'll never come."

"We'll get all that, maybe not right away. Your mother and I want internet too but for now we haven't time beyond the basics, *hijo*, and there's good hard work to do here."

"Grandma is going to miss me, *Papi*. She's kinda cool even though I don't understand most of the things she says. She and my sister are tight. I'm the *hombre* of the house. If I come up here they'll be alone."

"They'll come too when we've gotten the house ready."

Tomas shook his head. "I don't think so. *Papi*, I miss my homies."

"If, at the end of your vacation you want to do your junior year in Santa Rosa, that will be your choice. You're here for the summer with us."

"You don't understand anything. I'll die up here."

"Come on, let's tell Mom we're going to Redding and she'll have supper ready for us later."

From the moment the sun came up, Masha's only wish was to start a garden, plant tomatoes, basil, cucumbers, corn and the sunflowers from seeds her mother had sent and that she'd saved. The soil was still too cold for delicate vegetable starts but not for sunflower seeds. At the foot of the rickety steps from the deck, she scraped enough top soil and added compost to place ten precious seeds carefully in the earth. She'd keep the soil moist so they'd germinate.

She wiped her hands on her apron and returned to scrubbing the filthy kitchen and bathroom. The former owners seemed to have left as much bird shit as possible in cabinets—the mess felt like their final protest at losing their home.

When she finished scraping a particularly grease-encrusted iron stove, she put down her metal pads, pulled off her gloves and followed the warmth of the sun outdoors.

She discovered the gopher holes by stepping into them, wriggling out of her clogs to free her bare feet in the soil. They'd have to dig and place wire cages and maybe boxes to keep out gophers and a fence for deer, more work and expense. Don't worry, she told herself, you will make this beautiful and feed the family. The sunflowers will come early. Despite being sent away like an orphan—not words Masha would say but often felt, so long after—she understood she'd been given the life she'd never have had otherwise. She might have withered away like a plant that had failed to spread its roots. And there was no one else in the world she'd ever love as she loved Alex. The sunflowers were her own way to touch home and declare her life.

Their lives had been so free of time-keeping these past weeks. They enjoyed nights without TV or, before Tomas came, without anyone around. They sat outside on camp chairs, talked about past and future as they drank wine before going inside to make love. One night they made love outdoors under the full sky of stars, listening to the owl, maybe a fox, quiet as they could be in case someone was nearby. Masha never complained of the hard work. She seemed to glow with new strength and confidence. She was right, Alex thought, they needed time alone together to rekindle their spark. Soon enough they'd become scheduled again. Masha had an interview at Mercy Medical Center in Redding the following week.

"Hey *Papi*, are those zebras?" Tomas pointed out to the pasture in the moonlight.

"Yeah, your mother and I saw them coming up. Evacuees from fires. We'll be eating our own farm tomatoes before long. We'll be saving money."

"Mom will love spending money. She always spends," Tomas said.

"Be respectful, Tommy. Your mother is generous. She doesn't skimp on you."

"I know, but she still buys stupid stuff."

Packages of creams and cosmetics arrived in the mail. No matter how many times he told her she was beautiful without make up, that she needed nothing more than her good skin and her wonderful hair, Masha loved to buy these pink boxes and tubes.

"You have so many chances, *hijo*, that we never did, and you know how kids screw up and sometimes once is just enough to change your life in a bad way. It almost happened to us, long ago."

"What happened, *Papi*?"

"We screwed up. We were lucky a kind woman officer, a Latina, helped us."

"That's cool *Papi*, but can I get my driver's license? You have to sign."

"Finish the year, then you'll be up here. I'll take you out on back roads."

"They're all back roads."

"True, you'll learn about curves and watching out for aggressive drivers. You have two months to do your best in school and pull up your grades."

"I can ace the tests, I'm not stupid."

"Then do it, son, do it."

Alex sat to chat with his mother who always brewed strong coffee right up until she went to bed. Tomas vanished into his room. Adrianna was up studying. She wanted him to stay the night but he said he'd promised to be back home.

Adrianna came out to tell him good night before he packed up Ana Jesus' empanadas to take with him.

"Sweetheart, *hija mia*. Is everything OK with *Mami*?" he asked his daughter. "I feel badly not to be with her. Soon we will. The house isn't ready yet for her."

"Yes, she's doing great but we need to talk, *Papi*."

"OK, *hija*. What's up?"

"My brother's friends came by while he was gone. They scared *abuela* because she saw their tattoos. She thinks they're ms-13 and she's really afraid for Tomas."

"Who are Tomas' friends? How many came to the house?"

"Five, maybe six, probably not as bad as they look—hoodies so you can't get them to look at you or tell them apart. To me they act stupid but my brother is a copy cat and he does what they do."

"He's always needed his friends. He loves company. You were always the independent one with your own mind. He'd like brothers. We had big families at home but we can't afford that here."

Adrianna cleared her throat. "It's a good thing not to add to population, *Papi*."

"We're still young, your mother and I."

"Oh no, don't even say that," his daughter raised her hand in protest. "Mom won't want more kids, I'm sure. I'm glad to be done with looking out for Tomas."

"And *Mami*? You don't mind looking after her?"

"Just the opposite, I love your mother and she does more around here than you can imagine. She fixes real suppers every night. I love her to death."

"I'm so glad to hear your words. You've always been amazing and responsible but sometimes…"

"Distant, *Papi?*"

"Maybe to your mother. I always understood."

"That I've always had my plans, that I don't want distractions like Tomas does."

"I told your brother if he can pull a B-average, I'll sign for his license. He can't wait to drive. I get that."

"*Papi,* you've got your head in the sand. He's already driving but not with me. I'd never let him touch my car."

"Not your car?"

"Of course not and he's not going to either. There's a lot else you don't know happens, leaving me and *abuela* to handle him."

"We want you and *Mami* to join us as soon as possible." Adrianna didn't address her father directly. "He does respect *abuela* unless he's been drinking beer or is high."

"He's drinking? He's not old enough." Alex remembered he'd given his son several beers after their work. Tomas getting high?

"Adri, you and *Mami* keep Tomas safe two more months, then he comes with me."

"He's going to fight you on that," she said.

"He'll come."

"Please sleep here tonight, *Papi*. It's late to drive home. It's a five hour drive."

"No, *hija,* your mother will be worried. Is Tomas still on his phone? I'll just say good night and leave."

EIGHT

Alex was heating and then shaping metal scraps for a goddess, wings extended like the Angel of the Annunciation, that he planned to bring to Ditto and Carlos the next time he drove back from Malvina to Santa Rosa. He'd promised the goddess for their garden gate but it had taken longer than he planned. He missed the state-of-the-art plasma gun he'd been the master of at Carlos' garage but he made do with the MIG, a basic welder's tool. Standing back and looking at where the angel's eyes seemed to be needing something luminous, he heard an engine stall, then die. He turned to see the grey truck with the primer spots that had driven them off the road. No mistaking it nor the driver, bearded, wearing black leather, reflective shades and a red MAGA cap, who stepped out and moved toward him.

Alex pulled up his welding mask and with his free arm motioned Masha who'd come around from the back to go inside.

"What can I do for you?" Alex picked up a hammer to defend himself but the man in the red cap seemed to have no memory of road rage.

"Dunno. Folks who drive past say you're an artist."

"I do some welding with scraps and things I find around. I welded chassis and fenders at work. Hardly call that art. This is a hobby. They call it junk welding."

"What you doing there? Looks like she could fly off."

"Well, it's an angel for a gate. I hope it looks like she can fly."

"Fucking does. I'm wanting an eagle," the man said.

"What kind of eagle?" Alex laid down his hammer.

"Coming down for the kill." He drew a crumpled colored page from his leather vest. An eagle, talons out, hovered. "Nothing pussy. Name's Ray Lawson."

"I'm Alex, Alex del Calvo."

"I don't want no angel. I want a badass eagle."

"What do you want it made of? I don't do color and I lost some tools when our storage was broken into. Up here, I've picked up some metal sheets, found a whole box of spoons that could make great scales for a snake or claws if I cut them."

"Yeah, I want my eagle like a snake. I heard you got ripped off."

"How'd you hear that?"

"Not much secret around here, del Calvo. Folks are desperate. Hard times."

He nodded, remembering Mrs. Robinson talking about the cannabis growers going broke, and all the big hoops with torn plastic he'd seen on back roads.

"I can bring scrap and some tools. Give me a list. No problem. I want the sculpture for the front lawn." Ray coughed then lit up a cigarette. "Lawn! Fucking trash yard needs an eagle to protect it from folks who got nothing. Riches to rags."

"I'm looking for work but I have time now, once I finish this. I'm looking for eyes to put in this angel."

Ray came closer. "Yeah, I can see that. Eyes."

"I'll make a few sketches from your drawing and show you before I start."

"I'll come by tomorrow with metal. Tell me the tools you need."

"I can make do with what I have. I'll bring my heavy tools up when I come back from Santa Rosa next week. I just don't want to see them ripped off."

"I can see that doesn't happen." Ray stepped into his truck and gunned it.

Alex began working on sketching eagles. He missed the internet but getting connected had to wait until he made some money. When Ray came by, he hauled strips of sheet metal from his truck, darker in streaks. They carried the sheets and then some copper into the garage. Copper cost a lot of money and he couldn't weld it with his equipment here. Alex supposed Ray didn't pay for it so he thought he'd see if he could get one tool he really needed, a jigsaw to cut the metal.

Ray also brought pieces of sea glass, green and blue that looked as though they'd been polished by waves. "The wife used to pick them up on the coast of Oregon. She said, 'Go on, bring it to him.'"

"Thanks, perfect for the angel's eyes but something else for your eagle."

A day later, Ray brought him glistening mica.

"Yeah," Alex said, "those are it."

Alex never thought of establishing a relationship with Ray who came by every few days bringing treasures, like ravens or crows that picked up shiny things and gave them to someone they liked.

Alex brought out chairs into the front yard.

Ray stroked the eagle's iron wing without gloves and cut his palm but all he said was, "Bitchin' sharp, I still got red blood," and coughed. He looked around and squinted. "You know you got a deal here. Folks that lived here fucked up big time."

"We wondered about the birds."

"Never liked what they were into, parrots and other fucking beautiful birds they got brought in. Felt sorry for the birds. You saw it in their eyes, I mean, fuck, birds got a raw deal. Should have been free in the jungle."

"I never liked zoos."

Ray laughed but in a moment his eyes darkened and he stared at Alex. "You think we're all fuck ups. Should be in a zoo?"

"No, I didn't mean that at all. I was talking about myself not liking the idea of zoos because when I was a kid we never went to one."

"Just don't get ideas you're better than us."

Alex felt again the man might be dangerous. If he had anything to do with Ray, he couldn't be afraid or the man would sense it, smell blood in the water.

"My wife and I started with nothing," he said. "We were scared kids, foreigners. I definitely don't think we're better. We've worked for all we've gotten. My wife studied at night and she's a nurse now. She just got on part time at Mercy Regional. I was illegal for years but I got a trade, made myself useful, got my citizenship. I'll find an auto shop around here once I start seriously looking."

"Other folks losing everything here and you come in with big bucks."

"Not big bucks. Saving from salaries, two kids, not easy." Alex knew he couldn't give an inch and he didn't want to. If Ray wanted to throw a punch, he'd give the bigger man all he could in push back. "Do you know where we come from, Ray?"

"Foreign. Folks wondered." He pointed his hand somewhere in the distance.

"Yeah, places out there you wouldn't want to be. More trouble than anything you'll ever know."

"OK, OK man, chill."

"I'm chill."

"Is there somewhere more fucked up than this socialist fucking state?"

"Damn right, Ray, where people make life hell if they don't kill you first."

"You don't think government is fucking us over? Open your eyes, man. What Washington does to us is a crime, every day. We're not taking it anymore."

"We avoid politics, Ray. Serves no one good. Mouth shut." Alex gestured with his hand that he's sealed his lips.

"Hey no offense, little guy, just saying the truth to your ears."

"You seem to have time. You laid off?"

"Laid off! I don't fucking work. Don't insult me." Ray coughed a laugh.

"No offense meant. You married, kids? We have a daughter who probably won't want to come up here but I'm bringing our boy in a few weeks. Living with us, we hope we'll keep him out of trouble."

Alex expected derogatory words about his wife, women, but Ray's expression changed, softened, another look came in his eyes. His voice lost its angry edge.

"Two boys, doing time."

"Sorry to hear. I don't want that for my boy."

Ray pulled himself up and went over to his truck. "You want a hit? Local shit. You wouldn't believe the inventory. Boom and bust like I said."

Ray lit a doobie and offered it to Alex who shook his head. "All right man, you do yours, I do mine." He took a deep hit and coughed. "Shit for my lungs."

Ray's eyes narrowed and Alex saw the darker expression again, the look that reminded him of the first time Ray and his companion had run them off the road. But then the darkness seemed to go inward, not flash out.

"My old lady never gets out of bed. Bad back, all skin and bones. Not her fault our boys are trouble. She did what she could while I was gone."

Alex waited for an explanation.

"Don't ask me anything."

"OK."

"You're one lucky guy. I seen your old lady. A great rack on her."

Alex tensed, ready to pick up where they'd left off before Ray's mood had changed. "Don't go there, Ray. I'm a proud man, proud of my wife. No words, please."

"That was a compliment. And all I'm saying is that if you look around you'll see how our old ladies can't keep themselves up. Folks lose hope and so they don't keep things up. They don't like new faces coming in, reminding them."

"I'll be getting back to work on your bird."

"Just saying, we don't like to be disrespected."

"You're the only person I've met except Mrs. Robinson in town and I'm minding my own business right here."

"Bitch has her nose up everyone's butt. Hey, you do as you like. The eagle is looking great and I like a man who's not afraid to speak his mind even if he's fucked."

By the time Ray came late the next day, Alex had made every detail of the talons from the rake's tines sharp and deadly, and buffed the metal so it shone. He'd epoxied in the two glittering chunks that seemed to give off a different vibe from the blue and green glass in the angel's eyes.

"This is fucking bad." Ray took a roll of cash out of his pocket. "You're an artist, man. How much I owe you?"

"Hundred for labor. You brought materials. Make it $150."

"A steal. Extra fifty. I'm serious, you're one goddamn artist, you know that."

"Thanks, Ray. I'm glad my first paying customer is pleased. I've spent most of my life looking up at the undersides of trucks and cars and dreaming of making something." Alex didn't say 'express myself' because he thought Ray would laugh at that.

"I'll pass the word."

"Thanks. I was trying things out, more like a hobby. I'm happy you like it."

"Anything you need, just say the word."

Alex asked about sturdier fencing. "My wife wants to adopt a pair of goats she saw tethered with a sign. She said they looked miserable and she's a rescuer."

"Animals won't last long without a big dog. Folks around here, a man sees a chicken and he sees food. Goats, good for stew."

"They'd steal pets and eat them? Masha is thinking of chickens, too."

Ray gave a snort. "Get a big mean dog, that's my advice."

NINE

Alex left the garage door open to the road for air and to keep his eyes on traffic. He didn't want to be caught off guard, though with each passing week, Ray's visits, and a wave from Bort, neighbor and cohort riding in the truck with Ray, he felt their lives were under less pressure.

In the morning, Alex sketched out a vulture that a friend of Ray's wanted perched outside his gas station and auto repair in Hayfork, an hour south. Since he hadn't yet found work, Alex drove the road to the other side of a range of low and daunting mountains with roller-coaster curves. On the other side was Hayfork, center of the cannabis trade when it was flourishing only a few years earlier.

As he descended the last curve and saw the flat land ahead, he saw the hoops and greenhouses with broken glass and torn plastic like sailing ships castaway after a storm. Maybe more like covered wagons abandoned on the trail that Masha had imagined. Or ribs of a whale they'd seen at the science museum in Golden Gate Park. Strange that such a recent past now seemed to belong to long-ago even ancient history.

From the road, Avelos Auto looked in better shape than the businesses around Malvina Falls. Windows were intact and had been washed. Closer up, he saw a dozen old and damaged cars and trucks lined up in the yard waiting to be worked on.

"Since my welder quit on me, I don't know what I'm doing ordering a statue," Freddy Avelos said as he shook hands.

"I've always worked in body shops, Mr. Avelos. Decorative welding is more a hobby until I get a job. We only moved here a few months back. House repairs kept me busy so I haven't looked around for work."

"I could use help. Call me Freddie."

"I wasn't thinking of asking. It's a hell of a drive."

He rolled out his drawings of vultures.

"Yeah, yeah…I like these. I want this vulture on a crossbar out front to scare the bejesus out of fuckers who mess with me. Show 'em they end up road kill, have their guts ripped out by my bird here if they don't pay. You wouldn't believe they drive off without a look back. Around here, a handshake and your word was all you needed. Nowadays, I have to take cash up front before I start. You did the welding where?"

"Santa Rosa. I'm an all-around car guy, except for the new ones that you have to go to school to understand."

Freddie, who had a big belly, laughed until it jiggled over his belt. "Round here, those Prius' and the like, folks don't like them. They don't last long on our roads. I'm dying for a good welder. You could start tomorrow."

"Thanks, Mr. Avelos, but I couldn't make it every day. I'm thinking more like looking for a closer shop, maybe Redding or Weaverville. There's a shop in Lewiston."

"Yeah, that's my cousin Ricardo, a real nice set up in Lewiston. Called Rick's."

"Lewiston? First place I was going to go. Ten minutes from our home. I drive past but nothing much looked open."

"Yeah, not doing better than we are. Still, Ricardo needs good work just like I do and folks will start coming. Have a seat, friend." Freddie Avelos went to a refrigerator and brought back two cold beers.

"Where you come from, son, family ties?"

"El Salvador. My cousins in Santa Rosa took me in when I was fourteen."

"My people come from the Azores…some stones God dropped in the big ocean."

"My cousins in Santa Rosa work for a Portuguese farmer and his wife who've been on the land all their lives They're getting old now. They're from the Azores."

"*Hermano*, what's their name?"

"Mateos."

"Beautiful, we're cousins, too. See we're all cousins, and any friend of my cousins is a friend of mine. When can you start?" Freddie Avelos slapped Alex' hand. "I thought there was something meant to be when you came in."

"Appreciate that but like I said, it's a big drive to get here."

"You get used to it. You want to go back to the old country?"

"My country's not a good place right now. My mother just got here. I still don't know how she made it but she did."

"I didn't get to see mine, bless her soul, before she passed." Freddie wiped a tear.

They talked more, easy talk, no tension. By the end of the second beer Alex had agreed to work one day a week in Hayfork. Avelos would call his cousin in Lewiston about work closer to home.

Ray came into the garage. Alex kept on his face mask, made his seam and lifted his hand from the trigger. "Making a vulture for Freddie Avelos."

"Birds seem to be order of the day."

"You're right. Thanks for Freddie, he's taking this and offered me work."

"Fly away, fly away." Ray flapped his hands at his side.

"Do you mean fly away, like what?"

"Like get away from all this." Ray pointed around him.

Alex wiped perspiration from his forehead and looked at Ray, still talking. The man definitely did not look happy, worse than usual.

"You OK?"

"It's where you are, how you see things like my wife says. Me personally, what I got to look forward to? Dying from fucking lung disease."

"I'm sorry to hear that. Your cough never sounded good." Alex looked at the joint burning in Ray's hand and waited for the next cough when he sucked in the burn.

"Don't be saying pity shit or I'll kick your butt," Ray coughed out.

Alex nodded. Ray's mood was definitely dark. There wouldn't be small talk.

"Open your eyes, man. There's too much evil, man, too much, all around. Dark forces. The end is coming because it can't go on."

"Are you talking politics or an asteroid hitting earth or what, Ray?"

"Get yourself armed up, man. Came to talk to you about this."

"That's dark in itself but tell me more so I can follow you."

"Getting armed." Ray started to cough again. He backed up into the outside light. "Just take it for what it's worth that I'm looking out for you as long as you don't fucking do something stupid."

Ray couldn't keep talking without spasms of coughing.

"Susan's been wanting the bench fixed so we can sit on it."

"Let's make it happen. You want to work on something?" Alex asked.

He got an extra head gear to protect Ray's face. After a last toke, Ray stubbed out the joint and put the gear over his head.

"Gloves." Alex handed Ray big heavy gloves.

"Best way is to sketch on this grid with chalk." Alex rolled out butcher paper with grid lines. "Then we'll see what we need."

"I got the top but legs won't hold. Needs new legs."

"You draw what you want and we can weld them. Heat is magic, you heat anything high enough, you fuse it."

"How did you learn the tricks?" Ray was leaning close, breathing a bad breath.

"I taught myself, trial and error." Alex pulled back a little, trying to make his movement natural. "Heat makes the molecules relax and you can bend metal any way you want, like the wings. For finer welds like copper, you got to do it carefully but I can't do that up here."

"Alchemy, man."

Alex nodded. "Yes, you find the words, Ray."

"Used to be a reader. After all the shit in Iraq, my brain got fried but it's coming back. I can feel my hands twitching to try my hand again."

"You welded? I knew it somehow but you didn't say, you let me just go on. Where'd you work?"

"Where?" Ray laughed behind the head gear. "Inside a big room. Got paid 40 cents an hour."

"Prison?" Alex pulled up his mask. "We can put these back on. Tell me more."

"Like my youngest, minimum security, long time back." Ray pulled up the mask. "It wasn't that bad. I shut out all the shit inside the walls and they kept me safe. Learning to weld, even the noise calmed my mind."

"Welding can do that."

They sketched more with chalk until Ray had made a sturdy-looking bench on the paper. "They'll be good supports. What you got to do is penetrate with the weld to fuse and you should have a sturdy bench."

"I know that, bro." They slapped hands.

"When you bring the bench we'll get the legs done."

"I don't like to leave Susan long alone."

"I used to worry about Masha but thank goodness she seems better. It's her garden and all the trees that give her some peace."

After Ray left, Alex thought about the strange conversations they were having, confiding one moment, turning into near confrontation with the defensiveness and lurking anger coming out the next. Ray made him be more honest than most talk he usually had. Ray's bullshit detector was always on. Then there were his words, I'm looking out for you. But getting armed? He never owned a gun. He didn't want any kind except the one he welded with.

Alex thought of how he considered himself a pretty good welder, a fixer of broken parts, maybe a fabricator who made gates and smaller pieces. Was he going further expressing himself with that magical combination of heat and metals? He liked it a lot. He put back on his gloves, his protective mask and picked up the rake tines to work on Freddie's vulture. Details made anything come to life.

TEN

Alex began attracting visitors, a half dozen men, sometimes with women or a child hanging behind, to watch as he cut, soldered and welded the metal pieces for the threatening birds. Spectators stayed at a distance from the sizzle of the flame but they seemed to love seeing sparks fly as he melted and bent the sheet metal into curves for wings. Two brothers from Michoacán, big men with shaved heads and tats of snakes, dragons and bleeding hearts, chattered with a natural comedic rap in Spanish. They had a manic kind of energy that Alex supposed came from being high. They wanted two dragons but Alex told them it might be several weeks when he started part time at Richie's Auto, Freddie's cousin's, in Lewiston.

Alex didn't mind the audience but he was glad when all the rest cleared out and he could sit with Ray, drink a beer and talk.

"Someone teach you to weld when you were inside?" Alex asked.

Ray took a deep breath, then a cough.

"One brew?" Alex asked though it wasn't yet noon. Ray did not drink water.

"Next time I bring the Venom, this is piss." Ray drank, still catching his breath.

"Sounds lethal. I'm a light weight."

"I'll get you trained," Ray replied.

"You were talking about Jonathon and welding."

"Yeah, if he hadn't been on his shift and got me into the

shop, I might've turned out like my old man, full-blown asshole. I'm only half." Ray coughed. "Three-quarters."

Alex wanted to refute, but only asked, "Jonathon?"

"He was a big guy, he turned Christian when he married, maybe he was fifty then, no kids of his own but volunteered to help young punks. Said he'd 'raise me.' He meant welding but I was always thinking maybe something else. I had a suspicious mind."

"Did he try to convert you?"

"No never, not a word. We talked personal, fathers who were mean drunks. At my house, if my old man didn't get his fists into someone at the bar that night, there were us kids at home. This big guy confessed he'd never learned to read, that they'd graduated him reading second grade level. He always felt like he was being laughed at."

"How'd they graduate him?" Alex remembered his own difficulty learning English and how easy it had been for Masha with a natural ability he didn't have.

"He said he was big and they wanted him gone. Of course he fucked up for a while, never lived anywhere, odd jobs where he didn't have to read because he was afraid to look at pieces of paper. Ended up meeting the woman he's been married to most of his life and she had religion."

"Didn't anyone teach him to read?"

"His wife tried but he must have something cross-wired. He can see anything three-D. What happened when I was inside and I was using the library, I started reading to him because he said he always felt like he'd never known the rest of the world you learn about in books. He said it was like living only a slice of life while others seemed to get the whole pie, travel anywhere in space and time."

"Masha's more a reader than I am."

"I read *The Hunchback of Notre Dame* and *Three Musketeers* to him. Great books. I was about to start *Cannery Row* when my time was up. Pretty funny. They were letting me out early for good behavior but I didn't want to be on the loose. I was alone without Jonathon until I met Susan."

They were sitting quietly now when Bort showed up again.

"You still hanging out here?" he asked Ray.

"Yeah." Ray crushed his can.

Bort was their nearest neighbor and had been the passenger with Ray when the two men ran them off the road, but he didn't seem to remember any more than Ray had. That was where the similarities ended. Bort didn't like him, Alex could feel it. He came by because of Ray, like a jealous kid who's been dropped. The man's face with its flat red nose, pustules and tiny eyes seemed to radiate waves of angry heat. Masha warned that the man's pit bulls scared her if she walked by their rubbled yard with its State of Jefferson flag hanging from a tree, but when she'd fixed a scraped knee of one Bort's sons who'd fallen off his bike, the mother seemed OK. Maybe it was a start.

With no offer of a beer, Bork left Alex and Ray to continue talking. The temperature was perfect, sunny and cool, not a cloud in the sky.

"Named my youngest Jonathon."

"That was respectful."

"The little guy hated the name and called himself Reno after we went to see Susan's family who lived there. He must have been five or six then. He'll be out soon."

"You stay in touch with Jonathon?"

"Yeah, sometimes, though we're not ones for writing and I don't trust the phone. He's an old guy now but he'll live longer than me."

Vandals broke in the first week in June before Alex was bringing Tomas to stay with them for the summer. He and Masha had been gone most of the day, Masha at the hospital in Redding and Alex in Hayfork. He arrived home first to find the front lock sheered off, and the door swinging open.

He picked up a shovel from the porch but the thieves were long gone. Whoever they'd been, they were careless, probably looking for cash or drugs, leaving chairs upended, nothing much stolen because there wasn't stuff worth easy reselling. They hadn't messed with welding tools he kept hidden under tarps in the garage along with the TV for Tomas. They did manage to find twenty dollars Masha kept in a kitchen drawer.

"What next?" Alex struggled to put things right before Masha got home. He swept up broken glass and retrieved the new TV still in its box. Why had these kids—he assumed the vandals were kids—pissed on the doorstep but not taken the TV? The affront reminded him of the storage unit, the recklessness and contempt that felt personal.

"I don't know. We won't tell Tomas." Masha sat with a glass of wine that night.

"No. We've got the TV which is what he cares about. We'll lock up everything."

The next morning, Masha was gone before Bort stopped his truck and watched Alex working on the snapped-off door hinges.

"Dumb fucking kids. Like we told you, you need protection. Lose much?"

"Not much. How did you know this happened?" Alex was suspicious.

"No secrets for long and these kids have big mouths." Bort spat.

"Mostly they made a mess looking for drugs and cash. Didn't take tools which I would hate to lose. I'm not going to make an insurance claim, not worth it."

"You folks have fucking insurance?" Bort's little eyes narrowed. "Don't you know that they can implant a chip in you and then you're a hostage of Washington?"

"I didn't think of that."

"Just saying, information like that goes right up onto their spy drones. You need protection. That's why I'm here. We're calling another meeting."

Before he left to drive to Santa Rosa to get Tomas, Alex started making a drawing for the Michoacan brothers who wanted the dragons. Any allies he could make were a good thing. He thought about fashioning a shape somewhere between a realistic amphibian, like an alligator, and a fanciful monster from cartoons he'd watched with Tomas. He sketched a swooping shape of the body with its upright tail. He was thinking of putting patina on scales. He had pieces of grey sheet metal that might take a glaze.

He was lost in his work and enjoying the quiet when one truck and then another rolled to a stop in front of their drive. Green flags with State of Jefferson and the double XX in yellow, some with coiled rattlesnake and DON"T TREAD ON ME. Red hats. He saw several of the men carried rifles and fought an impulse to grab a heavy tool to defend himself, then to say he was about to leave and ask them to come back later. None of that was possible. The Citizens were here.

When Ray pulled up, Alex relaxed enough to get out into the open.

"You remember I was talking about getting armed?" Ray opened the gate, leaving the others standing by their vehicles in the street.

"I do, but what's the party? Anything happening?" Alex tried to compose his face.

"We come as aid and assistance. Heard you got robbed."

"Yeah, second time, including the storage."

"You need a gun and a big dog for when you're not around."

The Michoacan brothers got out of a truck.

"I've never owned a gun and we don't have a dog," Alex said.

"Time to get both," Ray said.

Bort, leaving a distance but close enough for Alex to smell his rank odor, said loudly. "We can get you what you need once you prove your worth. You got a record?"

"No, I don't have a record."

"Cause you're better than us?" asked a tall, lean man with a scar. "You're nothing but a fool."

"You join Citizens Watch. The punks won't come nowhere near you," Bort said. "They're dumb ass stupid but not that dumb."

"Do like the man says. You're with us then," Ray said.

"Do I have a choice?" Alex turned to Ray.

"Not if you're smart and want to live up here," Ray said.

"Ray's got a soft spot for this guy." Bort turned to tell his friends. "Any one of you fuckers against a first round vote to consider?"

Alex heard murmurs but saw no hands raised. He didn't like guns. In hospitals, Masha saw kids shot by their siblings when a loaded weapon had been left within reach.

"What do I have to do?" Alex found his voice.

"Like we said, we watch you for now. You got flags?"

Alex shook his head. He didn't know what he'd do if he was told to fly one.

"Every man his own sheriff, their own cop, together we're an army," Bort said.

"Fucking way it should be," came a shout.

"We don't answer to no fuckers out there, taking freedom from us," said the man with the long face who shot his rifle into the ground. There was a small applause.

"Freedom to exercise your god-given rights under our Constitution," said Bort.

"Who's out there making America great again?" the scar-face called.

There was a roar of laughter and a doffing of MAGA caps.

Our Constitution, thought Alex. Do they even know a word of it?

The smell of cannabis now filled the air.

"Anyone got weed to share?" A small man wearing a dirty jockey cap and baggy clothes stepped forward.

"Loony Gus come along to cadge." Bort pushed the smaller man aside. "Loony can smell weed a mile away, like a dog. He's our dog. You don't want him anyway."

Laughter all around.

The little man with bright blue eyes and few teeth they called Loony Gus skirted the group and came to Alex. "Court jester at your service." The man was fleshless, like a starved child in his oversize motley clothes. His body trembled. "Long time ago in the past the Jews were slaves in Egypt…"

Someone interrupted, "None of that Jew Hebe crap, Loony."

"Crazy Gus, guy has a brain if he'd use it but he always brings up the Hebe stuff and we don't like Jews or A-rabs," Bort said.

"There's a saying that the past is another country. You can say that again for me. I used to live in Paradise," Gus said.

"Burned to cinders a few years back," Ray said.

"Ever since my exile, I've been wandering."

The Mexican brothers made the *crazy* sign with their fingers. 'You ain't been nowhere, Crazy, 'cept maybe to *la luna*."

"I got special powers," Gus tapped his forehead.

"Loony will go on all night. Let's get this wound up," Ray said. "Calvo you in?"

"Where's blondie wife with the *chichis*?" one of the Michoacan brothers asked.

Ray raised his hand. "Keep your fucking trap shut."

Ray's words counted. The guy stepped back.

"You'll hear from us when we need you," Bort said, "and since you got that special thing with Ray, you report to him."

"We don't advertise, we don't march around, we're just here all around you," Ray said in a quiet voice he supposed was comforting, but Alex didn't feel comforted.

Alex told Masha about the gathering and the proposal to get a gun. She sat down heavily at the kitchen table. Alex poured them glasses of red wine.

"You know more people shoot each other with their own guns," she said.

"I know. They made an offer I couldn't refuse, *mi alma.* Comes with the territory, their territory, living here. We'd rather have them with us than against us."

"You won't have to use it, will you? You'll keep it locked away somewhere before you bring Tomas here."

"Absolutely. They said I needed one of those flags."

"Let's look up these Citizens and Jefferson," she tapped on her phone.

"They're not all bad. You know Ray has a good heart and you said that Bort's wife wasn't as bad as you thought. I'm sorry you missed an odd little guy they called Goofy Gus. No it was Loony. Seemed out of place but what do I know about who comes out of the woodwork around here?"

"Alejandro, look at my phone. Is the price too high living

here? They are not like us. I should have done research on these people. They're in California, Oregon, Idaho."

"I don't agree with them but I think a lot is bluff, Masha, and someone like Ray, he hates politics. He just wants to be left alone and sometimes I agree with him."

"They have guns. Guns are dangerous. And who are you going to shoot?"

"I'm not going to shoot anyone."

"If kids come to steal, you'll shoot kids?"

"No, but I'll have it and they'll know."

"Do we wear little badges?" she asked.

"We wouldn't do that."

"They won't take the vaccine. They even hate us, nurses, docs. They scare me."

"I'd choose other neighbors but we bought ourselves into this."

"I know, I know. I wanted it too much."

"Masha, we've got our house, you've got a garden, Tomas will be here."

"Men in gangs killed your father. You want to get Tomas away from gangs."

"We get on with our lives."

"Not our people," she said.

"Not our people."

"I know Ray is different."

"Yes, Ray is different," she said.

Alex now worked without looking at the people watching him; the welding mask and the grinding he made cutting metal gave him a noisy solitude. Instead of being watched with their curiosity, he felt the people who came were just waiting for an accident or something to happen. The few times he looked up he was surprised to see Bort sitting by himself in a camp chair smoking a big joint.

"Want a cold one?" Alex removed his mask.

"Never say no. You want some mellow smoke?"

"Thanks, brew's enough."

Alex didn't like getting high even with friends; the few times he had with the cousins, a ghost seemed to be leading him into the past he didn't want to visit.

"What's the story on the State of Jefferson?" Alex thought he'd never get Bort in such a mellow mood.

"First time in my life I voted for anything."

"What did you vote for?"

"Severance, man, severance."

"I know the word but what does it mean here?"

"Getting the fuck out of California."

"Moving away?"

"Why should we move, shit brain?" Bort's pacific mood vanished. "It's our land, us against them."

"Just asking."

After a long swig, Bort narrowed his eyes. "You want to know?"

"I do."

"Means we don't pay no taxes to CA no more, giving those queers in SF all the money, nothing to Communists and Jews in D.C., no vax, no tax. Give us our freedom, bust down the walls."

"Why Jefferson, the president?"

"Better ask Loony or your pal, Ray. What I can tell you is we got the guns and they ain't blunderbusses or whatever they used back then. We got weaponry, man. You just wait, it's a second coming. It's freedom."

Bort blew out his last gust of weed, folded his chair and climbed into the truck.

As he lay in the dark beside his wife, relaxed and warm after making love and comforting each other, Alex thought about freedom, the key word for these people. He was no philosopher but it seemed to him that the freedom that came with guns, obsessing about government on the websites and believing the buffoon president who still claimed he'd won the election he'd lost, wasn't what he'd call freedom. So you wouldn't take orders, wouldn't get permits for building or pay traffic tickets but you paid in other ways. Not a cop nor doctor nearby, roads in shit shape, no playgrounds for your kids. He couldn't answer his own questions and he needed sleep for tomorrow's drive to get Tomas. He could feel Masha's warm body beside him, still a wonder he nestled against.

ELEVEN

Ray handed Alex the shotgun. "Big gun for a little guy. Would have given you something smaller but this was what I had. Maybe better for a first-timer. You aim at the face and they back off. No one wants their nose blown off and you get respect. If that doesn't do it, aim front and center, right here," Ray poked Alex's chest, "and fire."

"Ray, can I ask you a question?"

"Fire away. Yeah, that's funny."

"Bort was here the other day."

"Yeah?"

Alex then recounted the part of their conversation about the State of Jefferson.

"What did you want to know. Should have asked me, not that shit brain."

"I want to know what it really means, the XX…"

"Double cross. It's a flag and it's the true state of minds here. Folks feel double-crossed so they make a new state to their liking."

"Rattle snake is clear."

"Yeah, stay back."

"The state troopers have guns, too," Alex said.

"State troopers, they won't stick with Sacramento. We're four states and counting."

Alex was surprised by Ray's smarts on politics that he said he knew nothing about. "But how do the Citizens fit in?" he asked.

"Local, on the ground, locals do the heavy lifting."

"Women go for this?"

"They best do. First person killed by the cops on Jan 6 was a woman."

"I remember, the Patriot Boys made her a martyr."

Before he drove off, Ray had Alex load and unload the shells but not do any practice shooting because Masha would have come out.

"Done the right thing. Simple as ABC."

"Ray, can I ask a question?"

"Shoot." Ray made a trigger finger of his right hand.

"Not that." Alex automatically flinched.

"No worries, you'll be able to hit anything with that thing. Question?"

"Ever think what you'd want to be doing if you could do just what you want?

"Are you gone like Loony?"

"You don't have to answer. I ask myself the question."

"What would I be doing if I weren't stuck up in this shithole?" Ray looked hard at Alex but not really looking at him with his grey eyes.

"Yes. What you want, really."

"You go first, fucker."

Alex had learned, not only with Ray but especially with Ray, that no-bullshit answers were the only ones.

"You'll laugh. I'd be a teacher like my father, but not in El Salvador."

"Guess not, that didn't work out well. Teacher! Fuck. Such a pussy job."

"I always admired my father, trying to get the best out of everyone."

"That's too high on the tree for me to reach."

"I don't think so."

"Fuck off, I'm no missionary."

"Chance for more education?"

Ray laughed and coughed. "Nah, they don't know nothing I don't or can't learn. I'd be back in olden times, blacksmith maybe, harness maker. I love that kind of thing. I can taste the whiskey in the saloons and I'd make sure there was law and order."

"Sort of close to welding, it is welding. You could do that." Alex didn't mention the Citizens. Their law and order was more vigilante—but that was old west, too.

"If I could breathe, if the fucking government hadn't burned out my lungs, I'd stand over that hot fire with a horse trusting me to make his shoes good." Ray coughed hard. "Maybe I'd make doo-dads with you."

Alex walked behind the house to find a secure hiding place for the gun but he thought it would be better indoors. What was the point of a gun if you couldn't get to it quickly? Getting to know the house inside out, replacing wood, scraping and painting, he found a niche for the gun with their documents they wanted to keep safe.

Masha had enrolled Tomas in summer school that started the next week in Redding. Alex hoped geometry would teach his son the basics that helped in everything he did, everything he himself wished he'd learned in school and had had to figure out by trial and error. He imagined Tomas could assist with the big welding pieces and try making something of his own.

You see a piece in your mind's eye before you start—that's the artist part—but I never got the basics of structure, he said to himself. So much to do with his son, taking week-end trips to explore and try the fishing, good things to teach him and share, more than just keeping Tomas out of trouble.

TWELVE

When Alex arrived in Santa Rosa and they were loading suitcases, stereo and video games, his son didn't protest about the summer away from his home and friends the way that Alex had expected him to. Rather, Tomas seemed eager to throw everything into the truck, pack up and leave as soon as possible. He kept looking out at the street as if he someone might drive up.

"Your grandmother and sister will miss you," Alex said. "Don't you want to go back in one more time and say goodbye?"

"*Papi*, I already did. Adri's studying and *abuela* is doing her stitching."

"We wanted her to have rest finally. To rest her eyes."

"There's no stopping *abuela*."

"That's true but I'll just go in and give her a kiss."

"I'll check I didn't forget anything." Tomas disappeared into the house, leaving Alex wondering what was happening.

Three weeks into summer school, Tomas was doing his homework and asking Alex for help with the math. This was a second surprise. He and Masha expected foot-dragging and reproaches but Tomas behaved like a grateful pup coming in from a storm. He was also taking shop and a drawing workshop and called them both cool. "I see what you mean about geometry. I never learned it before, *Papi.*"

When Masha stayed over in Redding some nights for late shifts, Alex fixed supper for Tomas and they shared a beer. The June light lasted until nine so they sat on the porch whittling together around an outdoor wood fire.

"Why can't Mom lay off me, Dad? Always why this, why that? You don't hassle me with questions."

"I'm leaving it to you to say what's on your mind. Your mother is tired from work where people are dying and she just wants a chance to hear about you. She's always ready to help."

"I get that but I don't need her worrying. Sorry, *Papi.* I'm not a little boy."

"We're both proud of you, son. I love seeing you work with your hands."

"You didn't think I could." Tomas was whittling on an owl he'd carved out of a large oak branch that had fallen.

"We both are making birds, that's interesting." Alex ran his fingers over the rough feathers Tomas had made.

"Yeah. And *Abuela* makes birds and butterflies with her stitching."

"You know your mother came to America all alone when she was really young. She was sick and needed care she couldn't get. She has an older brother who stayed with her folks in Ukraine. Maksym. I've told you about him. She worries about him a lot."

"I know I have an uncle over there but Mom never talks about him."

"His name is Maksym. Your mom doesn't know much

except that he's been in trouble and that's hard, being Ukrainian with the Russians there."

"I can relate."

"How's that?"

"I mean they get listened in on."

"True, and even with Skype or Facetime where she can see her mom, she doesn't say anything to get the family in trouble."

"You came alone and you didn't have anybody."

"I had my cousins Carlos and Ditto's family. They took care, they got me work, and we're guys, *hombres*, it's different for a woman."

"Your uncles say you were always tough like a brick," Tomas said.

"A brick? That's pretty funny. Anyway, the little town where your mother came from, everything will be poisoned for centuries with radioactivity. They call it an exclusion zone. Photos I've seen of the site show weird-looking dogs, mutants."

"Mutants are chill. Like zombies?"

"If you're not there. We'll watch *Chernobyl* one night when Masha's at work and you'll see the government cover ups and stuff."

"Like it is here, government talking shit?"

"What are you saying, son? It's nothing like here."

"Government lies about everything. I mean, being vaxxed. I wish I hadn't been but they made us. I don't want the new one."

"*Mi hijo*, you've been hearing too much nonsense that

people around here believe. They don't read anything that's true or proven science." Alex saw his son look away. "OK, no lectures, but California, the United States, is nothing like Russia or Ukraine or Salvador, believe your father. Ask your mom about not getting the boosters."

"I don't want to ask her anything. She'll just get crazy mad."

"Why are you being so hard on your mother, son?"

"She gets under my skin. Like my sister does. Like, I love 'em but they can be such bitches. Sometimes Mom scares me."

Alex felt a wave of shock. He stood up and glared at his son by their porch light. "I've told you we don't use that language around here. Kindness, *hijo*, with your mother. She needs that. Was it Adrianna that made you want to come up here?"

"Not exactly." Tomas kept his eyes on the owl. When he started to speak, his voice was so low that Alex leaned forward to hear.

"I love my bros but I didn't want to spend the summer with them. They were into shit I couldn't go along with but if I was there, they'd have made me go along."

"What kind of shit, *hijo*?"

"Ripping off stuff at building sites. You know that part of town that got wiped out by the fires?"

"We thought it would burn clear over to the Fairgrounds and get us but it didn't and we were so lucky, Tomas. We still had a home."

"Yeah, massive. Now they're rebuilding so there's tools

and stuff, and 'cause it's close to the freeway, some guys, you know, they grab stuff and then they take off."

"You're telling me your hombres are thieves?"

"The really bad dudes come up from the East Bay and they totally clean things out. My bros, they just pick up stuff lying around." Tomas avoided his father's eyes.

"Probably have guns, too?" Alex asked.

Tomas still didn't look at his father. "Guys who come in from Oakland, yeah."

"They're all doing the wrong thing, the totally wrong thing preying on people trying to recover. That's really sick, Tomas. It's called stealing, it's *malo*, evil."

"I know, *Papi*. Don't tell Mom anything, OK?" Tomas kept his eyes averted.

"So you wanted to get out of there because you knew it was wrong and you didn't want to be part of it?"

"Yeah, it's wrong. You could get hurt."

"And arrested. And you'd be hurting the folks you stole from, like we had happen to us up here, more stuff than you knew about, especially more than we wanted Adrianna or *Mami* to know. I keep what you tell me to myself and you do the same. I'm happy you're here, Tomas, and that's most important."

"Yeah, and I kind of like what I'm learning, I mean, from you, *Papi*, and the kids aren't that bad, a little dumb but not bad. I miss my bros though."

"Your life is up to you, son. I want you to be informed, so read different things. My best advice is, don't believe everything you're told or read until you judge yourself."

"And be a man," Tomas said quietly. "I want to be a man like you, *Papi*. What did you and Mom do that was screwed up?"

"Screwed up?"

"You said you guys did something stupid, screwed up, when you were young."

"Oh that. We were lucky that a good policewoman helped us."

"Police? You, *Papi*, Mr. Do Right?"

"It was long ago, Adri was a baby and you weren't born. I don't think your mother would want you to hear some of our mistakes. I'll ask her what she thinks."

"It's OK."

"I know you'd have liked to have your own brother. Could still..."

"Don't be gross, *Papi*. I'll just chill."

Tomas put on his head phones and went into his room.

Alex thought they'd overcome something and he felt heartened. Another time they'd talk about what was wrong in the way these folks thought about the government. And the vaccines. Another time. And if his son asked again about stuff they'd done when they were young, he probably would tell him about the night at the Lizard Club. Just thinking about it brought back the smells of their trailer on Moorland, baby milk, baby diapers. And the sex, a smell that he and Masha always had between them in the sheets. She hadn't cared about anything but having him. Their bed smelled like being in the wild.

Their trailer on Moorland Avenue had seemed an improvement over sharing rooms with three other young men, but once Adrianna was born, they had no space to be apart from her crying or babbling. Masha clung to her ambition to become a nurse and had been studying chemistry and biology from her high school books so she needed quiet. Alex remembered that any hour Masha had free, she went over the periodic table. At the end of his day, all he could do was stay awake for supper.

There weren't many times for fun, though he accepted having most of his waking hours at work. He admired Masha for her persistence with her books and knew their patience would pay off. The day Adrianna turned one, Masha begged to get out for that single night and celebrate the birthday with Alex' cousin Ditto who managed the Lizard Club on Santa Rosa Avenue. "Please, we never go out and have fun anymore. I just want to dance. I bought a new blouse."

"You did? How?"

"I've looked after Mrs. Rodriguez' babies. I saved for it. I walked to the mall."

"What do we do with our daughter?"

"She comes with. We'll be an hour or two. She'll sleep in the car."

Alex was dubious as they bundled up Adrianna and strapped her in her car seat. When they pulled into the back lot behind the bar, green and yellow neon lights from the flashing lizard tail kept the car from being too dark.

Adrianna was sleeping, though he worried if leaving her was safe. "She'll be fine," Masha said, and Alex gave Adrianna's small fingers a tickle; the baby squeezed back. Masha gently placed a pacifier in her mouth and kissed her warm forehead.

"Alex, leave the window more open," said Masha. "The air is good for her."

"Not too much, we don't want her to catch a cold." Alex lowered a back window by inches and clicked the doors locked. Then Masha pulled him toward the club.

As the evening progressed and they drank mojitos and Masha smoked some weed, time became as fluid as their bodies yielding to *rancheras*. "I am so happy with you tonight," she whispered in his ear. He forgot everything, holding her tightly against him.

Around midnight, Masha stepped out of the club to breast feed in the car. When the baby fell back asleep, she crawled out to fasten her blouse and somehow hit the button that locked the keys inside. Alex always warned her to keep keys out of the car because the doors locked so fast. She managed to jam her hand down along the wedge of window they'd left open until her fingers reached the button.

Masha came back in and asked Ditto for something for a headache.

"This fixes everything, *guapa*," Ditto said. She took the pill with a beer and soon everything was good again, better than ever. She let her hair fall from the clip and Alex was aroused as they pressed together. With them, it was always like the first time they'd kissed under the oak trees on the campus after their class. Not only their lips were two halves finding the whole; their eyes, dark and hazel-flecked with gold, were meant for each other, a reflection of their selves, the other half that made up for all they'd lost. Sometimes caring for their baby, Alex' difficult work schedule made Masha's anxiety turn into erratic behavior but desire always brought them back together.

After they danced, Alex said, "Let's go cool off and check on Adri."

He led Masha to the car where the baby was sleeping quietly. Alex moved the bundle to the seat up front, threw a blanket over themselves in the back. They made love like the teen-agers they still were.

They were asleep under the blanket when lights shone in their eyes and they woke to two policeman shining flashlights in their faces. The baby started wailing.

Grey light was filtering in through the glass. Adrianna was crying and with each wail, milk oozed from Masha's breasts. Before she could reach back and take her baby to nurse, a policeman's voice ordered them both to stay where they were. "Neither of you move," he said. "I'm calling Protective Services."

Moments later, another car pulled into the parking lot. Alex stepped out with his hands up under the flashing lizard that looked ugly in the colorless morning light. He slowly and carefully lowered his hands to show the policeman his license.

"You can't take a child inside these premises," the officer said.

"We didn't take her inside, sir."

"Then where was the child while you were inside? You both been drinking?"

"We were taking a nap before we drove home. I have to change for work."

Masha nudged him. "I need to go to the toilet." Her breasts were leaking circles through her shiny new blue blouse.

"My baby is hungry and I must go to the bathroom," she said.

"Ma'am, you come out. The child stays put."

The policemen roughly pulled Masha from the car.

"What are you doing to my wife?" Alex tensed his fists.

"Let her go, Frank. We've got the place covered. No way she gets lost."

When Masha returned to the car, Alex was talking to a young woman in a black uniform with a badge on her chest and a heavy-looking gun belt on her hips.

"Ma'am, stay where you are, right there." The woman put her hand up to Masha who felt her legs ready to buckle from fear.

"The child is yours?" she asked Masha.

"Yes, Adrianna is our child. She turned one year yesterday," Alex answered.

"Would you stand back, Sir. I asked the woman. Is she the mother?"

Masha was sobbing. "My baby! Where is my baby?"

Alex's jaw tightened beneath the dark stubble of his morning beard.

"She is my wife and mother of our child." He turned to Masha. "I'll do the talking."

"Watch out, Officer, he's going to hit her," one of the law enforcement men said.

"Never in my life do I hit a woman." Alex shook his head.

"Do you know that the baby hasn't been changed and is wet? You two seem not to be paying attention. My name is Officer Tamra Torres. May I see your I.D, sir."

She spoke to Alex first then to Masha who saw her husband relax his fists a little when he heard the officer's Hispanic name and her soft accent.

"We take good care of our baby," said Alex. "She's very healthy."

"After I see your I.D.'s, I want proof that she's your child."

"Look in her eyes, miss," said Masha. "You see she is ours, Alex and me, we have the same eyes. Adrianna has twice times our eyes."

"You have your driver's license, sir?"

"Yes, Officer." Alex showed it again to Officer Torres. "Everything's in order."

"And your wife? Does she have identification?"

"She has a learner's permission."

Masha searched in her purse, and brought out a folded paper.

"I see your residence is on Moorland Avenue. Where was the child born?"

"She was born in Sutter Hospital in Santa Rosa, California," Alex answered.

"Proof of residence, any bills or cards that you're carrying?" Torres asked.

"In our home. We pay our rent, the PG&E. I work two

jobs. My wife stays home with the baby. She will take classes to be a nurse when our daughter is older. Our baby is never alone."

"She was tonight and not in a safe place. Ma'am, your baby needs clean diapers. You can go back inside and change her. Sir, do you have a legal car seat for the child?"

"Yes, it's in the car, Ma'am."

"Have either of you ever been deported for criminal offenses?"

"No. I have my green card and I will be applying for citizenship, we both will."

"If there are no problems with your record, with either of your records, you can go to work, Sir, but I'll take your wife to your residence for the birth certificate and proof of residence. I'll secure the child in your seat. Where are you two from originally?"

"I am from El Salvador and my wife is from Ukraine. Masha, my wife, got special medical status when she came because of the nuclear explosion near her town."

"When did I read about that?" Officer Torres asked.

The officer asked Masha to come closer. "Ma'am, you've hurt your hand. Did anything happen?" Officer Torres looked from Alex and back to Masha.

"No, Officer," Masha now felt her swollen fingers throb. "I'm all right."

"You didn't notice these bruises, Sir?"

"What happened, Masha?" Alex turned over her swollen wrist that was now blue.

With Alex and the officer looking at her, Masha described

locking the keys in the car when she came to nurse the baby and forcing her hand down to open the door.

"I warned my wife about automatic locks," said Alex. "*Mi amor,* is there pain?"

Masha shook her head. "Only a little."

"Were you drinking this morning?"

"No, last night we drank some beers. I am the cousin of the manager of this bar. I didn't want to drive home so we slept."

"In your car?"

Alex nodded. Masha felt cold with fear.

"Mrs. del Calvo, you direct me to your residence."

"You will be my guest." Masha remembered she hadn't done dishes before they left, and she wished her hair looked better. There was nothing she could do about the big wet splotches on her blouse where her milk was still leaking.

"My wife speaks better English than I do," Alex said.

"That's good, we'll understand each other just fine."

"Will they give back my baby?" Masha was shaking.

"We've done nothing wrong, Masha. It will be all right. We've gotten through worse. We're safe here."

"I want my baby. She must eat."

"I'm already late so Masha, please, you go with this kind woman who doesn't want harm to come to any of us."

Alex passed the breathalyzer test, walked straight on the line, and after the officers confirmed the car registration, they let him drive off to work and left Tamra Torres in charge. She gave Masha permission to nurse. Both women let out a sigh of relief at the sound of the baby sucking.

When they entered the trailer park, Masha crouched down to avoid any eyes that might be watching and see her in the police car.

Alex heard the rest from Masha as soon as he was home and found her huddled in bed with the baby at her side. All she told him seemed to confirm the faith he had in his new country but Masha was in shock. He washed up quickly and sat beside her. He knew he wasn't as sensitive as she was and that she reacted differently to surprises or trouble. He always reassured her because she was more vulnerable and easily upset.

Masha told him in tears that she'd felt so embarrassed in front of the officer. "My new blouse was ruined and I had to nurse right in front of her because Adri screamed every time I took her off my breast. I felt like an animal, so primitive."

"Not primitive. You were doing what mothers do, *amor*."

"Like an animal, Alex. I have a brain, you know."

"Of course, a good brain. I'm sure she didn't judge you."

"She was kind enough to tell me that she'd hated having to express her milk for her baby when she went back to work. She told me to find a rent or utility receipt to verify our address, and the birth certificate. She didn't let me take Adrianna inside. I was afraid that our baby would disappear with the officer who was talking on her radio in the car. I realized how I loved our child."

"Of course you love her, we both do, with all our hearts."

"I picked up the first envelope from the bills on a shelf and then I opened the trunk with our papers."

"The birth certificate?"

"Yes. Then the officer said to me that she'd been born here in Santa Rosa but her parents came from Mexico and they had started out poor. She was grateful for her education. 'I know that you don't want to risk anything happening to get you in trouble. You're both young. I've seen folks your age make a small mistake, too much to drink, a temper that flares and then we come into the situation where you have a problem. Is there anything you want to tell me?' I said there was no problem and then I cried."

"*Mi alma,* I'm sorry," Alex said.

"I told her, my Alex is the gentlest, kindest man in the world. He is the best father. I didn't say how he danced, and how we love each other."

Alex blushed. "Thank you, *amor.* Anything else?"

"She gave me her card and said to get in touch if we needed help. She said she wouldn't file any papers and if the court got in touch, she would come forward for us."

THIRTEEN

Once she started full time at the Redding hospital, Masha's shifts were so exhausting and heartbreaking that at first she didn't talk to nurses or staff. After she showered, scrubbed with disinfectant soap, and handed over the records to the day nurses, she headed in a daze toward the parking lot and started for home. Vaccination rates were the lowest in California inland counties that the regional hospitals served – Butte, Siskiyou, Lassen, Shasta, Tehama, Modoc and their own Trinity. Desperately sick people came in only when they were gasping with defiant breath that the virus didn't exist. Mercy Medical wasn't on the front line for new treatments and so many patients were dying of Covid, at first the elderly and immune compromised, and then young people barely in their thirties, dying without any family member beside them.

Masha also had patients who were sure they were sick because getting the vaccine was contagious; they themselves weren't vaxxed, they told her, because chips were embedded that would control their minds, but a cousin had gotten the shot and given them the virus from the vaccine. On another shift, Masha worked to save a young highway patrolman from Red Bluff who'd been convinced he'd be sterile if he vaxxed. "My wife will be too, if she gets it from me. My boss Jake reads everything."

"Trevor, dear, if you want to be a parent you have to live. You're strong so don't talk more and we'll let the oxygen do its work," Masha told the young man as she rubbed cream into his dry skin. He was going to be intubated if he agreed. "You want to live." She kept stroking his arm and he nodded. Slowly his eyes closed. Tears dampened his lashes. When he was out, she kissed the soft young eyelids, and then they wheeled him away. As she watched the gurney go, she thought he'd probably caught it from his boss.

Masha and Luisa Fuentes, the Filipina nurse with whom Masha began sharing long nights, were often the last touch the poor souls would have before the doctor noted the time of death and closed the curtain on their lives.

They began getting sodas and snacks from the vending machine and going together to rest in an airless storeroom off the ward where they collapsed onto two narrow cots.

One night Masha fell asleep but was awakened by Luisa's quiet sobbing. She pulled herself up from her cot and held the smaller woman in her arms as she cried.

"Tell me, dear, what is it?"

"If I die, my daughter won't have seen me for two years. My son won't even remember me. He's only five now."

"Where are they? I thought you lived in Redding."

"My husband and I live in Redding but my children are with my mother in Manila." In between sobs, Luisa told Masha about the separation from her family and Masha told her how she hadn't seen her mother or father since she'd left Ukraine.

"Luisa, you won't die, you'll be with your children."

"God willing, but if we get sick with this virus, no one can save us. Sometimes I am so afraid." Luisa hung her head over her hands and breathed deeply.

"We are careful, we've had one vaccination. This is harder than anything I've ever done," Masha replied.

"Before I leave, I sit in the chapel and pray for the souls we lost," said Luisa.

"I'll go with you. I want to pray for Trevor, he's so young."

"Some of the poor people are hard to pray for."

"But we have to." Masha linked arms with Luisa.

As they walked toward the chapel, Luisa said softly, "Did you hear the man in fourteen? He could hardly breathe but made sure I heard him say he wanted a white nurse. He didn't want brown skin to touch him. I called Darlene to make the call to intubate him but she was running from one room to another. Finally I got Frances."

"I try not to take some patient's words personally."

Almost as bad as hurtful words from patients were hints from their own staff, even the hospitalist—a retired GP brought back in the crisis. The man said 'illegal' and 'Russian' referring to Luisa and herself. Darlene, who had narrow little eyes and rough hands with patients, had whispered something about 'the black one.' Masha knew she should have said that Luisa wasn't black but a golden honey brown, much prettier than Darlene's pasty white.

"Some of the nurses get fake vax cards," Luisa said.

"I've heard that, but why would they do such a thing?"

"They don't want to be told what to do or their husbands forbid them from being vaxxed or they get it from the internet."

"That is really crazy. They can infect patients who have cancer or heart attacks," Masha said. "I think it's a crime we should report."

"If we reported them, they'd get onto us in some way and we'd be shorter staffed than we already are."

"That's the last thing we want. We need more help."

"We won't get more good nurses up here. Who wants to come?"

"I thank God for you, Luisa. Except for you there is no one I can talk to."

Before sleeping on their cots, Masha and Luisa hugged and made the sign of the cross over each other. By the time they'd had four hours sleep but before their next shifts, they sat again in the small chapel and prayed silently. Masha realized how easy praying came to her and how she missed going to Resurrection Chapel where she and Alex were married, but now, to get to Mass on Sundays, she would have to drive back to Redding. When she had two days rest, she didn't want to budge from bed, the garden, her kitchen, her bed that maybe Alex would share with her before he drove to work. In her day of rest, she always made her call to her mother to reassure her they were in no danger and to hear Nadya's reassurance that things were 'normal.'

FOURTEEN

Luisa Fuentes revealed late one night that her husband Jorge had been a doctor.

Masha, half fallen asleep, turned on a light in their storeroom-rest space.

"I'd rather it be dark," Luisa said.

"Your husband was a doctor?" Masha turned off the light.

"A dermatologist. He did his residency at Hopkins. He could have done facelifts for the elite but that wasn't Jorge's way. He chose to return home to work in a clinic in one of the poorest parts of Manila, a slum where he saw every kind of skin disease. He got in trouble for treating people who don't share the president's politics. I was working with him by then and we were in love but I suspected he was taking drugs."

"What did you do?"

"I tried protecting him, especially when we were having our first child."

"Sounds scary. Alex has always been protecting me."

"You're fortunate. With this president, they were shooting addicts. We never knew if gunmen would come storming in, shooting. Jorge insisted I take a job at a hospital to be away from the clinic."

"He wanted you safe."

"He'd been medicating himself to stay awake. Then he'd have headaches and take something for them. He hid it from me at first but as he needed more, I found out. Even though he was a doctor and not a street person he'd be in bad trouble."

"How did you stand it?"

"Work, child…two children by then, love, faith, fear."

"Did he try to quit?"

"He did. He went into anonymous drug programs but they find you when you're not a government sympathizer. They find you. One place gave away their list. They probably had no choice with a gun pointed at them. That's when we left."

"How long have you been here?"

"Almost three years. I haven't had any problems because they need nurses. Jorge slips through the cracks practicing in clinics but ICE is going to catch up. He's a strong man but the drugs, you almost can't beat them. They beat you. Your own secret police."

"Meth and speed, they're bad, heroin…all of them you just crave more and more. I really hate those drugs." Masha was thinking of her brother, how her mother's evasions when she asked about Maksym had to be more than fear of listeners.

Luisa shook with tears and Masha stepped over to her cot in the dark to squeeze herself down beside her friend.

"You can cry, no worries."

"I feel so helpless. I love him, he's a fine man and a wonderful doctor. We have two beautiful kids we have to get over here somehow."

"How did you come here to Redding?"

"I googled jobs in the Emirates—many Filipinos go there as nurses but you hear some bad stories. We have cousins in Oakland so we decided on California where they need health care workers. When we arrived, we stayed with family. Jorge went through a supervised detox that was anonymous. When we wanted to find our own place, we couldn't afford to rent in the East Bay so we came up here where it's cheaper."

"We couldn't afford the Bay Area either. Alex lived first with family, too. Then his mother arrived. She's a sweet woman but we had no room for ourselves."

"Jorge's motivated to stay clean but he needs regular work, to see patients consistently to help them. I suffer everything with him. He's the love of my life."

"Alex is the love of my life and he's such a hard worker and good father. He's a better parent than I am."

"You're the mother, you love your children."

"Of course, but he has more feeling for them, more natural feeling. It's his nature to be loving. I've always wanted to do better. Sometimes I wonder if he's happy with me. Maybe he'd prefer a gentler woman like you."

"You're just tired or you wouldn't say that. I hope we all can meet one day."

Masha felt something reverberate in her, like a bell no one else could hear. "Thank you, Luisa, maybe so. We are the same age, Alex and me. Actually, I'm months older but he looks younger and girls turn eyes at him. I look middle-aged."

"Masha, you don't, you are beautiful. Your hair is like a golden chain."

"I need to get hi-lights but there's no time and Alex always says better to save. Look." Masha pulled up the top of her scrubs. "Baby fat. I never lost baby fat since Tomas."

Masha squeezed the small roll around her waist. "You're much trimmer."

"I have more worries. You are just right as you are."

"I am a person who worries. My life has always been worry. Before I had Adrianna and Tomas, I worried about radiation I'd been exposed to. Maybe my children will have mutated cells. I lit candles to our Virgin Mother. She answered my prayers. My children are perfect so now I worry about Alex, that he doesn't love me so much."

As close as they became at work, Masha never accepted Luisa's repeated invitations to sleep at her home when they finished a shift together.

"I'll go home for the night, thank you."

"We're back for morning shift and you wouldn't have to drive."

"It's not bad, but thank you. I will another time."

"Masha, are you worried that you might come into my house and find my husband high or maybe he's OD'd if he's found the wrong stuff? It won't happen. He will be normal and charming. No worries."

Masha laughed. "Of course not, and thank you."

"Remember it's an open invitation. I'm grateful to have you as a friend."

Masha crossed herself. "Thank you, Luisa. I'm sorry you've problems."

"Don't feel pity for me, Masha, that's all I ask. I cannot stand pity from a friend."

"Of course, no pity, I feel the same," Masha replied.

When Masha had made supper for Alex and Tomas, she left them watching soccer on the Spanish station and went to bed. The sound from the living room was muted but she couldn't fall asleep. The quiet brought back all the suffering of the day, the wave after wave of patients the ambulances were bringing on stretchers into the sick bay. But not only the virus was killing people she nursed, some were crushed in car crashes, or OD'd on something they smoked that was laced with the Fentanyl, or had hideous gut wounds from guns. In the midst of Covid, she tended women whose husbands beat them. She was lucky, she knew, to be loved and safe but she wondered about human beings, if they could continue in such a way, building those reactors that exploded and spread poison, ignoring the news about the oceans full of oil and plastic in mother's breast milk. And what about the people, the countries, waging war against neighbors who had shared their lives until they became enemies? She covered her ears with her pillow and waited for Alex to come to bed and make her forget all else. Her last thoughts were for Trevor, the highway patrolman. Tomorrow would be critical for Trevor. If he made it through the night, his own immune system would begin to kick in and fight. There was so much unknown about the virus that prayer had to help.

FIFTEEN

Loony Gus showed up at the del Calvos on a Saturday when Alex and Tomas were in Redding for supplies. Masha walked out the door to see what was disturbing Daisy, a large tawny female mix Alex had brought home from the shelter. They were keeping Daisy chained until she got used to staying on the property and Alex finished the fence, though the big friendly dog didn't seem inclined to wander from her new family. She barked loudly at the few cars passing on East Staunton. She also barked at squirrels, quail, raccoons and the occasional feral cat—false alarms that sent someone to the window or door. She was barely more than a big puppy with huge paws she offered so even Masha wasn't afraid of her. Even her ears seemed uncertain whether to stand up or flop over. The shelter people told Alex she was a shepherd lab mix. "Can't understand why people dumped such a sweetie on the road. Frankly, Mr. del Calvo, I like dogs more than the people around here."

"She's big, that's what we're supposed to have." Alex took the dog's leash, paid the fee to adopt and Daisy leaped into the back of the truck without hesitation.

Now when Gus whistled, Daisy's growl stopped and she leaped off the porch and ran toward him until her chain stopped her. By the time Masha pulled the dog back, she was licking the stranger's hand.

"Gustav Greenberg, aka Gustavo, and you may have heard they call me Loony Gus, a sobriquet of their choosing."

He extended the fingers wet from the dog's mouth. Masha

declined the handshake and motioned him to come onto the porch and sit while she stood.

"Sobriquet?" Masha asked.

"Nickname, answer to it or get a fist."

"Glad to meet you, Gustavo. Will you have a drink or water?"

"If you insist, I accept with pleasure, kind lady."

When she returned with a glass, Masha saw his thin body and even his nose couldn't stay still.

"What a blond *shiksa* you are!" Gus said.

"No way to talk, Gustavo," Masha said.

Gus slapped his hand over his mouth, and then said hello in Russian followed by Spanish, which made Daisy prick up her soft ears.

"How do you know Russian and Spanish?"

"Wandering Jew," answered Gus. "Some Leviathan you got there."

Again he said words in Spanish and Daisy cocked her head. Had Daisy come from a Spanish-speaking household, Masha wondered. They could try some words Alex would speak to her.

Gustavo walked close to Alex' dragon, and without turning back to her, launched into a description of deep sea creatures, Ahab's white whale, mythical beasts, a giant squid as large as a ship, so much fantastic life of the deep that Masha couldn't keep up.

"What can I do for you, Gustavo?" she asked when he seemed to have finished his bestiary. "You do have a wonderful way with words."

"Came by to visit. You folks are outsiders like myself, exotic plants."

"I take that as compliment rather than insult, Gustavo. Another time we can talk, but I'm ready for work. My husband and son will be back soon if you can wait."

"You don't have spare change in the meantime, for a good cause, funds for the general good." Gus began an even more twitchy movement with his torso and legs.

"Gustavo, forgive me, but do you take drugs?" Masha leaned forward as she would to any patient to look more closely at his skin beneath the dirt. A rancid smell came from his clothes and she could see his pupils were too large, too glittery. She stepped back again.

"It's a long story. Right now my organization has immediate needs." He brushed away what seemed like cobwebs before him. "Oops, I mean organism." He laughed, his mouth a jack o' lantern of jagged teeth, black spaces between.

"I can't give you money for drugs. I can make you a sandwich if you're hungry but I can't give you money."

"Your husband swore to the brotherhood, one for all etcetera."

"He didn't swear to give money for drugs."

"They get you in for life, Beauty."

"I warned him but he's got the gun now. I'm more worried about having a gun in the house than I am about the kids who stole a few things. I don't like guns."

"I concur. You live by your brains if you are able. These idiots, they blew it all when they had it." Gustavo shifted from one leg to the other. He rubbed his hands over his cheeks, then, as if performing some ritual, he opened his palms and made a circle over his face.

Masha squinted at him. "Did they buy things with the money?"

"Sure but they also listened to a shark who told them to invest in stocks."

"Stocks in what?" she asked.

"Big market in machinery to clean the weed."

"To tell you the truth, Gustavo, I thought hippies would be here, nice people who couldn't afford to live anywhere else, peaceful, with kids. I don't care for marijuana myself but it's nothing like the danger of other drugs."

Gus laughed. "Go down to the Haight and watch the hippies licking up drugs on the pavement. They've fallen into the same shit hole I'm in."

"Gustavo, have you tried getting clean? You can do better with your brains. You're like an encyclopedia. I can open any page."

"A-Z but I'm an addict, honey, you know, a squeaker, a tweaker, a shit load of sneaker. I can pay you in some powerful weed. Won't form a habit, just give a good trip."

"Is it meth, Gus? That is bad, the worst up here." At Mercy, Masha would treat their sores with antibiotics and then release the skeletal men and women knowing they'd either be back sicker or they'd be dead.

When Gus didn't answer, she asked, "Where do you live?"

"Nooks and crannies. I manage as long as I don't go far away."

"I know how to get you in touch with rehab in Redding.

They send good people there. The state pays for it, no charge to you."

"Too late, my pretty, too late. And Goldilocks, this may not be paradise for you any more than it is for me."

"What do you mean, Gustavo."

"I see beneath the pretty smile, I see your real feelings. Your aura is clouded, you have worries. You are not a quiet soul. Your needs are not being met."

"That's true, Gustavo. Right now, I have to work. Come again, we'll talk some more and I'll get you to eat something."

Gus made another unannounced visit during the week. Masha, home alone again trying to catch up on sleep, didn't hear him nor Daisy right away. She'd stayed after her shift to check in on Trevor; he wasn't going to be removed from intubation any time soon because one lung had collapsed but he was fighting the virus.

"Who's there?" she called, tightening her bathrobe around her waist.

"Madonna, a messenger to announce an annunciation. Are you ready?"

Daisy, who seemed to like Gus' redolent body smells, was already licking residue of food or dirt from his hands and arms.

"You light up the sky." He bowed, then looked into her eyes with such yearning that she had to resist bringing him inside for a bath. She wasn't worried being alone with him but she didn't want indoor exposure to Covid and anything else he might have.

"I'll make you eggs, bacon, some bread with honey?"

"Eggs, beauty, but G-D forbids the *treff*, the bacon, and I live in fear of the great hand coming to smite this poor soul."

"OK, butter and toast, milk and sugar in coffee?" Again he nodded. "I'll be right out. Just sit, Gustavo. Daisy likes you."

"I wouldn't be alive if dogs didn't like me. I talk to them and they understand I am a friend and that I was one of them in a former life. I also confide in mountain lions but snakes, *sh'lange* in the old tongue, don't get along. I'm working on that."

As she walked out on the porch with her hands balancing the plate and the coffee, Gus reached around the tray and touched her breasts.

She almost dropped the food. "Gus, back off, get far enough away or I'll close the door on you."

"Goddess, I just wanted one touch of the softest flesh that G-D created on earth."

"Sit there." She motioned a chair several feet away and put down the tray. She wasn't particularly shocked. She had male patients who wanted to nurse from her breasts and called her Mother. She considered it sad but not unnatural if they were frightened and wanted life's most immediate comfort.

She herself had been bottle fed because of radioactivity and wondered if she always yearned for a closeness with her mother they hadn't had in the chaos that followed the explosion.

She poured coffee, milk, sugared it, handed Gus the plate with eggs and toast.

He took a sip of the coffee, raised his fork to the eggs, put it down.

"Gus, eat, please you must eat. You are so thin."

"You have seen pictures of my people against the wires in their striped suits of the camps? That was thin. I am tuned to perfection by the outdoors."

"Gus, what do you live on?"

He scratched his head as if were trying to remember an elaborate menu.

"Dumpsters mostly but this county is terrible, the worst I've ever had to endure. The food these folks throw away most dogs wouldn't eat unless famished, and as I said before, I am half dog myself."

"Gustavo, I'll drive you to the hospital where I work. I'll make sure to look after you. You have reason to live and you might have natural immunity."

He shook his head.

"Gus, why do you waste this precious life?"

"Your concern is appreciated, sweetheart, but it's misplaced." He rubbed his head again. "All in here, the train wreck."

Gus went on a verbal rollercoaster through the beginnings of language, color returning to his pallid face and thin aquiline nose as he looked up at the sky and recited what sounded like a song to Masha.

As a girl where I was a Flower of the mountain yes when I put the rose in my hair like the Andalusian girls used or shall I wear a red yes and how he kissed me under the Moorish wall and I thought well as well him as another and then I asked him with my eyes to ask again yes and then he asked me would I yes to say yes my mountain flower and first I put my arms around him yes and drew him down to me so he could feel my breasts all perfume yes and his heart was going like mad and yes I said yes I will Yes.

"I don't understand some of the words but I can see the woman and the flowers "

"All one sentence, Beauty, the greatest seduction James Joyce has to offer and now I shall take my leave."

"Gustavo please, eat a little more. Get it all down."

Gus pushed his fork against the congealing eggs, stabbed a few curds and brought them to his mouth as obediently as a child.

"Did you hear about the lobster extravaganza here? Had them flown in, claws red as blood. Badasses with bibs. Made me sick laughing for days."

"All money from marijuana? Did they put any in the bank?"

"Canisters, Beauty, they buried cash in canisters."

SIXTEEN

"Sis, you won't believe what this yard was like." Tomas led his sister and grandmother around the house to where the sunflowers reached nearly ten feet tall and corn grew only a little lower, with beans wound around and lush leaves of squash in the shade. He sounded so proud that Alex couldn't stop smiling.

"It was all stones and shit, sorry *Abuela*, but it was so bad. Mom and I read about how Indians planted with corn and beans and squash growing together so we tried it."

Tomas broke off bright zucchini. "They're happy here."

They walked on a paving path to the door where a climbing rose was starting to show its pale colors. "Too bad the azalea are just about over. They're part of the rhododendron family, but by July, they're gone."

"My goodness, what you know, bro." His sister slapped hands. "Full of surprises."

At the door, Masha greeted them with frosty glasses of iced tea.

"Come in, come in. It's a long drive."

Inside they marveled at the large windows that let in so much sunlight and the wood beams Alex had scraped, sanded and stained.

"A very long drive. It took us nearly five hours without stopping," Adri said.

"Worth it to see you. And you, *Nuera*, so healthy here, so *linda*, like your flowers," Ana Jesus hugged her daughter-in-law.

Alex asked if after they drank something cool and rested a bit, they'd like to go for a drive into the forest to see the river and reservoir that had become Trinity Lake.

"*Abuela* would probably like a break from cars. I'll come," Adrianna answered.

"Come sit by me." Masha said to her mother-in-law. "I want to hear how you're feeling. Your hair is shiny and thick." Masha touched the bun on Ana Jesus' neck. "Would you like anything to eat?"

"No, water is fresh. I'll rest."

Alex took his daughter on a tour of town with its boarded-up main street, and then beyond so she could see Mt. Shasta, the encircling forests. He drove along the Trinity River that crashed over rocks in the winter and now flowed hushed into Trinity Lake.

"We had a big storm or two but we needed more steady rain."

Adrianna shuddered. "It's all changing, *Papi.*"

"You still aiming to be a doctor?" he asked.

"Of course, even more. I shadow Dr. Shira Cogan at the clinic where we brought *abuela* when she first came. Remember that woman who took care of her?"

"The short little doctor with the earrings who was so good to *Mami*?"

"Dr. Shira has followed up with *abuela*. She called several times and now that I volunteer at the clinic for pre-nursing experience, I keep her up to date. Dr. Shira saw to getting

Ana Jesus glasses and vitamins. She's had immunizations for free."

"We can pay. We don't have to be charity."

"I leave donations every time."

"That's good. You know your mother didn't believe the woman would be a good doctor but I liked her. I'm glad you're volunteering there. It's a place with heart."

"Exactly, *Papi*. Dr. Shira is a Ph.D. psychologist as well as a medical doctor, but establishing all the credentials here takes time so she's working nights at Sutter and the clinic before she can start a therapy practice. I like her a lot and she teaches me about medicine, and more."

"You're a quick girl to learn, like your mother." He saw his daughter's expression—I'm not at all like my mother—and ignored it. "I didn't know *Mami* needed glasses." Alex thought of all he didn't know about his mother.

"I noticed she was holding her embroidery up to her nose. At the clinic, she stood in a hallway—it's all basic there—and she could see OK at a distance but when she held anything near, it became fuzzy. We laughed about it and Dr. Shira ordered glasses. *Abuela* says she never saw so well."

"I'll pay for these services," he said.

"You don't have to. I cover it, everything's good."

"I'm proud you're following in your mother's footsteps, helping people. It's why we're in America, so you do better than we did. Are you still waitressing at La Fiesta, *hija?*"

"Not waitressing. I've been promoted to a hostess with a raise."

"You're not working too much? Do you have time for a young person's life?"

"Every time you ask that, I tell you the same thing. I love my pre-nursing classes and our quiet life, *abuela's* and mine. Our lives are full and they're extra peaceful now that Tomas has been with you."

"You've seen he's good."

"It's amazing."

"But you, you don't want a *novio*?" Alex felt his cheeks grow hot. "Girls read books with stories about love and…"

He felt his daughter's cool hand on his cheek. "Oh *Papi*, you make me blush, too. I read medical journals and chemistry and anatomy texts. I'm going to accomplish my goals, and boys my age, well, they're without drive. At La Fiesta, I have to get dressed up, Mexican girl clothes, and they act like A-holes, sorry for the language. They're noisy and rude and they feel privileged to say anything they want to me. I ignore them."

Alex nodded. "You have time. Masha and I were a different generation. We didn't really have childhoods or choices as you do. More than that. We had strong feelings and we had only each other, until we had you two."

"I was waiting to bring this up, *Papi*, but now's as good a time as any. I know you'd like us closer, but for now, we can't live here, *abuela*, me. I couldn't study or work and she's making friends in the neighborhood. She's got a small sewing business going. She babysits, too. She likes to earn."

"I'm not surprised. It's not ideal for you here but there will always be room. I want to see you more."

"It's a long drive."

"It is. I wish it weren't so far. Would you like to go sit by the lake?"

They looked out at the unbroken still water of Trinity Lake edged by deep green.

"It's lovely and we'll come again but today we have to drive back."

"Not all that way," Alex protested.

"You do it at night, remember?"

"OK, we'll start back but I don't like the night driving."

"I know, I don't either. What's that, an airstrip out here?" Adrianna pointed to a flat black-topped strip cut into a clearing.

"For the cannabis growers to fly in and out. They're not using it much now."

"But cannabis is legal, didn't growers want that?"

"You'd think so but it's complicated. Corporations, maybe the cartels, may they burn in hell, have taken over is what I hear. When it was only legal for medical use, growers made plenty but now the prices have dropped. They blame it on government."

"Along with everything else. I hope Tommy's not involved in anything?"

Alex shook his head. "No, thank god."

"He does seem to know about plants." Adrianna covered her father's tendony hand with hers. "I'm glad we got off together and had a chance to talk."

"You're so grown up. Happens so fast, just babies and now look at you both."

As they waited at home, Ana Jesus was working bright threads to repair a torn blouse for neighbors in Santa Rosa, embroidering a pansy over a tear too large to sew together, and Masha, after finishing preparations for supper, sat in the chair beside her, sewing project in hand. Masha could hardly believe Ana Jesus was the same woman she'd cared for only six months back, the old woman in such fragile health that Masha feared she wouldn't survive the virus if she caught it. Even then, there was a fierceness in her small body, a fierceness that must have scared off any number of threats and kept her going through what she endured. Masha wondered if there had been other men in her life since she'd lost her husband when she was so young.

"Pretty stitch you are making," she said.

"Yours also." Ana Jesus looked over to see the cross stitch on curtain hems.

"My mother taught me and I still remember," Masha said. "It's not like yours which is artistry. Like your son. He makes art of whatever he finds."

"My Eloy, also," Ana Jesus said.

"Eloy?"

When Ana Jesus didn't answer, Masha felt she had to fill in conversation. "Alex told me names of your two younger sons. Eloy and…"

"Gilberto, living in Costa Rica with his brother, safe places, thanks to God."

"One day Tomas will meet uncles Eloy and Gilberto. Maybe your two sons will come here. We can take a vacation…one day anyway."

Ana Jesus sighed. "*Espero que si*. I hope. You have a brother, *un hermano?*"

"Yes. My mother says he's very good with computers."

"Your mother, is she well? What is she called?" Ana Jesus asked.

"Her name is Nadya, Nadya Sergeiyevna. In Russian and Ukrainian we use our father's name after our Christian name. Her father is also named Sergiey. It's a popular name. My father is not in good health and I don't think my brother is either."

"I am sorry."

"Thank you. I miss them and I am worried about them."

Masha didn't say she worried about nearly everything that was happening in Ukraine and Crimea; her mother never said anything specific because international calls were tapped, but beyond being secretive, Masha suspected her mother avoided talking about her brother. She knew he had computer skills but did he use them legally or was he a hacker or a troll where crime was the only way to make money?

"I missed Alejandro, my oldest, my first born. Everyday I missed him but when he sent photographs of you and the children, I knew his life had been saved for good."

"My mother says the same. She had to give me up to save me."

"I'm sorry. My heart goes to her."

"Thank you. I understand Adrianna is helping you with immigration papers?"

"She is such a smart girl with a good heart. She finds kind people who help me."

"She loves you," Masha said, while feeling hurt that her daughter and her grandmother had an ease with each other that made her feel left out. Adrianna never had been as affectionate with her as she was with Ana Jesus.

When Alex and Adrianna returned, their daughter said they wouldn't be able to stay for supper.

"But I have fixed borscht, beets from our garden. I thought Ana Jesus would like to try Ukrainian cooking."

Ana Jesus said, "We should stay."

When they had finished the borscht, bread, a salad of their own tomatoes and pickled zucchini, Adrianna helped her grandmother up to leave.

Masha took hold of her mother-in-law's arm.

"You must come to sit before you leave. It's a Russian custom that before anyone leaves we sit together."

"Mom, we're in a hurry and you don't like the Russians."

"Not too much of a hurry to sit. It's our custom also. Come, Ana Jesus, for a safe journey and to come back soon, please sit beside me and hold my hand."

On the couch facing forward as if already on the journey, Masha reached out for Ana Jesus' hand. Adrianne quickly took her grandmother's other side.

Masha asked Alex how his mother could have sent him on the dangerous journey by himself.

"Neither of our families had choices."

"I had a sponsor, a living place. I didn't like the Svetlovs but I wasn't on my own like you were. Until I met you, I was an obedient girl." Masha gave Alex a wink.

"I led you off the narrow path."

"She said your brothers were doing well. Show me that picture again of all of you."

Alex, the tall boy in the middle, looked proud of his gold and red *futbol* team shirt, while the two smaller boys flanked him, holding hands. The man standing behind them was wearing a suit, tie and a beret.

"He looks French, so debonair," Masha said. "And look at your mother in the flowered dress. She was so pretty. How sad to lose your father."

"My brothers didn't really know our father and what a good man he was, so respected as a teacher. But at least they didn't see him dragged off."

"One of your brothers is a photographer?" Masha said.

"Gilberto saw a camera and he discovered his vocation. Since he turned sixteen, he's been making a living going to the rain forest as a guide with foreign people. Our baby Eloy is in school. Maybe he'll be our first graduate."

"You could have been the first," she said.

"Adri will graduate for me. Your mother didn't send Maksym out of Ukraine to follow you. My mother gave up all her boys to make them safe."

"I don't think my mother wanted Maksym to go. She preferred him." Masha dried her apron and took a sip of wine. "Let's finish this bottle and I'll clean up."

"Masha, you've cleaned up enough. The borscht was wonderful. Everything was." Alex poured the last of the red into her glass.

"It's hard for me to accept our daughter working around men who harass her," he said.

"She didn't tell me anything but she knows how to take care of herself." Masha sipped her wine. "When I tried to buy her nice dresses, she said, 'I'll go to Goodwill, don't spend money on me.' But I wanted to. She's my daughter." Masha hugged herself. "I wish we were closer. She will go much higher than we have."

"That's what we talked about today. She wants to be a doctor."

"I don't think she'll move up here with us. It's not for her," Masha said.

"We may not stay forever, either. For now, we have each other and Tommy."

Masha, up early while Alex still slept, brought her phone outdoors. When her mother appeared on the screen, Masha pointed at the sunflowers where pollen shimmered with the dew. "I planted for you," Masha said.

"They are planting *soniashnyk* to clean the village from radiation in soil. One day, maybe we go back," Nadya replied.

Masha thought of what her mother still called the 'village,' a cluster of five-story apartment buildings hollowed out by abandonment. In the square, Stalin was still pointing his finger in blame while ghostly shadows of creatures crawled around the statue's feet.

SEVENTEEN

At first they loved the autumn dry heat under a sun so bright and hot that Masha had to shade the ripening tomatoes from scorching. A second planting of flat beans almost popped out of their pods under cloudless blue skies. Then the winds picked up and turned the skies smoky from fires breaking out in the dry forests in Trinity and Shasta counties. The white-capped cone of their snow queen was reduced to a grey shadow within grey. Alex and Masha searched their phone apps to find out where the fires were moving. They saw the glow from the north at night and understood from three years of fires in Santa Rosa that the blazes weren't far.

Masha's shift didn't begin until noon but she was staying in bed as long as she could. Alex left coffee in a thermos. He was in Redding to buy new hoses in case they needed extras. They felt haunted by the fires they'd escaped in Santa Rosa that had come so close. Neighbors helped neighbors leave in the middle of the night and brought food to share at the evacuation center. The best chefs prepared special meals for them in the Fairgrounds Center. Everyone became closer, listening as the Santa Rosa radio station stayed broadcasting while flames crackled around it. Whole blocks less than a half mile away went up in flames. They returned home with smoke and fear.

When she heard the rumbling of a truck over gravel in their driveway, Masha peeked out the window, suspicious that someone had seen Alex leave and come with harmful intentions. She heard the gate open, Daisy bark, and then silence.

She saw Ray, a thermos and two cups in a cardboard container. She heard a knock on the door. Ray must have expected Alex to be home. She never saw him without Alex and though he was the exception to the hostility they faced, she didn't know what to say.

She wrapped her robe tightly, gave her hair a brush and went to the door.

"Hey Ray, how are you?"

Stepping back a few paces, Ray seemed surprised to see her. "Just lookin' for the old man. Sorry if I got you up."

"No, it's good, Ray. I needed to get up." She fanned herself. "It's getting hot already and the air is terrible. Let's sit down." She sat on the step before the open door. "My legs feel like lead and I…I'm having a hard time, Ray. Alex and I can't forget the fires we went through before we moved here. We were all traumatized by them."

Ray coughed. "I get it. Smoke doesn't do these breathers any good."

"Alex told me your lungs give you trouble. You go to a V.A.?"

Ray shook his head.

"They'll finish off the job they started."

"What do you mean?"

"They'll kill me to shut me up."

"Ray? The V.A., the hospitals for vets?"

"Shit yes, get rid of the witnesses. They burned such shit where we breathed it every day, piles of it. Poisoned us and then denied it, which is the lying bullshit you expect. Like Agent Orange didn't make cancer. Only one reason I hate government."

Masha looked away. They sat in a silence neither tried to fill.

"I gotta go. Just thought of checking in."

"Alex maybe told you I get depressed sometimes. I like company. Glad you stopped by."

"Never said a word about it." Ray looked down. "I get real down sometimes."

"I'll be right back. Don't leave, please. I'll get dressed fast. Drink your coffee."

"I brought two cups," he said.

She ran inside, pulled on underwear and jeans, bra and shirt, braided her hair and pinned it up. She could shower at work when she changed into her scrubs.

The toaster bell went off and she brought a tray with jam and butter.

"Thanks Mrs. del Calvo." Ray sipped his coffee and chewed the toast.

"Masha, please. Can I ask you, Ray, how you manage when you feel down? Do you have meds?" Masha asked.

"I've had too many fucking pills to fuck around with more. I used to get high."

She nodded.

"Used to be when it was bad after Iraq, I shot up. I don't do it no more, only weed, occasional little party with some coke but I'm careful not to indulge too much. I go shoot my gun off up in the woods."

"I work in a hospital, Ray. I do know about drugs. Your friend Gustavo was here not long ago. He's quite a character."

"Yeah, Loony, he's too far gone. My wife takes Oxy for her back. My buddies die, I come home from fucking Iraq with no more than a cough and she's got a back that's killing her. Susan got me clean."

"You did it yourselves?"

"It wasn't that bad. Being high never did much for me." Ray stared at the paper coffee cup still half-full. "Haven't talked about this with your old man. We've chewed the fat about everything else. You don't need to say nothing."

"Of course. I've wondered how you deal with some of the folks around here?"

He laughed. "Dumb as fence posts. No one messes with me. You two, be careful what you say, who you're talking to. Words are like fire, trouble starts with a spark."

Masha nodded. "Susan? Tell me about Susan. She sounds like a strong woman."

"Got a big heart. Used to take in ladies when their old men knocked them around, but then we'd have trouble and the skirts would go back to the beaters anyway."

"It's awful. We send these women back to get beaten up or worse."

"No worry about Alex, sweetheart. No worry."

"Why do you say that?" she asked. "He's never laid a hand."

"I didn't mean that. I just have a feeling you worry about him."

"You're intuitive, Ray. Alex is my worry. It's been hard

up here, not with Alex, but the rest, the folks and what they believe. We're really different. I do get down. What do you think about the fires?"

"Bad. Winds are high, everything's tinder."

"I know. What are we going to do?"

"Fight it, lose a lot of trees, people's houses. It's bad. You know, sometimes if I am ready to pop my lid, I roll a fat joint and go sit under my tree."

"A special tree?"

"Just a tree, a big oak. I like being there. I mellow out. There might not be time now."

"I know and I have to get to work."

"Sorry," he said.

"Oh Ray, don't be sorry, I'm so glad we talked." Masha decided she'd dare a hug and she came in quickly and pulled back. She'd never seen him look bewildered.

"I wish I had a tree," she said. "I haven't figured out how to shut up my brain. Worry about my kids, about Alex, can't turn it off."

"I got two sons. One is fucked and I don't think he'll ever be right, but Reno, the youngster, he's getting out of Lompoc soon and I got good feelings about him. He's not about to make dumbass mistakes again. Your boy, he's at a risky age."

"I know but we think he's been making a real turnaround here."

"I'm keeping my eye on him. You go on now, Masha. Thanks."

"Thanks to you, Ray. I feel better, really do."

EIGHTEEN

Two days later, the county schools closed because of the smoke. The blaze in Trinity forest would become unstoppable if it joined with the thousand-acre conflagration northeast in Lassen National Park.

They kept the news on the TV most of the night. Tomas begged his father and Ray to go with them on a volunteer brigade battling the Trinity Complex fire. "*Papi*, I gotta go with you guys. No one will be in school and I don't want to be with the girls."

"It's good to be with girls," Masha said.

"Mom!" he answered in disgust.

"We'll take care of him, I promise," Alex said. "It will be a long weekend."

"My shift starts tonight so I won't be here. Who feeds Daisy?"

"We can get that covered. Bort's kids will come over," Alex said.

"Those kids are not reliable. Our house will be empty for anyone to come steal and you are going into danger."

"Offer the kids a little money. We're only back-up to support the professionals. I promise, we'll be safe. Ray is an old hand."

"You told me his lungs were bad."

"I know, I brought that up but he said…you can imagine how well he takes to being made to feel weak."

As Ray, Alex and Tomas drove east toward Redding, the blackened sky and a flaming red blotted out the mountains. "Like a black dragon swallowed them." Tomas, crammed into the jump seat, pointed north. "Or like a volcano, like Jurassic Park."

"Good imagination, kid." Ray coughed and gunned his truck to keep a BMW from getting into the middle passing lane ahead of them. The shiny black sedan, like a racehorse on the outside rail, cut ahead. Ray gave the driver the middle finger. 'Let's go Brandon!" he yelled as the car with a Biden sticker on the bumper sped away. "You smell their socialist shit a mile away."

Alex felt embarrassed by Ray's politics in front of Tomas—if you could even call knee jerk reactions politics. The man wasn't stupid, so why did he support crazy notions like the stolen election and conspiracies of every kind? Only one time as they were working on Ray's bench, Alex tried introducing facts of the election, the electoral college, to which Ray spat on the ground.

"You're still sucking tit on fake news." They'd dropped the subject and Alex pulled his mask down.

They picked up vouchers for the Star Motel and the next door Mexican restaurant. The single bedroom was small, one double, one single bed crammed together. On their beds lay instructions where to join Cal Fire in the morning.

Alex and Tomas didn't get many hours sleep the first night, not so much because they crowded each other's space but because the nasty sound of Ray's coughing kept them awake. Alex knew Ray shouldn't be where smoke would make his lungs worse.

In the middle of the night, Alex stepped outside into the smoky gloom. From the porch of the motel he could see the steady line of headlights of cars moving in slow motion south on Highway 5.

By the time they were back at the Star Motel after twelve hours digging trenches and cutting undergrowth in scorching heat, they all drank beers as if the brews were water and Alex didn't say a word to his underage son. If Tomas was old enough to be on the lines, he could drink with them. Memories of the hours when day seemed as dark as night, when everywhere they looked they were seeing a negative on burning film, made for more sleepless hours with the smells, the burn in their noses, eyes, lungs that coughed up brown sludge and a thirst nothing quenched. They'd watched helplessly as an old van trying to make its escape ahead of flames caught an ember near the gas tank and blew up. They heard the boom, the screaming from the couple trapped inside. In minutes, the heat had bent and reduced metal to puddles of grotesque shapes Alex couldn't have made if he'd tried. Later in the day as they were driving back to the motel, the charred remains still smoldered and medical crews were taking DNA to identify the dead.

While her husband and son were only a dozen or so miles away, Masha saw patients with smoke inhalation and burns at Mercy and kept phoning Alex for updates. The hospital was far enough east of Highway 5 to be safe for the moment but they were evacuating the most critical patients to Ukiah and Santa Rosa just in case the Lassen fire burned southwest and the two fires joined.

"Like *Chernobyl*, feels the end of the world," she said to Alex who didn't like the quavering sound of her voice.

"Try not to think of that. Have you heard anything from *Mami* and Adri?"

"They are OK, they are safe. But the smoke is bad there too."

Alex hacked and Masha peered into her phone to see him more clearly."

"You are not sick, love?" she asked.

"I'll be fine. Ray knows a guy, Carl, he got burned and they brought him in. We last saw him being taken off in a stretcher in Weaverville."

"I'll ask. His family name?"

Masha heard Ray's voice. "Callan, Carl Callan. Keep him safe."

"Oh Alex, I know this young man. He's not good," Masha said. "How is Tomas?"

Alex turned his back to Ray and spoke into the phone softly. "I'll tell you everything when we're home. Tomas is fine. Ray's not vaxxed and we're together so that's a worry but what can we do? Can you check on Carl?"

"Goes by Curly," Ray said and then collapsed in coughing. When he got his breath, he called out for Alex to tell Masha, "He's one of the inmates they let out from Lompoc where my boy is. He's low risk and he gets time off for fighting fire. I knew his old man. Curly's not a bad kid. Can she get me in to see him?"

Masha spoke loudly on the phone. "No one allowed in or out, Ray. That's rules."

"Fucking government rules," Ray shouted as Alex clicked off his phone. "This country is in the hands of shit commies and liberals. He'll be OK?"

"Ray, what are your sons' names?" Alex asked.

"Reno and Colonel. Reno, I told you he's in Lompoc for small stuff. He could have turned up here with Curly but he's just eighteen, otherwise he'd be here."

"How old are your kids? "Tomas asked.

"Reno, he'll turn eighteen inside right before he's out. He wasn't old enough to be charged as an adult and put in with the hard guys. Colonel, he's older, I think he's out in Wyoming. I haven't heard from him. He's twenty."

Just then the siren went off to alert the fire crews to get their food and be ready for transport back out on the line.

"America is fucked man. You can't get a burger without it being foreign."

Ray swore as he shoveled in a burrito.

"America is where I can have a family, my own home, it's what we're out here fighting for, Ray." Alex didn't want to argue but he had no patience right now.

His cell rang again. "Don't tell Ray," Masha said, "I just

looked in on Carl. He may not make it. Covid, burns, organ failure. They coded him once, brought him back. The young highwayman I told you about, he might make it but I don't know about Carl."

"Can you keep track of him for Ray?"

"I will pray. Please, Tomas, my baby. May I talk to him a minute?"

"We gotta go, Masha. Our boy is a strong young man. You can be proud. Everyone said, 'You have a future fire fighter here.'"

"No, no fighting of any kind."

"We're not on the front line." Alex saw no point in telling her this wasn't the complete truth, nor that Tomas was hanging with the group of young men who'd been let out of jail to fight the fire, like Ray's Curly.

Just as they were getting into Ray's truck, Alex answered his phone one more time. "Where are you going?" she asked.

"We're going to a place called City Junction on the Trinity River. Very bad burning there."

"I'm so worried," she said.

"I am more worried about Ray. He's coughing his lungs out. He said to me, 'If I don't make it, don't think I was just some dumb fuck.'"

"He's a good man. Please tell him Masha knows he's a good and intelligent man. He's my friend, too."

"Ray saved my life today." Alex stood outside the motel room to call Masha. He debated whether to tell her anything but since he was safe and had had his burns treated, he continued. "Pushed me out of the way of a falling tree, held on to me, fell on top of me to put out the fire on me. Then he stripped me and…"

"And what?" Masha's voice quavered. "You have burns?"

"Not serious."

"Did you get antibiotics?"

"Got those."

"You must get antibiotics."

"Masha, we already have. And pain meds. They're sending us home soon. Big equipment, bulldozers, lots of aircraft coming in. We'll be more in the way than useful."

"Thanks be to God. Tomas, can I speak to him?"

"He went to watch TV with some other young guys, so it's just me and Ray. I can tell you a happy story."

"Yes, please, a happy story. Then I'll tell you good and bad."

"We were sent up a narrow road in a pine forest, where we were going to stage from. Remember I told you we were heading to City Junction."

"Is there a city there?"

"No, there's almost nothing left of a mining camp, just cabins and vacation homes, and a Buddhist temple of some kind where we cut away bush before we went up a steep road. The pros were ahead, we were following them."

Alex did not say that flames were catching from embers everywhere in the dry brush. "Near the top of the road, we met a woman driving down the mountain with her son who waved and leaned out the window. We could see he was a simple fellow, like a big baby, round face, big smile. He had a red lollipop and didn't seem aware of danger. The woman must have just decided to leave and try to get west to the coast. 'God Bless,' she called out her window and continued down the mountain. She'd handed our crew her keys and told everyone to make themselves at home. There was a swimming pool she said to use. Can you imagine what that water looked like to us!"

"You were in the middle of fire with a Mongoloid boy and a swimming pool?"

"No, no, we just stopped to let her pass and saw the boy, well he really was a man. The fire captain said they'd been to her house more than once because the woman's son had a delicate heart and needed help. All that day, crews used water from her swimming pool. Saved her house."

"That's a good ending but I worry about you and Tomas and Ray."

"We'll be home soon, I promise. How's Ray's friend? The good and bad."

"Carl passed. No way to save him. But my poster boy Trevor, better. He's breathing on his own."

"I won't tell Ray. He's not in a good way, I mean he can't stop coughing and he won't let the docs see him except for his burns saving me."

"We evacuated some people. You can say his friend isn't here."

"For now, I just might. Cal Fire says we're gaining control

and winds have dropped. Like I said, bulldozers and air support coming tomorrow—the big guns. It's only been three days but it seems like forever since I saw you. Love you, *mi alma*."

"Love you more than everything. Get sleep, drink water and suck on lemons."

Alex slept some that night with a good feeling about Masha regaining her composure and strength when she had to be strong.

Early morning the motel lights went off and so did the AC. "Power's gone," Alex said to Ray who was coughing so hard that all he could do was put his hand up.

"I have a bad feeling about Carl. You don't hear nothing?"

"Not being vaxxed makes you vulnerable."

"It's about freedom, man, says right in the Constitution. Freedom." Ray wheezed.

"Have you lived where there's freedom for anyone to point a gun at your head?"

"Called Hell's Angels. Don't make me sorry for keeping you breathing."

"Makes me angry, Ray, that you're risking your life. The fires and…"

"You want to talk about angry!" Ray shouted then collapsed coughing.

"No, I don't, Ray, let's get some rest."

"Fuck government," were Ray's last words before he

turned his head to the wall to cough.

Alex thought of SSI that Ray must be receiving, and how he could get free healthcare from the V.A. if he'd go there. He supposed Ray's mind worked in such different ways, turning what was good about government like their citizenship papers, to upside down bad for Ray. Alex felt himself shaking his head in a silent conversation about how anyone could be so wrong-headed and stubborn that he'd refuse the free health care he needed. Did Ray's wife share the crazy conspiracy theories? He knew her name was Susan, and that she had health problems, but that was all. Ray never invited them to his place nor introduced them to Susan. They were never going to be two dining out, going-on-vacation couples. The thought of Ray in a leisure suit sitting at a restaurant with a white tablecloth made Alex smile and fall asleep.

NINETEEN

Masha answered the phone at the nurse's station. She expected another call to let the staff know that patients were being returned from evacuation but the moment she heard the hoarse voice on the line, she knew it was Alex. "*Amor*," he whispered.

"Is everything OK?' Alex never called her work station, only her cell. She feared hearing the worst. She sat down but didn't look at her screen.

"You, Tomas? And Ray? You all OK? How are the burns? Are you keeping them clean and changing bandages?"

She heard some affirmative answers but Alex seemed far away.

"Your voice sounds weak."

"It was a long long day and I'm beat but they've gained a lot of ground. The bulldozer operators are the most fearless men I've ever seen—I guess all the men are. The air crews fly right into the smoke. Nothing will keep them grounded even though it's dangerous with so little visibility. It's an air force. Can't wait for my own bed and you."

"Oh Alex, hurry home. Why didn't you call from your phone?"

"My battery is recharging and I'm using the motel landline."

"O.K. that's good. How is Tomas?"

"Our son is fine, he showed courage."

"I don't like hearing courage. I like safety."

"Ray and I kept him close. Just thought you'd like to know

before we go to sleep. Tomorrow may be the last day we're needed."

"Some patients have returned. Less danger now, thank God."

"That's good. They're getting containment in Lassen, too. They've got engines from Nevada and Washington, even some Aussies is what we've heard, so fewer untrained like us are needed."

"Fucking good Aussies," Ray said in the background.

"Hey Ray, thanks for keeping boys safe. Love you, Ray," Masha called.

Ray coughed loudly.

"Doesn't sound good," Masha said.

"None of us sound good. I'll tell you what it's like to be in a hellfire hurricane when we're home and having a glass of wine. That will be soon."

"You talk as if it will be over. Well it's hell here too and I can't imagine it over. We're the burn unit, the ER, the ICU all in one, there's not a ten-minute break. Third degree burns, where you've lost your skin and it looks like charcoal."

"It must be some of the folks staying and defending their homes and then having it all collapse down on them. Embers travel hundreds of yards and start new blazes."

"You didn't ask how I am feeling."

"I'm sorry, Masha, I'm always thinking how you're feeling. Sorry I didn't ask."

"I'm just beat up from the strain worrying about you out there and folks here, it's very bad. I'm not a burn specialist but we're doing everything. Really good is that our boy Trevor is making a recovery. He's talking."

"Remind me, who's Trevor."

"Trevor. T R E V O R. Alex, I've been talking about him for weeks, he's a young highway patrolman, a vax denier, but I've grown to care so much…" She began to cry.

"Masha, I want to hear everything you do to help these people but…"

"You never listen to me. Maybe you're jealous of Trevor."

"Masha, stop. You are a wonderful nurse, an angel. And I've got to go."

Masha kept talking to the mouthpiece where no one was listening. "We keep them alive first of all. Then we treat for dehydration and infection as best we can. The body without layers of skin, you get so cold. And the children. I was holding a boy, five years old, in my arms, holding him under warm water and trying to peel off the charred skin while he was screaming. Makes me cry for my father. How was he treated? What he suffered!" Masha cried quietly and looked over at the two nurses watching her. "I couldn't live if anything happened to you," she whispered into the silent phone.

Masha turned her back on the others. At the coffee machine she made coffee for herself and Luisa. Lots of sugar, another two dollars for candy bars. They had so many more patients they'd never have a break for dinner all night. When was dinner anyway, behind them or ahead? They lost all track of time under the bright lights.

Alex hadn't told Masha what happened on the fire line nor after they returned to the Star Motel off 101. He was glad he hadn't because she didn't seem in any state to listen—it had almost become an argument, the last thing he could handle.

He and Ray had been lying on their beds, drinking beers alternated with sodas, anything to quench their thirst and stop coughing up black phlegm. They were waiting for Tomas to return so they could go to the Mexican place where Ray would make a stink about the food and Alex would finish up his plate of enchiladas, beans, rice, extra tortillas because he was so hungry.

Tomas said he'd be gone five minutes to say good bye to the young men from minimum security facilities being shipped back tomorrow, a group of a half dozen or so housed in another part of the motel with an officer. He hadn't returned in half an hour.

Alex got up, walked to the door and opened it onto a smoky darkness, a thickness so heavy in the air he could hardly see a foot ahead.

"I could go get him. I'm getting pretty hungry," he said.

"How about chili dogs and chips in the Kwikstop. Let the kid feed himself."

"I don't want to eat without Tomas," Alex answered.

"You might wait a while. Those boys were giving him a farewell party."

"What do you mean?"

"Remember we were taking a break, and then we saw those young guys charging back up the hill like it was the battle of San Juan. Those kids were given speed or meth, I'd bet on it, whatever they got their hands on or were given, they were high as kites."

"Aren't the boys being watched? They're on a kind of parole."

"While in the line of fire, no questions asked, anything to keep the kids going. Military does it all the time."

"I'm going to find Tomas. He was flirting with drugs before we moved and it scares me worse than anything." Alex put his shoes on and pulled up his hoodie over his nose. He opened the door and almost collided with his son who came reeling toward him, mouth grinning, eyes all black, shining pupil.

"Hey *Papi*, how you two guys hanging?"

Before Alex knew what was happening, Ray was off the bed and had Tomas by the collar.

"You little shit. What have you been smoking?"

For the next minutes, Ray became the enforcer while Alex stood by, too stunned to intervene. Ray hit Tomas on either side of his head, knocked him down, knocked him against the door and held him there as he opened his pocket and shook out pills from a bag and something wrapped in a blackened kerchief.

"You got rock out there!" He held a dirty looking chunk up to Tomas.

Alex could see his son was in shock, that all he could do was try to scuttle away from Ray who caught him by his ankle and jerked him back

"You little shit. You fuck yourself up when you got the great family and you think they deserve this?"

Tomas was sobbing now. "The guys said I'd need something for tomorrow because they're being taken back."

"Not going to happen, kid."

"I won't take them," Tomas pleaded.

"No, you won't." Ray shook Tomas one more time, then went into the bathroom and flushed the toilet. He came back shaking the empty baggie. "You get in here."

Ray proceeded to hold Tomas' head under the faucet until he begged for release.

"Modified water treatment…very modified," Ray said as he dragged Tomas back into their bedroom and handed him a towel. "You, you don't leave our sight. I see you with those mother fuckers and I will break your balls, I swear."

"Tomas, what were you given out there?" Alex asked.

"I don't know, Dad, just took stuff, they said it was for energy."

Ray, once started, seemed unable to control himself hearing Tomas speak. He was rubbing Tomas face in the rough carpet when Alex pulled him off.

"Enough, Ray, he got the message. Tomas, change and we're taking you for some food then we're back here to sleep. Hurry up, I'm hungry."

"You heard me, little fucker?" Ray let Tomas scurry to the bathroom where he closed the door.

"You gotta know how to deal." Ray popped another soda. "Not that it did my kids any fucking good."

Alex was about to say something when a subterranean cough shook Ray.

"I'm grateful, man. Let's eat the chow and then get some sleep."

TWENTY

On the drive back to Malvina, they kept windows up against the smoke that burned their raw lungs. Alex would try to hide from Masha how much toxic matter they'd breathed in but it was Ray he worried about. Ray never stopped coughing as he drove. Alex would have offered to take the wheel—something Ray would never accept yet Alex kept a close eye to make sure he was holding steady.

By the time they reached their house and Alex and Tomas pulled out their knapsacks, they could hardly stand up from the accumulated fatigue. What had been four days and three nights seemed a lifetime of fire, heat, smoke and being together.

"Take care *amigo*," Alex called out as Ray pulled away.

"I didn't get to say goodbye," Tomas said.

"Ray doesn't go in for that," Alex answered.

"I don't hold anything against him. He's a stand up guy. I heard his words."

"I know you did and he wouldn't have done what he did if he didn't care."

"I could feel it even when I was on the ground that I wasn't going that route." Tomas looked away. "And drowning in the toilet."

Alex and Tomas let two days pass before they drove to Ray's. They admired the eagle on the pedestal he and Ray had built together. They hesitated before pulling apart wires that held the gate together. They read the sign, DOG ON DUTY, then replaced the wires in case there was a dog meant to be kept in. No barking, no dog appeared so they walked toward the door. The bell didn't seem to work. They knocked. They waited and knocked again.

Finally a thin woman wearing a large man's faded shirt and dark glasses opened the door just enough so she could see them and they could see at least half her face behind yellow hair straggling over her forehead.

"Hello Susan, we're friends of Ray's."

"I know who you are. Ray isn't feeling good."

"We wondered because he hasn't come by." Alex stood at a distance from Susan so she wouldn't think he was pressing to come inside. "We usually see him. Tomas, my son, brought him something. We're sorry he's not feeling well."

Alex and Tomas had replaced Ray's red MAGA cap lost in the fire with a black one that had a comet streaking across its brim.

The woman took the cap. Her hands were shaking. "Thank you. I'll tell Ray you came by. Like I said, he's not feeling so good today. Last night…he just coughed."

"I'm sorry about that. We cough a lot too…all that smoke we breathed in. My wife makes us teas with honey and herbs and has us breathe steam. She's a nurse. She could come by and see Ray."

"He'll be fine."

They could hear a sound of hacking and spitting from a room further back and out of sight.

"Thank you, Susan. Just tell Ray we're thinking of him. I'll come again."

Susan nodded and closed the door.

Alex gave the reason for the second visit to bring Ray news about how much of the fire was contained, that City Junction had been saved, and more about the woman with the Downs Syndrome boy whose home had escaped the fire. Much of the forest around Ruth Lake had burned and Alex wanted to show Ray pictures on his phone. The fire storms had decimated some hillsides as if bombs had been dropped on them, while on others just adjacent, green-branched pines stood as if they'd never been in danger.

At the door, Susan wore no dark glasses but rings under her eyes were almost as black. She didn't greet them in an unfriendly way without welcoming them in.

"There's a reunion of the local firefighters happening in Redding and we thought Ray might want to go," Alex told her. "It's not until a week from this week-end."

"I'll let him know," she said.

"I brought a six-pack for him." Alex handed over the Serpent Venom.

"I'm sorry I'm not more hospitable. I don't sleep much."

"We didn't take it that way," Alex said. "We've all had a hard time sleeping."

"Ray still can't see you. Don't take it personal."

"We're concerned. How's he doing?"

"Just a minute, maybe he'll have a message for you," Susan said.

There was no chair, no porch to wait on so they stood in the littered yard looking out on the eagle that now seemed ominous.

When she returned, Susan had combed her fair hair and

tied it back. She partly covered her mouth when she spoke but Alex saw she was missing teeth. Had Ray hit his wife? Alex wondered for a moment and then realized that he was creating a stereotype that Ray didn't fit at all. Ray wouldn't hit a woman any more than he would.

"He's just not good, can't get his breath. He says thanks for stopping by with brew. Maybe it will help. He says he's got a terrible thirst."

"I'm so sorry to hear that, Susan. Like I said, Masha, my wife is a nurse and she'd like to help. She knows Ray."

"The Russian?"

"She's from Ukraine. Do you think he would see her?"

Susan shrugged. "They told him at the V.A. that he has COPD, lungs that don't give him enough air since Iraq. No doc admits it was their burn piles outside his camp that made him sick."

"He talked about it. The V.A. should be treating him, it's their promise to him."

"He was there, fighting for our government's oil. Hated every minute."

"Doesn't the V.A. give him care for free?"

Susan shrugged. "He's quit going. No government, any size or shape."

"I know that about Ray, but for his health…"

"You tried telling him what to do?" she asked.

Alex shook his head.

"Ray shouldn't have gone to the fires." Tomas spoke for the first time.

Susan sighed. "Son, he made up his mind you wouldn't

go without him. He said it was his duty because you've been good to him."

"He saved my life and he turned this young man's mind around," Alex said.

Tomas shuffled his feet and kept his eyes on the ground. "He did good for me. He made it different, being here, for my Dad and me."

Susan wiped her eyes. "The only way he's making it is with my pills. He's helping me get off them because he needs the Oxy more than I do."

"I really think my wife should come or I could take Ray into Redding."

She shook her head. "Never going to happen. They'd make him take the vaccine and he won't do that. He's sure it will kill him."

"What do you think?" Alex asked.

Susan lifted her thin shoulders and dropped them. "It's his life."

"What can we do to help, Susan?"

"I still believe in prayers," she said. "I was baptized in the Church of Christ."

"We'll pray and we'll be here tomorrow. We can't tell you all that Ray's done to help us. He really has saved us more than once."

"Ray has a big heart but he doesn't let most folks know it. His life's a book, a long book you gotta read slowly," Susan said.

"We want to know more, we only just began to be friends," Alex said.

"The guy is my rock—I mean after my Dad," Tomas said. "We love him."

Susan backed inside "He's a good man." They could hear her sobbing.

That afternoon, Masha didn't wait for Ray's approval to visit. When Susan stepped out of the house half-challenging, half-receding, Masha asked, "You have chairs?" and set down her nurse's bag.

Reluctantly Susan went inside and when she returned, she was dragging a folding chair. Then she went inside for another. Masha saw the woman was so thin that various tattoos on her butt where her jeans slipped down seemed to be falling off her white bones.

"Ray isn't going to see you." Susan pulled out a crumpled pack of cigarettes and offered Masha one, lit for herself.

"Tell me how he is," Masha began.

"Tell you what? You a reporter?" Susan coughed phlegm then spat on the dirt. Masha would have liked to be sitting further away.

"Reporter? No, Susan, I'm a nurse and I'm a friend of Ray's, very grateful for all Ray did in the fires to keep my guys safe but now your husband needs hospital care."

"And I told your husband that Ray won't go to any hospital, not V.A., none."

"The V.A. has his medical history, they know Ray."

"They deny the burn piles, Sister, so what's the point?"

Susan reached in her pocket and brought out an empty pill container. "Can you get me more Oxy, that's what we need if you want to help."

"Susan, that is not the kind of help I can give. I'm not a prescriber. I can listen to Ray's breathing and heart. I'll check his vitals. That's all I'm able to do but the hospital can do everything that I can't, including giving drugs."

"No, no." Susan stood as if to bar Masha from the door. Then she sat, slumped.

"Fires were bad for him."

"I know. I'll do no more than see him for two minutes. We're friends."

Susan ground out her cigarette in the dirt, quietly opened the door, leaving it for Masha to tip toe in after her, follow through a darkened hallway toward a very bad, sour smelling room, a smell Masha recognized, the closeness of an unaired room where someone very sick was lying. The smell was hopelessness.

Ray's eyes didn't open when Masha leaned close but he knew her voice and he nodded. His eyes had sunk in his eye sockets. He'd lost so much weight that his beard projected from a jutting chin, almost like pictures Masha loved of Abraham Lincoln, her favorite person in American history. When she reached over to take his pulse, Ray didn't resist His heart was racing, his temperature at least 102, maybe more, she estimated from touch, but before she could put on a blood pressure cuff or place an oxymeter on his finger, Susan pulled Masha back outside.

"You done enough, Sister."

Outside, Masha couldn't keep herself from saying, "I can't bring you pills without a doctor seeing Ray, Susan, but I might be able to get portable oxygen to help his breathing. How old is Ray and how much do you think he weighs?"

Unspoken between them was Masha's certainty that Ray didn't have long to live.

"He was fifty on fourth of July. Pretty funny. Ha! I'm five years older. His old lady. He always treated me fine." She swallowed a sob. "He loves you guys and he doesn't love anyone else around this shithole. He said to me, 'I feel like a person with Alex and the wife too.'"

Masha handed her a tissue. "Can Alex come sit beside Ray? It would mean a lot."

Susan shook her head. "Ray doesn't want pity."

"Alex won't pity, he will be strong for Ray, be with him as a friend."

Susan seemed to consider this, then shook her head. "No."

"What will you do, Susan? You also need help."

Susan let a big sigh escape and wiped her eyes again.

"We can help Ray have more comfort in a hospital."

She picked up her chair and left Masha sitting alone.

Alex brought his own folding chair, sandwiches and fortified milkshake that Masha had sent for Susan. "Please get her to eat. She looks starving. You know the person who cares for others must keep living."

Alex sat until the sun was going down. No one came out

of the house. He left the brown paper bag on their doorstep. Before he drove off, he saw Susan open the door and bring the bag inside.

Alex helped Masha roll the oxygen tank over the dirt to Ray's front door where they knocked for a long time before Susan answered. Alex looked around but didn't see Ray's battered grey truck—that truck that had run them off the road, had driven them to the fires, and had become the most wished-for vehicle arriving at their home.

"You can't smoke, Susan, near the machine. I'll show you," Masha said.

"You just missed him."

Masha glanced at each other and back to Susan.

"Missed him? Did someone come get Ray?" Alex asked.

"No, took his truck. Got himself dressed, drank a beer and grabbed his keys."

"But he was in no condition to drive," said Alex. Masha nodded.

"When the man has made up his mind no one could stop him," Susan said.

"Which way did he go? How long ago?"

"Headed north."

They drove less than a mile when they saw cars parked on the side of the road. People were standing at a distance from Ray's truck, still smoking but not yet on fire where it had crashed against the oak that impact had split down the middle.

"Don't look." Alex tried to cover Masha's eyes but she was getting out of the car, pushing her way through.

"We have to pull him out."

They saw Ray, twisted at an angle, head to one side, eyes still wide open staring at the sky as the back wheels of his truck spun and smoke began to billow from the engine.

"It's going to explode, get out of the way quick," a voice called behind them.

Masha still tried to move forward but Alex grabbed her arm, pulled her with him. Ray wasn't going to have done anything halfway and they had to get far back.

An explosion of red and orange flames sent them all back.

"We've got to put out the fire! Everything here is tinder," Alex yelled at everyone who edged closer. "Get any sparks you can and stamp them out. Use your hatchets."

Masha held herself together until they were almost home and then she began crying, softly at first, then sobbing, bent over on the front seat, her head on the dash.

Suddenly she sat upright. "The tree was Ray's favorite tree, the one he sat under. Why would he hurt that tree?"

"He never talked about a special tree," Alex answered.

"It was his special tree. I don't know if he meditated or anything but he liked to sit quietly under it."

"He told you this?"

Masha nodded. "Ray came by to see you a little before you went to the fires. You were in Redding buying hoses, I think. We talked, we really talked." She began to cry. "Too much, Alex, too much, all this. I can't bear it. Too much pain."

Alex hurried to their gate and helped her to the porch.

She was gasping, then sobbing, then gasping again for air.

"*Amor*, what is it? I know you liked Ray. The man made his choices."

"No, it's not bearable, the fires and the dying people. Too much," she kept repeating, sometimes in the language he knew was Ukrainian.

Alex stroked her hair. "We are here, the three of us. I'm thinking of Ray and Susan's sons, Reno and an older boy he called Captain or Colonel. I might be able to get in touch with Reno because Ray said he was in Lompoc."

"Lompoc?"

"Prison in the Central Valley. He's young, barely older than Tomas. I'd like to meet the young man to tell him about his father."

Masha continued to sob. "How can it be, Alex, to die without being able to see your children? Did we make a big mistake coming here?"

He held her tightly, reassuring her with words, whispers, touch, kisses, that they would never leave their two without telling them they loved them. "We'll be OK."

"But you could have died in the fires and how would I know?"

"Masha, we'll grow old together and watch the trees we planted full of fruit for our children, our grandchildren."

She sobbed harder. "That will never be. Adrianna will never come. She only wants to stay far from me. What have I done wrong that my daughter doesn't love her mother? Remember how I cherished her?"

"Of course I do and she loves you. And I am yours for life, *mi alma*, my soul."

"I can't go on like this."

"Like what, *amor?* Living here? We'll move. Just tell me and we'll sell and go."

"I don't know, I don't know." Masha kept shaking her head. "Sometimes it's all too much to bear. Everything is a stake to my heart, Alex, a stake to my heart."

TWENTY ONE

Dogs kept tied outside the clinic, usually thin and raggedy dogs tied with a rope, belonged to street people. Dr. Shira Cogan brought bowls of water and snacks from the staff table for them. "I regret, dogs aren't eligible for care," she laughed as she looked at a man's terrier with open sores, "or I would examine her. I'll give you antibiotic cream that will help."

Every Tuesday and Thursday morning, Adrianna shadowed her mentor everyone simply called Dr. Shira. She followed the short wide woman down the narrow corridors and into the small examination rooms of Jewish Health Advocates. Even though the clinic was located in the middle of an industrial block off Highway 101, a surprising number of walk-in patients showed up. They came from everywhere in the world in need of TB tests and physicals for work, vaccinations for flu and Covid, all kinds of emergency medicines that generous donors had purchased to give out at no cost, and especially help for their children.

Adrianna marveled at how newly arrived immigrants like her own grandmother, sick and with no papers, were never questioned by the staff. Each person was treated with dignity. The unsheltered children carried tattered stuffed animals along with coughs and fevers. Adrianna and Dr. Shira spoke a functional Spanish to the parents of children with teeth decaying from sodas and sugars. "How can we help?" Dr. Shira asked. "There's no cure for the diet," Adrianna answered but Shira only said, "We try."

"How is Grandmother?" Dr. Shira asked.

"She's taking the neighborhood by storm. She's friendly and loves getting out and complimenting people on their gardens. They tell her names of plants she remembers and will plant. She's without fear. I can see where my father got his character. She's always willing to babysit and making sewing alterations. Sometimes she's paid."

"Good. That's American way but here, all free."

"It's amazing here." Adrianna wasn't officially allowed in treatment rooms because of HIPPA privacy but Dr. Shira, not one for rules, brought her along to learn.

"Privacy!" Dr. Shira had a hearty laugh when she returned from the meeting with the director who reluctantly agreed that Adrianna could assist, though 'highly irregular.' "Make sure she locks door from inside. We never know if we might be the target of some hate crime. Large packages always come in the service door out back, never front." The director repeated the instructions and gave more.

Dr. Shira raised her heavily painted eyebrows as she mimed the director, then told Adrianna, "We help people. If we have fear, we run away. Fear is the worst."

"We do have the word *Jewish* and the symbol of a star outside."

"Dear girl, I wasn't afraid as a Jew in Russia so should I be afraid in America? In Petersburg, hooligans threw my husband to ground, smashed glasses, threw instrument in gutter in front of Marynsky Theater. Husband got up, his cello had survived, and with no glasses played Tchaikovsky by memory that night."

"Really? He was a musician in Russia? I thought he was also a doctor."

"No, no, he was cellist in most beautiful city on the Neva, St. Petersburg. My husband is still cellist. In Petersburg, he played for opera, ballet, Nureyev, Makarova, Baryshinikov. We knew them all. Here, he plays for patients and friends."

"I would love to see a ballet one day," Adrianna said.

"You will. I will take you. We miss culture of Russia but we are good here."

"You said your husband is playing?"

"Abram works in Sutter hospital, in ER, but sometimes he plays cello for patients. They love him. We are giving back, Jewish way."

"What way is that?"

"Service to others, young friend, it's called *tsedaka*."

"Do you have children?"

Dr. Shira shook her head. "No, no success. Maybe better, we leave no little hostages behind." She laughed heartily again.

"How can you afford to live in the county? You're not paid here."

"I am well enough paid for night duty work at Sutter. Husband also. I hear Abram play sometimes if we have shifts together."

"Wait, I'm not clear. Your husband the cellist is also an ER doctor?"

Shira laughed so loudly that an older nurse who did the TB tests looked in.

"No, he's not doctor. He's musical janitor, only janitor in Sutter."

"Shira, you are at it again, making us laugh," said the older nurse.

"Did you know my mother? She was an R.N. at Sutter until a year ago. "

"Your mother from Russia?" Shira asked.

"Ukraine."

"Pity, convey condolences from Russians," Shira said. "No, not at hospital we didn't meet. We met here. I remember mother with hair like yours, goldeny locks."

Adrianna touched her tight bun at the back of her head, something she'd done since boys in her class always pulled her braid. "I don't show mine off like she does."

"Show it off, show beauty off! If I showed you what's under this, how I am like *babushka* without hair." Dr. Shira fluffed out bangs while the rest of the complicated wig stayed immobile as if affixed with wax.

"At night, I take off wig. I am *babushka* at home, fat with little grey hair."

" I don't believe it."

"Good. I am opera star, *gitane,* gypsy if you believe, young one." Shira winked.

Adrianna felt the doctor had opened a space for her to talk about the personal, her difficult mother, her plans for the future, when the door bell summoned them.

Adrianna spoke through the grill to an elderly man who looked frail and confused but responded that he wasn't coughing and had tested negative for Covid. The clinic didn't ask for proof but let anyone in who didn't show symptoms.

"You tested negative today?"

He nodded. She took his temperature, normal, but noticed right away how strangely his eyes seemed not to focus on her as she handed him a mask and forms to fill out. A woman in wrap-around glasses and a parka pushed the man aside.

"He's legally blind, Miss. He can't read. You'll have to help him."

"Wait just a moment, please."

"I'm cold out here," the woman said.

Adrianna asked Dr. Shira what she should do.

"Take him into room two, ask questions. You fill out forms."

"Am I allowed to do that? I don't think it's in the protocol for a student…"

"Protocol!" Shira raised her expressive eyebrows then winked from behind the eyelash extenders like little brushes. "Go, go, help poor man. More important than protocol. Call me when ready."

The man's knees shook as they sat on chairs opposite each other. Adrianna tried to keep her own limbs from shaking. She felt torn between following Dr. Shira's example of leaning forward toward a patient and taking his hands to stop his shaking—confidence, Dr. Shira said, the human touch—but kept two feet between herself and the man.

Once she began the interview, Adrianna's sympathy overcame her anxiety. Paul told her he'd been living on the streets with his wife. They'd given their Social Security to their addicted son for food for his children. "Our grandkids. Wore us out. Now we have a roof over our heads, just cover rent with SSI. It's not much but they're walls."

Adrianna saw tears run from his strange eyes. "$1500 a month. Takes all we get so how can I pay for insulin?"

"I'll talk to the doctor. She might be able to get you insulin," Adrianna said. "We can get you Covid and flu vaccines if you haven't had them."

"They put embryos in the vaccines like I hear folks say? And chips?"

Adrianna checked 'not vaccinated' on the form. When she came to writing down a phone number, the man tried to remember. "Go ask her." He pointed behind him.

"I'll be right back." Adrianna left a rock to keep the front door ajar—against protocol—while she went looking for the man's wife. In the 'no parking' zone, she saw a man also wearing wrap-around dark glasses behind the wheel of a white Lexus.

"How long are we going to have to wait on him?" The wife called from the back.

"I don't know, Ma'am. You might want to go park across the street."

"We're fine here," the man said.

"We need your phone number for your husband's records."

Again the man behind the wheel answered and Adrianna wrote it down.

After she brought Shira the clipboard, Adrianna told her about the expensive car. "They were homeless but the wife was waiting in a Lexus. Do we give them free meds when they have that kind of car?"

Shira raised her heavy black eyebrows. "You asked?"

"The man seemed to be telling the truth and grateful to be taken care of but his wife and the driver weren't nice. Did he make up the story of diabetes to get free meds?"

"I'll look at him. No one makes up stories of diabetes, blindness, young friend."

"But if we give meds to people who can buy them?"

Shira's black eyes narrowed. "Learn to listen with heart. You give, no regrets."

TWENTY TWO

Alex proudly opened the passenger side for Masha to step into his all-terrain-drive Subaru Forester, newly painted dark blue over the dents he'd smoothed. The Subaru had been towed to Freddie's after the driver met a redwood tree head on. Repairs were going to cost the driver thousands but the man, bruised and with some cuts, never took off his shades to look at the estimate. He lit a cigarette. "Send me the numbers." He handed Freddie a card and made a call on his cell. All they heard was "Fuck all," before the man walked toward the unmaintained airstrip.

"He could be dead," Freddie said to Alex as they looked at the smashed front end of the vehicle. "He should be thanking God on his knees. Instead he's waiting for a plane. These people. World is full of them. Let's have a beer."

Weeks passed without any sign of the driver. Alex and Freddie both tried a dozen times to reach the number on the card to give detailed estimates before beginning work. Finally a recorded message, "This number is no longer in service," made Freddie slam down his phone. "Del Calvo, the wreck is yours. Get it going and it's yours. Take the time you work on it off your hours but you can use everything I have in the shop."

Alex was thinking of this windfall and the hours he'd spent on the excellent vehicle when Masha said urgently, "I feel sick."

Alex realized he'd been taking the mountain curves too quickly.

"I'm sorry, love."

"Stop, for a minute," Masha said. "Not for the view. My stomach is…" She jumped out onto the gravel pull-out and turned her back so he wouldn't see her throw up.

"I dressed so pretty, now I'm a mess." Masha sat back in the car.

"I'm used to this road. I know it's pretty bad. I'm sorry." Alex handed her a bottle of water and a paper towel. The water in the bottle was already warm. She wiped out her mouth without messing up her eye make up. She wanted their first day off together since the fires, in their new car Alex was proud of, to be romantic.

"You look fine. We're almost there."

As the prefabs and squat business warehouses with their metal roofs came into view, he turned to Masha. 'We're almost here. It's not a pretty town."

"I can see that. A very long drive you make, Alex."

"Once a week isn't that bad. I like my boss and he could use more help. I'm saved by the fresh bread I buy when I'm here." Alex had planned on stopping in Hayfork at Nateena's to buy supplies for a picnic to Ruth Lake. It was to be a special picnic.

"The same store where you buy the good bread?"

"I eat it during the day. I always try to save some to bring home but I can't stop before I finish the last crusty bite."

"You've brought some. It probably is better hot."

"Tastes good to me any time."

"Really?"

"Yes. Nateena's bread is special. But not just her baking.

Anything you want to know about raising animals, you can ask Nateena. You still want chickens, don't you?"

"I suppose. Nateena, an unusual name." Masha felt herself on the alert; some way that Alex said the woman's name and praised her came too close for comfort.

"I think she's Indian. She looks it," Alex said.

"Feathers in her hair?"

"No, you'll see. She's told me that the sourdough starter has been in her family for generations so I guess they settled here before Hayfork became a doper's town."

"Nateena sounds as if she could do anything."

"We can get wine, cheese, her fresh bread, everything for our picnic." He reached over and squeezed Masha's hand.

"I know. We haven't been away on our own…"

"Ray's death just took the joy out of everything."

"And the dangers. I felt ruined. Still haunts me but then I think of who we saved. I suppose I'll never hear about Trevor. I hope he'll tell his family that health care isn't bad. We saved his life."

"That was good news.'

"Like the woman with the Downs boy."

When Alex turned onto route 299 they passed more prefabs and shacks covered with tarps, more State of Jefferson flags with their coiled rattle snakes, more hoop greenhouses, torn plastic flapping.

"I wish we could help Susan but she just disappeared," Masha said.

He nodded. "I think she'll come back."

"I hope Tomas will feed the animals and water the

tomatoes and sunflowers."

"He will and we'll be home tonight," Alex answered.

He's such an optimist, she thought. When Alex saw the black scars from the fires, or a chimney standing in a heap of rubble where a home had been, he managed to point out new growth that had already sprouted up after a first light showering of rain.

The only person in the feed store was a slender woman in jeans, crisp white western shirt, a suede vest decorated with beads. A long braid of black with strands of grey came to her waist. Alex spoke of Nateena as if she was a middle-aged woman or a grandmother but despite white in her hair, Masha judged she wasn't past forty. Her skin was a smooth coppery brown without wrinkles and her jeans fit snugly over slim hips.

Masha caught the sparkle in her black eyes and the shine of her moist lips when she saw Alex.

"Come in, Alejandro. So good to see you. Are you working a second day?"

"No, my wife and I are having a day off and a picnic," he answered.

"Bread's just out the oven, hot, how you like it, so the honey will melt on it."

Honey? The hair on Masha's neck seemed to stand up with 'honey' and 'how you like it.' She couldn't take her eyes off Nateena's turquoise and silver earrings, the hunk of turquoise at the hollow of her neck. Alex saw this woman once a week!

"Nateena, my wife Masha, Masha this is Nateena."

"I've heard so much about you." Nateena extended a firm grip from a brown muscled arm and more silver bracelets and rings.

Masha barely touched the hand. "My husband speaks well of you also."

Masha's heart was beating so hard that her breath barely filled her lungs. She focused on the goods on shelves as Alex stood talking to Nateena. From the cooler section, she pulled out several packages of cured meats and three packs of cheeses.

"Nateena bakes every morning." Alex took a loaf wrapped in brown paper from the counter.

"You've told me." Masha placed the bread on the counter. "We don't need this."

Alex looked hard at Masha who stood facing Nateena and the register.

Nateena started adding up. "You forgot the bread."

"Masha, you will love the bread."

"I prefer crackers. Not so fattening." Masha pushed the packet of Triskets and two bottles of wine toward Nateena. "This is good."

Alex turned with a puzzled look to Nateena. Before he had time for further conversation, Masha walked out the door.

He started the engine without speaking.

"That wasn't polite, Masha. I'm surprised."

"You know Nateena well?"

"She's always helpful and I admire the way she manages on her own. I wanted to share the pleasure of seeing her with you."

"You admire? Pleasure? Usually you are alone having this pleasure-giving conversation?" Masha turned her head away from Alex. *And when I looked my worst, my absolute worst, she thought, and probably I have a bad smell.* "I can't believe how insensitive you are."

As they left Hayfork in silence, she again saw the bare spikes of pines no more than spindles a bad fairy had left after the fires.

"Spikes to the heart, evil fires." Masha rapped her chest.

"Masha, what are you doing?"

"Is this Nateena always by herself, no husband, no family?"

"I never asked. She says she loves children."

"Loves children! Well that's wonderful. She'd like yours if you marry her?"

"Masha! Don't, please. Maybe Nateena does have a husband and a dozen kids, I don't ask, but clearly she's upset you."

"I don't trust her. Or you right now. The hot bread the woman bakes casts a spell over you."

"Masha, why are you making unfounded insinuations?"

"I'm jealous, you know that I am a jealous woman."

Masha continued to look out into the burned forest. "I am a boring woman to you. Just a wife. You just live with me because that's your way, you're loyal to family. You'd like a new life you'd find more interesting. I'm 'mother' to you, I know it."

"Masha, I do not want to hear one more word." Alex kept his eyes on the road and his jaw clenched. He never spoke harshly to his wife. He understood that Masha hadn't snapped out of the crisis of the fires and she still had nightmares that he and Tomas and Ray had never returned. The flames of her dreams became the flames at *Chernobyl* as if she'd actually seen it, she said, waking in a sweat one morning. He understood, but now she was crossing a line he had to stand firm on.

"Fires are a catastrophe. We've had a hard time here but you're going to try to control some of your feelings. We came out of it. Ray didn't. The trees will come back."

"I don't see green trees in my dreams. Only fire and smoke, black. Why do you see the best of things even when they're not?"

"I don't see anything good losing Ray. We both miss Ray."

"You will still be friends with that other woman?"

"If you're talking about Susan, we'd both like to know where she's gone. I'm trying to get in touch with Reno, the younger son."

"Not Susan. She did her best. It's the Indian I think of. Don't be so dense."

"We're back to Nateena?"

"Are you that unconscious of my feelings, Alex? You are that truly innocent?" Masha raised her hands to her forehead and pressed her fingers to feel her throbbing pulse. "I won't say anything more, I promise."

"You should never worry about me, all I am and have is yours."

"Oh, Alex, you're a good man. You're too good a man and that's why I worry. You think everything is all right."

"Our love is right, like the fairy story of the girl and the bears."

"Goldenlocks?" Masha smiled.

He laughed and looked over to see a smile on her face. "You are my Goldilocks, you are just right."

As they rounded a deep curve, thick flourishing woods mounted the hillside, a swath of forest untouched because the winds must have shifted and the demon in the fire had made a turn away from the sparkling blue lake.

Ruth Lake stretched so long they couldn't see from end to end, only across to another green shore. Alex pulled over into a parking spot above a pebbly beach where a picnic table had one leg coming loose. He went back to the car, found tools to right the table, hammered the leg in, then picked up a flat rock to stand it on. Masha began to lay out the picnic. She was still trembling with anxiety, trying to calm her breathing.

She watched Alex roll up his pant legs, unlace his boots and walk toward the water, stepping carefully over stones.

"Alex, it's probably too cold," she called from behind him.

"The sun has warmed the water. We're here at just the right time, the last warm day for us." He unbuttoned his jeans and pulled up his tee. He had a brown, smooth back, a waist that nipped in, firm buttocks under his jockey shorts—no sign of age that she felt showed on her. He was so handsome; how could women not want him as she did?

Alex splashed himself and waded to his knees. He didn't swim well while Masha was an excellent swimmer.

He turned and watched as she peeled down to bra and

panties, black and lacy as if she knew she'd be stripping for him. She loosened her bra, her full creamy breasts with their aureole of fine hairs around the nipples tightened and seemed to float on the water. His throat constricted. He wanted to call out to tell her how he loved her, to reassure her of his feelings she never seemed to completely believe.

She swam arm over arm, twenty then thirty strokes before she turned and waved.

"Masha, not too far."

"I will wash out bad thoughts. Water is my good place."

She swam further until the cold water began to feel warm and she floated on her back under the clouds.

She emerged from the lake wringing out her hair and smiling. "New woman."

Alex bundled her in his warm shirt, aroused again by her breasts, her nipples erect under the cloth.

"Did I tell you that the Svetlovs took me to a pool. They didn't want me to drown and lose payments they received for looking after me. Swimming and going to the doctor, they did that, but not even the money mattered when we stayed out all night, Alex."

"I remember. They looked like a pair in the Bible, pointing fingers at us sinners."

"A long time ago."

"Not so long that I don't remember our first time." He pulled her toward him. "My beautiful woman!" He kissed her breasts.

"Am I really? You love me?" She leaned in, draped her arms over his neck.

"I love you, my wife, mother of my children. You know that."

"I mean, love me, just me, not mother, wife, *me*, woman Masha?"

"Oh yes, yes, you." He kissed her deeply, then unscrewed the bottle, bought out two cups, and raised his to hers. They drank. The cheese and spicy sausage she'd bought needed bread but since they had none, they ate the Triskets and Alex said nothing.

With the sausage and wine on their lips, they made love on a blanket before they drifted to sleep in the warmth of the late autumn afternoon.

They dozed until the sun had gone down over the rim of the mountain.

"It's late. We have a long drive home," he said.

"We can call Tomas, tell him we are coming home late," Masha said.

Alex found his cell but there was no signal. "Maybe on the ridge," he said.

By the time they packed up, it was almost twilight. Alex looked at his watch. "We can try Tomas from the town but it's going to be long after dark when we get home."

"We can stay overnight at cabins I saw on the way. We'll get home tomorrow. I'll call Tomas and explain."

"You think he'll be OK? You saw a motel?"

"No motel, nice cabins. Tomas will be fine. No worries."

They drove back up the narrow dirt road into the burned forest.

"Dracula fire sucked blood," Masha said.

"Spikes to the heart, like you said."

Even from higher up, they got no cell phone signal. Both tried several times but no matter which way they faced, no bars appeared.

Journey's End Resort looked deserted but a light was on inside an office.

Alex got out and climbed steps toward the office. Before he reached the door, a large man wearing a red MAGA cap came out.

"You folks lost?"

"No, we're looking for a room for one night. It's late to start back home."

"Where you coming from?"

"We were at the lake." Alex felt a wave of hostility from the man but he'd learned to wait out suspicious strangers.

The man had a snake tattoo coiling up his arm.

"Where from? You're not from around here?"

"Malvina Falls."

"Never heard of it."

"I work at Freddie Avelos' garage in Hayfork."

"You don't say." He nodded and went back inside. "I got sheets and towels. Basic cabin. You put bedding on yourselves."

"No problem. How much for the night?"

"Hundred bucks. Cash only."

Alex brought out his wallet and handed over two fifties.

"There's wood for a stove in there. You'll find logs and kindling in back."

"Can we get cell connection here? I need to call my son."

"Nothing doing since the fires."

"You have a landline?"

He shook his head, walked away and closed the office door.

"He doesn't like us but he likes the money." Alex turned the key in the cabin door expecting the worst but the one room smelled of cedar as if they'd just opened a hope chest. There was a spotless kitchen counter and an old tub on claw feet in the bathroom.

"Much nicer than I expected but I worry we didn't reach Tomas," Alex said.

"I don't like it either but we tried. He'll be fine."

Masha bathed first while Alex made a fire in the wood stove because the warm bright day had turned chilly. When she emerged wearing only a towel, Alex handed her a glass of wine.

"This is our first night out in so long, Alex. I get envious when the young nurses say they have date nights with their husbands, all dick nights."

"Masha! Such a word!"

"Nurses' station, late night. Not Luisa or me but they say everything."

"Well come here and we'll have date night."

TWENTY THREE

Tomas took Daisy for a walk, and was listening to his dad's favorite Rolling Stones on his phone, expecting the crazy-sweet Subaru to pull in. His dad always had the luck so he didn't worry at first that they weren't home by dark.

He tried both their cells and left messages. He didn't get a call back from either his mother or father. The night seemed to close in on him. They never left him alone. Break-ins and muggings happened all the time around them; they hadn't had any intruders lately but druggies could come by any time. His father had taken the gun. If only he could call Ray for protection. He still couldn't get over Ray's death. It didn't seem real that the guy was gone. He missed him, even those minutes he was face down on the floor. He missed him and his Dad really missed him. He could hear Ray saying now, 'Hey you a little chicken shit or a man?' He'd be brave for Ray's sake.

He made sure doors were locked, living room windows facing the road closed and curtains drawn despite the room's stuffiness. Masha had left plenty of food for supper but all he ate were chips and salsa. Daisy lay beside him on the bed keeping vigil. He didn't believe he slept at all but when an owl hooted and he jumped up, it was nearly light.

An hour later he called his sister. "Adri, the folks never came home. They never called and when I tried their cells, no one answered. I'm kind of like worried."

"You're OK, Tommy? Nothing happened?"

"Nothing happened. I don't know where they are, Sis, and

I don't like being alone."

"Of course you don't but no worries, they'll be home soon. Call me at noon."

At noon, Tomas called. "Not here, no phone still. Come get me, Sis." The strength he vowed to show for Ray vanished and he almost told his sister he was more scared in broad daylight by every sound from the main road than he had been in the dark.

Adrianna calmed her brother and promised that she'd start driving if their parents weren't home in two hours. As she waited, she decided to go to the sheriff's department before her classes because she started imagining everything bad that could happen to them, being robbed, kidnapped and held somewhere, off the road in a canyon or river. The wild west where they'd moved, with her mother always on the edge of going hysterical, made no sense.

"*No olvides los camarones.*" Ana Jesus called as her granddaughter pulled away from the curb. *Abuela* had promised a Salvadorean dish with prawns and rice for supper. She wouldn't say a word to alarm Ana Jesus, no mention of the law.

"Where do you believe your parents were last?" the young male deputy asked.

"I don't know. My dad bought a new car, I mean it was a banged-up all-terrain that he got running. He's great with engines, and with fixing the outsides." Adrianna wanted the officer to know her father was a capable man but didn't know more about his new car.

"Where did you say they lived, Miss?" The officer was filling out forms.

"Malvina Falls, Trinity County, west of Redding and east of Weaverville. I don't live there. My parents and my brother moved north last spring. My brother is worried something happened."

"Never heard of the place. Kind of far out for them."

"Like the song, 'You can't get here from there.'"

"Never heard of it."

"Freddy Fender. Officer, can we start checking for missing persons?"

"Just a few more questions. Why didn't you contact the authorities in Trinity County? Or is it Modoc they went to?"

"It's Trinity County, but maybe they went somewhere out of the county. It's all forest though a lot of it burned this summer. My dad and my brother were part of the fire-fighters. You're not going to get help from up there. They don't vote taxes for sheriffs."

"Let me get Detective Torres. She knows the area and I don't."

An imposing woman with slicked-back black hair and a determined stride entered the room. Adrianna judged her to be late forties. She brought a coffee for both of them.

"Good morning, Miss del Calvo. I'm Detective Torres. Let's start over."

Adrianna reviewed what she'd told the first officer and gave as much information about her parents' new vehicle as she could. She liked Detective Torres.

"I don't know the year but it's a dark blue Subaru and it's an all terrain vehicle."

"Easy enough to find that out, Miss del Calvo. Transfers are public record."

"My dad got the car when a man crashed it and never came back to pick it up at the garage. Dad and the garage owner waited months and tried every way to make contact."

"But your father registered it, I'm sure. He sounds like a careful man."

"I'm sure he did."

"How long have they been missing?"

"They were supposed to come back yesterday evening. My mother is rather anxious so they wouldn't leave my brother without letting him know. He called me this morning because they hadn't returned calls and he had to spend the night alone."

"Is he a child?"

"No, he'll be sixteen soon."

"Oh, I thought we were talking about a child. What's your brother's name, Miss del Calvo."

"Tomas del Calvo. He was at Montgomery High but he moved in with my parents at the end of last summer. He helped fight the fires. I think he'll stay up there."

"Has he been in trouble?" the detective asked. "Name sounds familiar but I can't place it. I'll have to go into my computer. Do you mind waiting?"

"My brother isn't the one I'm here about. It's my parents who are missing."

"We'll get to that. I've a nagging memory like a tickle. Back in a minute."

When Detective Torres returned, she was smiling.

"You won't remember me, of course, but I met you long ago, Adrianna. I knew I recognized the name. You were a baby when I met your parents. It's really quite a co-incidence. I was in Protective Services then and now I'm a detective. Your parents, they were so young. You were hungry and wet as I recall." Torres smiled at the young woman.

"My parents weren't neglectful."

"No they were just young. I always wondered how they were, and you, too. You'll be finishing high school if I've got this information right." Now that Detective Torres had solved one mystery, she settled in with her coffee.

"I passed my GED. I started community college summer school taking pre-med classes and doing volunteer shifts at a clinic for credit. Now I'm enrolled in pre-nursing. I want to become a doctor."

"Good for you!" Detective Torres reached over and slapped palms with Adrianna. "Tell me about your brother. I didn't follow your family's history so I only know you. I do remember your parents came as refugees?"

"Not exactly. My dad has never been arrested but he came escaping drug gangs and my mom had been exposed to radiation in the Ukraine."

"Now I'm remembering. They'd gone through ordeals."

"Good memory. My grandmother, my dad's mother, made it up here from El Salvador and we live together. She's gone through a lot, too." Adrianna thought that if Torres wanted to inform ICE about *Abuela* she could do so, but didn't think she would.

"Let's get back to your folks, Alejandro and Maria."

"I haven't heard anyone call my mother by her name before."

"It isn't Maria?"

"Yes, but everyone calls her Masha, that's a nickname for Maria."

"Oh, I'll note it in the file. Now keep on, please, tell me what you know."

"They've never been gone from home at the same time because they've got animals to feed. Many nights my mom works in Redding, she's a nurse. When she's gone, my dad is always home. I guess with my brother there, they felt they could be out for longer but they would have called, I'm sure, unless something happened."

"Your mother was about your age when I met her and I see the resemblance, the gorgeous hair. Your dad was already working two jobs, I think. A responsible father."

"He sure is and loves making things for people. He won't call it art but he's creative. For mom, it's gardening that makes her happy. They seem to like being together up north though it's the last place I'd want to be. I was surprised my dad would leave his mother so soon after she arrived. My mom has the last word with him and she wanted it."

"You know, Miss del Calvo, what I remember about your folks is they were in love. I'm happy to hear they still are…a bit of a sentimental streak in me, romcoms."

"They are, with my mom it's pretty obsessive. She's not the easiest person to get along with while my dad, well, he's just smooth and consistent."

"First generation here, you work hard, it's what you do to prove you're American. Next generation kids are different. None of us know what strengths and weaknesses we have until we're tested, do we?" The detective stood up and gave Adrianna her card.

"Like my grandmother, coming through such dangers at her age. She's amazing."

"You're a credit to all of them, Adrianna. Let's get back to your folks and then I have to go. To list them as missing persons, we'll have to wait because it's too soon for that. There's usually an explanation and they're together, so that's good. If they don't call by tomorrow, contact me, I'll get on it."

"Thank you. I worry because it's such a dangerous area but you make me feel better, just talking about it, as if you understood a lot more than you say."

"Detective sixth sense, Adrianna. The wild north?"

"Affordable. Huge forest and rivers. The fires, too."

"My husband and I got into a nice two-bedroom house years ago when it was still affordable. We couldn't buy now. We were too close to the fires but in the end, OK."

"I don't think my folks understood the country they were moving into. They've been broken into and vandalized more than once."

"Those counties up north are revolving doors for criminals. They get dumped right out of jail as if they knew how to survive as law-abiding citizens. Now that cannabis is legal, we worry about meth, the devil drug." The detective's screen pinged. "A recent batter, old couple in Modoc County, survived but injured. That's good."

"That doesn't give me comfort."

"Modoc, Shasta, Trinity…those folks want to be left alone."

"Except when they need help, then they come to the hospital. My mother's been working through the worst of the pandemic and then the fires."

"Sounds as if she must be stressed, almost PTSD."

"I think so too but she won't admit to anything."

Detective Torres stood up and extended her hand. "Adrianna del Calvo, I can't tell you what a pleasant surprise it is to meet the baby grown into a fine young woman who's going to be a doctor. You let me know when you graduate medical school and I hope you come back to serve the community. Really, I think your parents are just fine."

TWENTY FOUR

Alex and Masha didn't find Tomas waiting for them mid-afternoon the next day though Daisy appeared in seconds, wagging and squirming with pleasure. To Daisy, the parents' absence had given her the treat of sleeping on the couch and leaving dog hairs.

Alex hurried down the hall and knocked on Tommy's door where he could hear music pounding inside.

"Tomas, open up, we're home."

"That's cool, *Papi*. I'm listening to a cut. Be out in a minute."

"We couldn't get cell connection anywhere. I'm sorry we couldn't let you know," Alex said through the door.

"No problem. Daisy was really scared though. Call Adri. She was worried."

When Masha called, Adrianna, like Tomas, sounded cool, even distant.

"I don't know why you're upset. We're back—it was only overnight."

"Mother, you should have let Tommy know."

"We tried, Adri. There was absolutely no cell service. Tommy seems fine."

"Yeah, today, but not last night. I went to Highway Patrol where I met Detective Torres who remembered you and dad when you were young and I was one-year old."

"Doesn't sound familiar. Why did you meet him?"

"Her. You two must have been in some kind of trouble. Like with Tommy last night, you left me alone."

"Tommy is sixteen."

"A young sixteen and not even. What were you guys doing?"

"We went to a lake and swam and then it got dark."

"I mean what did you do when I was a baby."

"Nothing, I'm sure. I'll ask your father, he's got the better memory."

"Mom, will you ever be real with me. I mean real real?"

"That question makes me unhappy, Adrianna."

"I wish I could like being with my mother as much as I like being with you." Adrianna sat on a stool in Dr. Shira's office.

"OK, young one, tell me what is trouble. Be quick, please," Shira said.

"They didn't come home night before last and my brother freaked so I went to the police, and then my mother gaslighted me so I didn't tell her I was scared for them."

"Gaslight?"

"Means when you play with someone's head. Anyway, if I'd talked to my father, I'd have said how relieved I was they were home. I can't bring myself to sound vulnerable around her. She stonewalls everything."

"Stonewall? Another interesting expression. Any reason they didn't come back?"

"They'd stayed late, it was dark, she said. I can understand that. The roads are windy. Cell phones don't work. They found a motel. I bet she loved it all."

"Why don't you speak to her? She's your mother and she loves you."

"I know that, Shira. I was just feeling that you're fun and Mom never has been."

"Are you fun, little one, with your mother?"

"No, I always push her away. I didn't even like her reading to me because she still had such an accent. '*Piotor Raabieet*' she would call it. Come listen to *Piotor Raabeet*."

Dr. Shira started to laugh and caught herself. "Hurtful, not good of you."

"I never wanted to hurt but what she wanted for me, to buy me pretty dresses and go out with boys, be Miss High School something. She didn't get it that I didn't want that, that she couldn't live through me."

"We had no pretty dresses. I would have liked pretty dresses."

"I resisted everything. I don't know why."

"What is your real me that you want Mother to know?"

"I am directed. I like learning. I want to become a doctor like you. I see six, seven years ahead. You ask so many questions. Is that the psychiatrist hat?"

"Hat!" Shira gently patted her hair arrangement.

"I guess I should be paying you."

Shira stood up and paced the small room. "Boys? Girls? You like special person?"

Adrianna shook her head. "My father just asked me that as if I weren't normal. Right now, most males don't have goals like I do. I'd like to meet someone like Dr. Hashi, the

Japanese doctor who comes in. He's so neat and so polite. I like that."

"I know Dr. Hashi. Twice your age."

"That's about right for me," Adrianna smiled.

"And married, and frankly, dear girl, you will meet younger men."

"My folks have always been so crazy in love, I felt I never would find the perfect person, the way they are to each other."

A bell rang at the front door. Adrianna stood up to answer and Shira went to the wash stand to scrub and put on her mask.

"Adrianna, another time we'll talk about your mother and father, but while I still have on shrink hat, I have the last word."

"OK."

"You'll be happier if you talk with your mother. I mean, with good attitude. Give her chance. And no pity for self. Be stand-up girl." Shira doffed her imaginary hat, slipped a N-95 mask over her head.

"They want us there for Christmas. She loves to bake her Ukrainian specialties."

"See, my dear, good woman. Ukrainian cooking better than Russian."

TWENTY FIVE

Masha slept until ten after her night shift and woke to find coffee Alex had made still hot in the thermos. Why had she slept so late? So much to do, everything to be made ready for their first Christmas Eve with the family in Malvina Falls. Adrianna and Ana Jesus would be arriving by noon. Tomas had taken up snowboarding at Shasta and promised to bring home a tree to decorate together before they went to Midnight Mass.

Masha saw herself in the quiet church of her childhood, candles in the recesses of the white plastered walls. She was kneeling beside her mother, the incense and candle smoke heavy in the Church of the Holy Redeemer as the priest and his retinue proceeded toward the altar. Decorations were simple, green boughs and red poinsettia surrounding the illumined Mother and Child that glistened with gold leaf. By then the family had been assigned an apartment in Simferopol, close enough to take a bus to the Black Sea in the summer and stay in rest houses. She loved sitting on the shore and looking back at a lone Juniper or old pine that clung to rocks, then returning to her book. She didn't yet swim but her father had been able to enjoy some time in the water. Her older brother Maksym had pals who were Tatar as well as Russian and Ukrainian. They kicked a tattered canvas ball one of the Tatar's had stolen from a local team's field.

While she was kneading dough for *syrnyky*, the sweet and tender pancakes her mother made every year, Masha had to wipe tears from her eyes. Early that morning, her mother and father on Facetime thanked her for gifts she'd sent. Masha saw how dingy the room looked, even more with Christmas lights, garish in the gloomy dusk. They all gave and received blessings for the holy days ahead. Since the Russians had taken over Crimea, her family had been moved to a cramped apartment hardly better than Soviet communal living. Her father, Sergiy, sitting in a chair, her mother opposite with the phone, was thin and white as a ghost. Because of his health, Nadya said they no longer went to the church on the other side of the city where the family had worshipped. Then, in what sounded like unrelated news, Nadya told Masha that Maksym was in the hospital.

"Beatings he got from the Russians. We could not get along without you, our American girl. From you, we have money for tokens and to bring food to the hospital."

Masha wiped her tears. She knew 'tokens' meant bribes and regretted most of she money she sent went to these gatekeepers at the clinic. They gave their blessings again and her phone went dark. *So much sadness.*

While the ducks were in the oven for de-fatting and carols played on the radio, Masha did the kind of house cleaning she seldom had time for during the week. The fridge, the counters, even the cupboards emptied and shelving scrubbed. Her mood brightened with the cleaning. They might go snowshoeing at Shasta, nothing adventurous like the snowboarding that Tomas loved, but good to be in the snow. Finally she stoked the wonderful stove that gave the room such a winter fragrance and warmth.

She went to the guest bedroom with its coat of new

light blue paint, smoothed wrinkles from the blue coverlets on the twin beds for her daughter and Ana Jesus to sleep under. Furnishings cost more than Alex liked to spend but he was proud of her decorating and she'd been earning good money—earning at the cost of sleep and being home. So much she wanted to buy and to increase the monthly remittance to her mother and father.

The view outside the guest room gave onto the bare fruit trees and green pines. Little by little, as she cut back vegetation around them, a pomegranate had emerged, and what looked like a stump turned out to be a blood orange with enough leaves to keep it alive through years of neglect. Each discovery made her feel like an arborist archeologist finding life after centuries.

She was wondering whether to leave the ducks to cool on the counter before removing fat in the pan or whether to skim it off hot when Tomas burst in like a snowman in his gear, a frosting of white still on his head of thick black curls. "Got us a great tree, Mom, I'll bring it inside. Shasta was incredible."

"Snow?"

"Lots and I think it's coming our way. Where do you want the tree?"

"We need a bucket. Bring it in and we'll put it in the center of the room."

"Maybe in a corner. We don't want it to fall over and they're not like a tree you buy, they're thinner."

"Good thinking, son. Over there." She pointed to the corner beneath a window.

Tomas brought in the blue spruce and set it in a bucket of water. Masha stood back to see. "Thank you, son. Were many trees burned?"

"Depended where I was. Less on the east side but really bad other places. With the snow on them they really look like ghosts."

"The fires were terrible. Tonight we'll give thanks and prayers."

"It was bad, Mom. Sometimes I can still smell smoke and I wake up with my heart beating so hard. I guess it's normal."

"You and your father were in the middle of it and I know you have effects. I do, too, worrying about you, treating many burned men, but not like what you two saw."

"Ray did it all with us."

"I know."

"I've been thinking, Mom, I might take courses in forestry at Butte Community after I graduate from high school. I met some guys snow-boarding and we were looking at the trees. It's cool how much you can learn, like how the forest recovers and what folks can do to replant. They said I have an inside track as a volunteer fireman."

"I guess we know there will be more fires. I hope your study isn't dangerous."

"We're going to have more fires. And isn't what you do, Mom, dangerous?"

Masha nodded. "But you're my son."

"I'm almost legal age."

"And you're a good son." Tonight, she'd give thanks for the many ways her son was growing up and loving her enough to confide his plans. Maybe Adrianna will one day, she thought. Maybe distance will make the heart grow fonder as they say.

She and Tomas set the glittering star on top and lights on branches. They left decorating for when Adri came, bringing family ornaments from Santa Rosa. Outside the sky had clouded over and the air felt ripe for snow.

It began gently, a snow flake at a time, landing on Adrianna and Ana Jesus and on the boxes they carried tied with red and green ribbons. If the snow fell all night, they might awake in the morning to a white Christmas.

Adrianna unpacked new and old treasures of glass and ceramic ornaments the family had collected over the years. "Welcome, *bienvenida*, Ana."

"Gracias, Maria, so pretty here, very warm," Ana Jesus unwrapped her scarf.

"You've done so much, Mama, the house looks sweet and cozy. You two know how to work. You didn't tell me you had a wood-burning stove. I love them."

"It came with the house, part of the bargain, but in summer you don't notice."

Adrianna hugged her mother. "And we're all here." She brushed a warm strand of hair from Masha's forehead—a brief touch Masha felt blushingly grateful for.

Under a cloth cover, the duck fat was congealing enough to scoop it out from the cavities and from the skin. Should she put in her potatoes now or wait until they were back from a walk and enjoying a glass of wine before supper? Make gravy now or later? She was trying to decide when Adrianna walked in with a cloth-covered tray.

"Abuela made *papusas*." Adrianna wrapped her long arms around her small grandmother. "We have been eating very well with my grandma's cooking."

Before Masha could react to those words of approval for her grandmother and a treat that might be tastier than her pancakes, Alex came through the door and lifted his mother into his arms. "*Feliz navidad, Mamacita.*"

"*A ti tambien. Que dios te bendiga,*" she responded, blessing each of her son's fingers and making a sign of the cross. "*Hijo,* you have white hairs."

"Only snow." He shook off the flakes and made a little puddle on the floor.

"*Abuelita.*" Tomas flung his arms on his grandmother's shoulders.

"You are so tall!" she stood back, covered her mouth in mock surprise. "You'll become a giant."

"You're taller, too," Tomas said.

"I stand straighter now."

"Shall we go for walk in the snow?" Masha whistled and Daisy, a red bow around her neck, bounded to them. "This is Daisy, our dog who's supposed to protect us."

They walked slowly into the woods along a path only lightly dusted in white while Daisy went leaping ahead, sniffing, squatting to pee every few feet. When they lagged behind, she turned and barked at them to hurry. They didn't need to leash her because she never ran farther than a recall would bring her back.

They walked an hour more than they'd planned because the trees under snow seemed to catch a faint sunset glow behind the low grey sky. Arms around each other, they were singing Christmas songs when they came into the yard.

"We closed the door. Why is it open?" Masha rushed ahead.

Alex held her back at the door. "Let me go first."

He was shaking his head. "Oh shit! Pardon me but goddam those kids. I bet you I know who they are. I thought we were past this."

"I don't know what to do." Masha collapsed on the couch, head in her hands. Some ornaments lay shattered as if the intruders had been playing *piñata*. "It's one thing, then another. I don't know how to apologize, Ana Jesus. Sometimes I feel they are breaking us, like the ornaments."

"No, they are not breaking us." Alex knelt and pulled the tree back up, stood to kiss the top of Masha's head. "They don't break us, my love."

They all looked down where boxes in bright wrapping and ribbons had been. The presents had vanished. In the kitchen, drawers hung open and pots had been thrown around the room. Knives were gone, silver that wasn't silver lay thrown into corners. The ducks and the *syrnyky* were still in the oven with the *papusa*.

"I am so sorry," Masha said to her children and Ana Jesus.

"We are all well, no one hurt," Ana Jesus said softly.

"My god, Mama, we were only gone an hour. How can anyone do this? Call the sheriff, Papa." Adrianna helped her grandmother to a chair and sat beside her.

"No one will come," Masha said. "We will clean up."

"Come on, *hijo*, we have a few ornaments we didn't put up yet. I'm sorry about the presents. Nothing has happened for months, not since before the fires and Ray..."

"Because Ray is not here," Masha clutched Alex' hand.

"I know you've worked so hard but is there nothing to make you see you're making a huge mistake? It's only a house," Adrianna said.

Masha pressed her fingers to her eyes. "Please don't add more to this headache."

She tied apron strings around her waist and put potatoes on to boil. She poured off the last of duck grease to make a gravy. Then she began sweeping. Alex was vacuuming in the living room. Sounds of clean up were better than the carols she couldn't listen to.

Alex opened a bottle of red wine that the thieves had missed and poured glasses for everyone. They ate mashed potatoes and duck, roasted turnips and parsnips moistened by gravy that clung to their lips. They drank a second bottle of good Argentine Malbec that Alex had also hidden. Their voices rose, Spanish and English, and even Masha celebrated, wiping tears and grease from her face. Everyone was so full they decided to save the *syrnyky* for after Mass along with *abuela's* sweet *papusas*.

"We got you such a beautiful sweater spun from goats' wool, Adri. I'm sorry," Masha wiped a tear from her cheek.

"I'm sorry for you guys. Why don't you drive to town and get the sheriff?"

"Like your mother said, no one will come. In Redding

there's Highway Patrol but they won't come out this far. We'll find who did this and we'll get some things back." Alex was sure it was the two boys on a cross road, the only house after Bort and his family, boys who were not right in the head. Thank heaven they didn't find the gun. With Ray gone, did the agreement with the Citizens end? What if they all turned against him?

Snow was still falling when they reached Redding and turned east toward Our Lady of Mercy in time for Midnight Mass. They'd left Daisy on guard and Alex braced the door shut from inside and kept lights on.

The church shone with candles and fragrant pine wreaths decorating the altar. When the choir sang and they were invited to join in "Holy Night," the voices of the del Calvo family rose with the others. They waited a long time for everyone to receive communion and left with the feeling of solace.

As they were walking from the church toward their car, Masha heard a voice call, "Masha, Maria Sergeyievna, Merry Christmas and God bless."

Luisa, small and wrapped in a black coat with fur trimmed hood, stood beside a man wearing a cap white with snow. He had dark skin and dark eyes like Luisa's but an unhealthy pallor compared to his wife's rosy cheeks and bright lipstick.

Masha had never seen her friend look so pretty. "Alex, this is Luisa. Luisa, we have Alex' mother and our children with us."

"I am happy to meet you. I've heard so much about all of you out there in the countryside." Luisa extended her gloved hand to Alex, then the children and Ana Jesus. "*Mi esposo, Jorge.*"

Masha hadn't realized that Luisa and Alex looked like a matched pair though she always said they, husband and wife, were one and the same. A feeling of anger, resentment, almost hatred kept her from moving toward Luisa, Alex, and Ana Jesus, who were all speaking Spanish. They were far enough from her so she only understood the cheerful, intimate tone. Then Luisa leaned over to whisper something to Alex. Masha wanted to rip her apart, to get in between them the way she had in their ESL classes when the buxom twins flirted with Alex. After the shock of the break-in, didn't he understand she could not endure one more hurt? Wouldn't he show that he belonged to her? She turned away and walked to the car without saying goodbye.

The next morning, Masha cleaned up the rest of the evidence of home invasion before anyone else was up. She turned on the coffee maker, heated the *syrnyky* they hadn't eaten last night, powdered sugar over them and then more and more sugar.

When they were all seated at the dining room table, Ana Jesus said in Spanish, "We have more gifts than we lost. Let us name them."

Around the table, everyone named the gifts they had chosen for each member of the family and described them until it almost seemed that presents lay before them with ribbons and wrappings. Even Masha found her voice and described the sweater that they'd bought for Adrianna.

"*Niños, la familia* is why I am living still," Ana Jesus sighed.

"Maybe we will all be living together in Santa Rosa again," Adrianna said.

Masha shook her head. Overnight she felt a determination not to be defeated. *I am not a giving-up person*, she said to herself. *I won't be driven out and I won't have another woman steal my husband. I will die first.*

TWENTY SIX

Masha found most of their gift wrappings and boxes, some discarded presents, including the natural wool sweater turned dark with mud. A good washing and it would look like new.

Alex took the time for himself between Christmas and New Year to finish the dragon for the Michoacan brothers who brought copper, most likely pinched. Alex loved copper that glistened and shone with a special luster when polished, perfect for detail on the scales of the mythical beast. Unfortunately he couldn't use it without a more precise, high temperature welder. He might be able to fuse metals somehow, or even shape the scales and find a way to affix them—a shame not to have the copper and be able to work it in. He didn't really trust the brothers but wanted to keep them as allies.

When the vacation week was over and snow had melted, Alex didn't mind driving the mountainous road to Freddie's shop in Hayfork. The day went quickly with one battered vehicle after another sputtering in—these folks never got rid of their trucks and cars, nor just about anything else to judge from their front yards. He could also have counted on seeing half of these junked up yards with the only bright colors a MAGA or GO BRANDON or the double X X of the State of Jefferson. He drove past and tried to put the words out of his mind.

Just as he'd done for his Subaru, Alex gave old clunkers a smoothed-out fender and a paint job that took off years of corrosion and abuse. He accepted customers' thanks, replaced his earphones when the men gathered for a smoke, going on about conspiracies in Sacramento and DC. He understood however they got their information they believed it, and there wasn't any use reasoning or arguing. He liked Freddie who kept words and oversight to a minimum.

At the end of the day in deference to Masha's feelings, Alex didn't stop at Nateena's. Masha hadn't bounced back from all that had happened over the Christmas Eve break-in and meeting Luisa. She was working longer hours to send more money to her parents. He thought she was working too much. She was always tired and cranky and her hostility toward Luisa and even Nateena hadn't let up—subtle and not so subtle remarks about the women's appearance or character came out of nowhere.

Masha had always bristled around nice looking women who chatted, maybe flirted with him. Her jealousy at first flattered him, until it didn't. He learned not to bring women into the conversation. Instead he praised her. "Guys tell me what a lucky fellow I am." Recently, probably since Christmas, he couldn't predict which Masha he was with, the woman he loved with her soft moist body, a woman he always admired, or the frowning, troubled Masha insinuating that he wanted other women. She never forgot Kim, his cousin Carlos' daughter. Kim was one of the reasons Masha had rejected moving to Carlos and Ditto's property in Santa Rosa.

Now he looked at his watch. He had a full day ahead at Freddie's but when the phone rang and he saw it was Carlos in Santa Rosa, he answered.

"Everything OK, *Primo*?" he asked. Adrianna would have called about Ana Jesus.

"Grab a beer, Alejandro del Calvo. Got news, amazing news."

"Can't have a beer. I'm at work."

"That's OK. We'll have time for the beers."

Alex heard the excitement in Carlos' voice. "The old people want to go back to their island for their last years. Their own kids never wanted to farm. The Mateos could sell twenty five acres of flat land for a bundle, I mean a big bundle, but the money doesn't matter to them as much as keeping the land and taking care of the animals. *Patron* doesn't want developers to come in and carve it up."

"Wait, you're going so fast. Are you talking about Mateos' land, where you live?"

"It's not a done deal but they want to leave and they want us to take over and keep farming the land if the money can be arranged. They'll ask as little as they can and we've got savings. We can sell our interest in the bar and the auto shop."

"Sell off the Lizard Bar? The auto shop?"

Carlos paused. "Alejandro, we'll own land like we always dreamed. You can share everything with us and *Tia* Ana Jesus. We're family, *Primo*. If you have anything in cash to contribute, that will help."

"My god, congratulations. If I had a beer, I'd be raising it. Del Calvos, land owners like their grandparents and parents, all in one generation."

"The cows, the horses, goats, chickens, they include everything."

"We're almost a year in Malvina Falls," Alex started out but Carlos didn't seem to be listening.

Over the years, the brothers knew the habits of the cows and goats and had increased Mateos' stock. It was hard work with the other businesses they'd kept going, but the brothers relished the barbeques under Christmas lights hanging over their doorways all year. Alex remembered the elderly Mateos loved small children around, brought their home-made cheese from a huge round and a bottle of their fiery house-distilled brandy to celebrate holidays.

"We'll pay them off over time. The *patron* says, 'Don't hurry. God has time.' They're religious folk. We'll light a candle every day for the Mateos on their island."

Alex could hear Carlos popping another beer. "With your help, *Primo*, we will have the good life we've worked so hard for. We build Ana Jesus her own small house, a bigger one for your family. Your *madre* will be so happy."

A week later, driving the final curve into Hayfork, missing his morning warm bread and Nateena's good humor, he decided to buy chicken wire for the coup he and Masha were going to build. They were waiting for the weather to warm up before they brought chicks home, and he knew that Nateena would have whatever he needed.

Alex hadn't told Masha about the phone call. She wasn't in a state of mind to feel positively about land and farming the way he did. She loved gardening but she'd never become part of his family.

Nateena evidently sensed he was not his usual self when he left with the wire and a quick goodbye, hardly responding to her question about their holidays. He barely resisted turning around and going back in for the bread his stomach yearned for.

He applied himself to getting wire tied down in the truck bed and covering it with a tarp when he looked up and saw a beige Camry pulling away from the curb. Neither the color nor model were unusual but it was so like their Camry, the same dent in the same place on the rear bumper that he'd been meaning to hammer out. The first letters on the license plate were theirs.

Alex almost followed Masha as she must have been following him. If by chance the car had been stolen, he'd kick himself for not pursuing it. Deep down he knew his wife was behind the wheel and that she'd watched him go into Nateena's. She was making herself very late to work driving the rough windy road in the Camry in order to spy on him. He sat with his hands on the steering wheel in shock. Why would she do this? He remembered this morning had been one of her scowling, mumbling days when she looked at herself in the mirror as she dressed. "Nothing looks good on me."

All day he lost himself in the work that needed his full concentration. Before he left, he called Mercy Regional in Redding.

"Mrs. Masha del Calvo, please."

"Alex," Masha answered.

"Masha?"

"Hi Alex, how's it going?" Her voice sounded forced.

He had no intention of saying what he said next but the words were out because the question had been eating him all day.

"Masha, did I see you in Hayfork this morning? I didn't think it could be you at first, but if it wasn't you, did someone take your car? How did you get to work?"

Silence on the other end.

"Masha?"

"Got to go," she ended the call.

At home he made another call to Mercy.

"May I speak with Mrs. Luisa Fuentes if she's still there?"

"I see her now. Let me catch her before she leaves."

Alex heard background conversation, then a voice, "Jorge, is it you? You OK?"

"Luisa, sorry, this is Alex, Alejandro del Calvo, Masha's husband." He knew he was breaching confidence. Masha didn't make friends with women easily and she had seemed close to Luisa until the Christmas Eve Mass.

"Hello, Alex."

"Hi Luisa, glad I reached you."

"I was on my way home."

"Sorry to detain you. Can you talk a few minutes?"

"Of course. Let me step outside and find a bench." After a moment, Luisa's voice came back on. "Anything happen to Masha? She came in late but she's on another floor. She seems to be avoiding me. I haven't had a chance to talk to her."

"That's why I'm calling but I don't want you to talk if you don't want to."

"It's perfectly fine. You called for a reason."

"She'll be furious with me if she finds out I talked with you." Actually, he thought, she'll blame Luisa, imagine she made the call.

"I won't say anything, and since you called, I can tell you that I think she's been struggling. Since the fires, she's been obsessing about small things. I can tell you that when we had to leave Manila like criminals, I couldn't sleep for months. Trauma can do that. Is she sleeping when she's home?"

"We have crazy schedules so I'm not sure. It hasn't hurt her work has it?"

"Oh no, she's an excellent nurse, the best, patients love her. She gives shots and puts in drips they don't even feel. What did she say to you about Christmas Eve? I was glad to meet the family but ever since then, it's like she's giving me the evil eye."

"She believes you and I were flirting in Spanish."

"Really? I was talking with your dear mother as much as with you. She knows my situation with Jorge. I haven't a moment of time nor an ounce of flirtation in me. Masha's told you about Jorge?"

"She has. I'm sorry."

"We're doing the best we can. Every day while I'm away from him I'm scared. You know the AA 'one day at a time'?"

"I do. Masha isn't on drugs is she?"

"No, no, of course not. I was talking about Jorge. Let's get back to Masha."

"Christmas Eve before we came to Mass, we got broken into and stuff was stolen and ruined. It really upset her especially because our daughter and my mother were here."

"I've heard about the bad guys in your neighborhood. Masha told me about a friend who didn't make it. From the fires. She's been upset about his death."

"Ray had health issues we didn't know were so serious. We should have. His passing hit us both hard. I feel at fault for letting him go to the fires."

"Everyone was stressed, so many patients coming in with their lungs and bodies burned on top of the virus, and then we had to evacuate others."

"We were all on the front line," he said.

"It was a war zone. We walk around in protective gear like we were going into space, and sometimes we get hate from some patients we're trying to save. Enough to drive anyone crazy."

"There's more going on in her head than I understand. She is a more complicated person than I am," he said.

"Sometimes women are more complicated, especially when it's the menopause."

"She's too young and that's not what's happening" He felt offended for Masha. "I want to understand so I can help her. I love her." He tried to keep his voice steady.

"I know you do, Alex, no question. If I can speculate…"

"Please, it's all speculation. I'm afraid she's having some kind of break down. I'm in the dark about what to do. We made this move together. Maybe we need to go back."

"Maybe she's living a trauma of the past and it won't matter where she is. Another saying, 'You take yourself with you wherever you go.'"

"We used to talk about all of that but we don't talk now. We've all had trauma."

"Jorge, my husband, just wants to blot it out. Not a good way. I think you should encourage Masha to talk. She needs reassurance first of all, then you go deeper."

"You want to get home, Luisa. I won't keep you."

"Alex, I care about Masha. She's my only friend here. We were close."

"You know she was only a few months old when *Chernobyl* happened. She can't remember the explosion, fires, evacuation but maybe deep down she does remember."

"Her parents probably talked about it a lot. All kinds of ways to get PTSD."

"She skypes or she's on Facetime with her mother. She sees her father who's sick—he's always been sick. I've thought it was a good thing, seeing her family, but it's bringing up everything. She told me once that when she was in school in the Crimea where they'd been resettled…"

"She's talked about bullies to me."

"In first grade, the kids who'd been evacuated from the poisoned zone were called freaks and mutants. She has a brother and they were close when they were young but he's been in trouble. She got away and it seemed for the best then. We met. Everything was fine, better than fine."

"Alex, I haven't told Masha because we haven't talked since Christmas, but Jorge and I are leaving Redding. I've put in my notice. We're moving to the East Bay where there's a large Filipino community. Jorge can't be alone so much or he won't make it."

"Oh Luisa, I'm sorry to hear this, especially for Masha. You are a friend."

"It's not her but maybe a little bit, more about feeling comfortable in our skins. We like to be with people we can talk with. Folks with a little darker shade."

"I get that. She'll miss you. I know she already does."

"I'll try to talk to her. She has so much heart, so much *corazon*."

"Today she followed me completely out of her way to see the Indian woman who owns a supply store in the town where I work once a week. I told her I wasn't going to see the woman, but we need chicken wire so I went in and she saw me. There's nothing between me and the woman in the store. I'm hurt she doesn't trust me."

"She has other women rattling in her brain. Do you ever question her about it?"

"She bursts into tears. Never blames me, always the women."

"Blames me, I guess."

"There's no reason. She's not herself. Following me isn't normal."

"It isn't, Alejandro, I'm sorry. I should be getting home."

"Thank you, Luisa, for your time. I hope we see you and Jorge before you leave."

"I'd like that but it depends on Masha. You could try to find a therapist. Maybe no one around here but there's people doing therapy over the phone or on zoom."

"We'll be OK. *Gracias Luisa, y suerte.*"

TWENTY SEVEN

Masha fixed a spicy fish stew with peppers and potatoes and set the steaming bowl in front of Alex. "I'm trying your Mama's recipe. Probably she makes it better but I hope you enjoy it. Especially good with rain falling like music for us."

Outside the rain was heavy, more like a deafening sound, he thought.

Masha lit two candles and opened a bottle of Spanish red wine, then took off her apron and tucked her napkin under the fastening of a pink and white flowered blouse he had given her. With blush on her cheeks, her hair a graceful coil on her shoulder, she looked pink and pretty. How could anything be wrong with his wife as she poured wine with a steady hand and raised a glass to him? Alex wondered.

"My dearest!" she said.

"It's delicious." He tasted the stew and raised his glass again. "You're OK?"

"You don't think it's as good as your Mama's?"

"As good, even better." Alex wanted to forget the morning but he couldn't. He carried the memory with him to bed and Masha felt it. Instead of kissing his eyes as she always did, she kept her face turned and slept with inches between them.

The next morning, Masha caressed Alex awake and aroused him. When they finally separated their damp bodies,

Alex was the first out of bed to make coffee. He brought it back to Masha and sat by the bed. "*Amor*, we need to talk."

"Whew, got to change the sheets," Masha started to slide away but Alex caught her arm.

"We need to talk, Masha."

"Is this about seeing me in Hayfork?"

"It is."

"OK, I'll get dressed. Give me five minutes."

"I need to tell you that I talked with Luisa yesterday afternoon. I was upset. She knows you're avoiding her." Alex didn't look at Masha but at the rain coming down.

Masha set down her cup. "Why did you do that?"

"I couldn't stop thinking about seeing your car across the road and how it made me feel guilty of something I wasn't guilty of, and I needed to talk to someone who knows you and cares about you."

"Luisa? You called her and you spoke about me? You told her about Hayfork?"

"I'm worried about you, *mi vida*. She is also."

"She has no right to worry about me. What I do at work stays at work."

"It wasn't about work. She's a friend. I think there's cause to worry."

"You believe her more than you believe me?" She shook the table, spilling her coffee. "You could have asked me why I was there. I feel completely betrayed."

"I called you at the hospital before I talked to Luisa. You avoided conversation."

"Probably I was too busy."

"Let's not argue, Masha. Let's help each other understand."

"Do you two have more in common than just talking about me?"

"We have nothing more in common. I have met her once at Christmas."

"Now you judge me with that woman you whisper and tell jokes with in Spanish."

"Luisa is your friend, Masha. I needed her help. That's all there is to it."

"If I could only believe that. It's as if I committed a horrible crime."

Alex shook his head. "Believe me, please, and who said anything about crime?"

"You might have well have accused me of stalking."

"Masha, listen to yourself. This is blowing everything out of proportion."

"That's what I think. Luisa will never be my friend now." She stood up but Alex held her shoulder until she sat again.

"You're avoiding talking by making accusations, Masha. It's not helpful. Since it seems you don't know that Luisa is leaving the hospital and moving to the Bay Area, she won't even be at work. She'll be far from here and you'll miss her."

"I didn't know she was leaving but good, I'm glad she'll be gone. She's a sneaky person who can't even tell me she's leaving."

"I'm sure she would have told you about moving but you were avoiding her."

"She said I was avoiding her?"

Alex nodded.

"Well, that's true. After she flirted with you, I just couldn't talk to her."

"She didn't flirt with me. I didn't flirt with her. She knows how stressed you've been."

"I don't make mistakes at work, did she say I did?"

"No, nothing like that."

"But you think I'm a crazy person because I don't like your Indian woman?"

"Not my Indian woman." He sighed. "Please, Masha, be reasonable."

"Am I inventing things? I saw the look in her eyes when we went into her store."

"I went for chicken wire for our coop so you can have the chickens you want. I don't think you're crazy but there's things that have pushed you into thinking what is not true. Whatever it is, you're hurting yourself and you're hurting us."

"You're hurting me more with accusations." Masha looked at dregs in her cup and threw it, shattering the fine pieces on the linoleum. "Let's go away from all this."

"That was your special cup, Masha. The Ukraine cup you loved."

"You're calling me a stalker and you think I'm crazy and I've broken our love."

"You've been pushed beyond limits, you even said so."

"You make me feel worse because you're so calm, such calm words."

"I don't feel calm. I feel terrible about anything that's happening to hurt you."

"Why were you talking to Luisa?" Masha started to cry

quietly. Soon she was sobbing and shaking with gasps of air and tears. "My beloved Alex," she whispered.

"I'm sorry I had to speak with Luisa. She isn't to blame for anything."

They held each other. "I don't know what's happening to me. I was a bad mother. My kids can see it. They don't love me. I can't even help my own mother."

"You help Nadya and your children love you. You must stop seeing the worst, imagining unreal things. You gave all of us love."

"Why doesn't my daughter give me the affection she gives your mother?"

"Adri wants her independence, she always has, and Tomas is just finding his way to being a man. They're going to be fine. It's you, my love, I worry about."

"Alex, I don't know how to love them. If I didn't have you, I don't know what I'd do. I'd kill myself."

"Masha, never say that. Never. Never. We've been stressed for years. Moving up here seemed a way to simplify our lives, to give you the home you wanted. We didn't understand the people we'd be living with."

"I thought they'd be nice older hippies," she laughed and he did, too.

"That would have been better than these people with their anger."

"You think I have a complex because my mother gave me up like your mother gave you up? Some kind of abandonment complex?"

Alex looked at her sharply. "I never believed *Mami* gave

me up. She kept me alive by sending me away. Masha, don't go there."

"My mother is a stranger to me, Alex. Sometimes I feel they sold me and I weep for that thought because it's so bad for them under the Russians. No respect, always made to show their passports, sometimes they're not served in a shop because of their Ukrainian accent. They have no place else they can go. Sometimes I feel haunted, like the negative shadows on x-rays."

"Before the fires?"

"Since the fires, before the fires. Alex, you question me like a therapist. Should I go to a head shrinker that costs lots of money?"

Alex knew better than to bring up Luisa's suggestion of tele-therapy.

"Mama told me recently that the May Day after the explosion, after we'd been evacuated, the Russians made Ukraine and Belarus celebrate the May Day holiday with a big parade in Kiev. They said children were to come waving red flags. Maksym went."

"Were you afraid he'd get sick?"

"Of course. He's a gangster now so maybe that made him what he became."

TWENTY EIGHT

Until Luisa's replacement arrived, Masha had double shifts, her own penance for what happened between them. The supervising nurse had sensed something of a chill between the two nurses but she didn't ask questions and complimented Masha on her willingness to fill in when she was needed. "But sleep, Masha, you can start at noon tomorrow. We'll all feel better when this damn rain stops. I barely made it here myself," her supervisor said.

Masha drank the strong coffee Alex made before he left, brushed her teeth, her hair, slipped into jeans and a tee shirt. She was ready to plant but the rain was making her late. Damn rain, she said to herself. She wanted to feel her hands in the earth but it was so wet the seeds would just float away or rot.

Masha didn't put on her shoes. The soles of her feet and the skin between her toes squished in the mud. She walked toward the bubbling sound of the creek to see how full it really was. Amazingly high, she saw, nothing like the summer's slow trickle. Closer, the water seemed to be whispering Luisa's name, sibilants repeating *Luisssssa, Luisssssa*.

Thunder clapped to the northeast over Mt Shasta. Branches made swirling moving nests within the creek's turbulence, nests like a safe place, like a raft in a flood whose arms might hold her. *No fear*, she said to herself. *God is watching*. She crossed herself and slipped down the muddy bank to embrace the water and be washed clean.

The nest-like branches gave way and she sank with them.

Coming up, spitting out water, she fended off tentacles that ripped her arms and her face, lashing her on all sides. If only she could breathe, she'd fight back. Her lungs gasped for air and filled with water and she heaved up a cough the way the virus patients coughed up their drowning lungs, only a breath away from giving up. How horrible to think of them now under plastic tents with herself, a masked alien-like figure hovering over and suctioning. *No, no* she flung her arms up and raised her head above the whirl. *No, not me, not me.* The Falls that crashed and boomed over rocks were close ahead.

Arm over arm she made her way free of the branches, her mouth and nose full of thick brown water, reflex gagging it out, gasping for each new breath. Currents roiled against her and she swallowed more muddy foam. The bright blood streaking her muddy hands made her imagine the *Californio* girl escaping her pursuers in this torrent before the Falls. Those Falls. She remembered Tomas climbing and leaping up the rocks from boulder to boulder when the creek was a gentle trickle over the tumble of stones. Blood had run down his calves where rocks had nicked him.

Had the *Californio* girl tried to climb out? She must not have been as strong as I am, Masha thought, as she grabbed at a handful of branches that hung over the boulders. The first ones broke off but others held. She pulled herself hand over hand, gripped thicker branches until she felt her toes touch the bank. She began to claw her way up and vomited a gush of mud and water into the creek. She lay panting and filthy and grateful to be alive.

"What happened to your hands, Masha?" Alex asked. "And your face, your face."

She was wearing a long sleeved jersey but couldn't hide the bandages she'd had to wrap from her wrists up to her elbows nor the scrapes on her face with make-up.

"I slipped, the ground was so slippery."

"Does it hurt, *amor*?"

"Not really. I feel good. You're home early."

"I thought you were taking another shift."

"I called in with a sore throat. They needed me but not if I was sick."

"We lost power in Lewiston. I didn't want to wait until it was restored to come home. The roads are terrible. I'm glad you didn't drive in this rain."

"You worried about me driving?"

"Of course I did."

"Thank you. Alex, do you remember the legend we heard when we first came here about the girl drowning at the Falls. It's a tale, don't you think?" She was shivering.

"It's a legend but maybe something did happen."

"I tested the water. It was cold."

"Masha, you tested what water? The shower should have been hot. It's on gas."

"It nearly swallowed me up."

"Masha?" He came close, hands on her trembling shoulders.

"I slipped by accident."

"Slipped? Where?"

"Out back, into the creek."

"The creek? It's very high, almost over the banks. You have to stay back."

"I didn't go over the Falls like the girl who drowned. Maybe she didn't swim like I do." Masha laughed. Alex remained silent.

"Masha, something is wrong here. I'm confused and I'm worried."

"I'll do my best to make supper even with these hands." She wiggled the fingers. "Frankenstein."

Alex didn't crack even a small smile as he sat down. Tomas would be home soon and he didn't want his son hearing any of this.

They sat with their warm tortillas and cheese. Alex and Tomas added their salsa and refried beans but Masha just looked at hers. "I am tired."

"Me, too," Tomas said. "I'll go listen to some music."

"You're excused, son. Bundle up because it's cold in the back of the house." When they heard Tomas close his door, Alex stood up and led Masha to the crackling fire in the wood stove.

"Masha, it's more than being tired. We need help. We can't go on like this—I can't go on like this. I'm frightened for you and I don't like what's happening, especially since I don't understand. You really fell into the creek?"

She nodded. "I didn't try to drown myself if you're thinking that. Word of honor." She raised her bandaged right arm. "It was an accident."

"You have to talk to someone, maybe at the hospital. You must, Masha."

"No hospital. I won't be able to work if they don't trust me. I'm not self-harming. I wanted to cure myself, to live, and the water…remember Ruth Lake when it helped so much…water is good for me. Honest, Alex, I am better now."

"Now but tomorrow? The creek, my god, Masha. That's so…"

"Crazy? You want to say crazy, don't you? I'm not, I'm really not but it seems so long ago I felt myself. Maybe I wanted to baptize myself."

TWENTY NINE

Through Patrice Maldonado, a Physician's Assistant at Sutter Santa Rosa, Masha got a prescription for an antidepressant. Patrice also gave her the name of a psychiatrist who had openings in a virtual practice, everything via zoom. "Hard to find therapists who aren't full up with Covid. You're lucky, Masha, this doctor just got her license and she's a smart cookie. She's done some E.R. here," Patrice said. "The doc's husband comes around and plays his cello at night for patients, totally like a professional, like Yo Yo Ma." Masha thanked Patrice but didn't click the link for an appointment.

The contact was with Dr. Shira Cogan. Masha remembered the clown-like doctor at the Jewish clinic where they'd brought Ana Jesus, and where Adrianna now volunteered. Was this person the therapist Patrice had referred her to? She'd give it one session and then find someone else.

"You are more surprised than me, Maria Sergeyievna?" The doctor's dangly crystal earrings sparkled and made a strange halo facing Masha.

"Maria Sergieyevna, forgive me. When your name came on screen, I remember, you are mother of daughter Adrianna—very smart good girl—and *Señora* Ana Jesus."

"I am Adrianna's mother and the *Señora's* daughter-in-law, yes. I know you've continued to help her. Did my daughter set this up? I haven't talked to her about it."

Dr. Cogan looked confused a moment. "Set up? No, no. No connection." The woman with the big hair shook her head. "I take new clients."

"So it's really a coincidence?"

"Maybe I am Dr. Ruth, but more chic, no?" Dr. Shira shook her earrings.

Masha let herself relax enough to laugh at the resemblance. "How do you know Dr. Ruth?"

"Watching TV of course, Americans talking to Dr. Ruth. Do you want to talk?"

"Not really…"

"Not with me or another therapist? Shall we arrange a referral? Yours came to me because I'm just starting practice and you, Maria Sergievna, are first experiment."

"That doesn't sound hopeful." Masha looked down hiding her eyes; the doctor was giving her an out.

"Our hour is already paid by insurance, so how can I help?"

Masha paused a moment. "I started taking an anti-depressant." She named the medication. "It makes me feel numb to everything."

"Medication helps the depression? Or is it anxiety, Maria Sergievna?"

"I suppose it's both, but I don't like what else it does," said Masha.

"We have medications you like better." Dr. Shira wrote the name of an anti-depressant Masha had never heard of and held it up so she could see. "Less side effects but please continue prescription you take before you start another. Same class, SSRI."

"I know that, serotonin uptake inhibitors."

"Correct."

"I'm an R.N."

"Yes, I know. New med goes less fast through body, less side effects."

"I get off the one and onto the other?"

"Maria Sergieyvna, I will research and make certain. I believe no problem."

"Call me Masha, everyone does."

"And I'm Shira, Masha."

"I didn't know you were a psychiatrist, Dr. Shira."

"My specialty in Russia. Now California license has come. You are first person I do zoom with, not like in person but OK."

Masha stayed silent, looking at Dr. Shira's large eyes, magnified by her oblong rhinestone-studded glasses. Such terrible taste, Masha thought, typically Russian make up, too much eye shadow and mascara and hair like an old diva. Poor woman.

"I was spoiling my life. With meds, I don't act impulsively but I feel numb. I'm glad to try the new ones you suggest."

"Are you sleeping, Masha?"

Masha nodded. "The weather is so grey here, there's nothing to get up for. I go to work and clock hands don't seem to be moving. I worked at Sutter before we moved. Didn't realize how good I had it there."

"I also like Sutter, and also husband likes."

"Doctor?"

"Janitor."

"Patrice told me he plays cello."

Dr. Shira smiled and nodded. "Yes, Avram is a musical janitor."

"Do you think Adrianna knows I was referred to you?"

"No. *Departmentalizata.*"

"Close. Compartmentalize. My daughter thinks I'm crazy and she reveres you."

"Next week, same time? Monday is good? I'll send prescription for new med to hospital pharmacy in Redding?"

"Not the hospital. Redding Safeway. Monday morning is fine unless they call for an extra shift. Usually I know a week ahead but they're short-handed. Can I text you?"

"Yes. Thank you, Masha, for making choice. And please, don't begin taking new medication until I check."

"Thank you, Dr. Shira, for taking me on. I'm not a usual person."

"I'm not usual psychiatrist. We will get along fine."

THIRTY

Alex stopped in front of Ray and Susan's house to see if she might have returned but there was no sign of anyone inside. Since he intended to do a little work on the house whether Susan had returned or not, he opened his toolbox and took out his gloves. The first thing he did was return the front door to its hinges. He suspected kids had broken in, probably to get high. If they came again, they'd smash windows as long as the house stayed deserted, so he wouldn't replace cracked panes. One day they'd probably set the place on fire and he couldn't prevent it. He swept up shavings in case Susan did return.

He wished Ray had a grave where he could pay respects, not where a few ragged flowers lay against the tree, bits of glass, metal and a Jefferson flag streaked with mud from the rains. An ambulance had finally come to take Ray but Alex didn't know where. If Susan had Ray's ashes with her after she'd had him cremated, that would be at least something for her. Would she ever be back?

As Alex packed up tools, he heard a sputtering truck and turned to see Bort getting out and slamming the door shut before he announced himself with a hoarse call, "What you doing here, scrounging parts?"

Words enough to start a fight with Bort but Alex wasn't going to react. "Making repairs for when Susan comes back."

"Repairs? When you fucked him up, man."

Alex watched Bort inhale his joint and hold the smoke. Exhaling cannabis made the air musky but better breathing that than Bort's rank breath.

"You made him go to the fires. Killed him."

A passing truck slowed down to look at them. Bort gave the driver the finger as he had from Ray's truck that first encounter.

"Citizens told him he shouldn't go with you, that you weren't one of us. You come in, Ray dies. You cast a dark spell over that man."

"I feel as bad as you do about Ray." Alex knew there was no explaining more.

"And you knew the man how long? He just didn't see it. He told us you got our protection and we didn't see nothing coming back."

"You never asked and I didn't have a choice, did I? It's Citizens or…"

"We don't ask. You're in or you're out and I'm saying you're out. I vote you out, gone, and stay out of stuff around here if you know what's good for you."

"What's this about, Bort?"

"It's about the bad vibes you bring. You and your big blond get the shit out of here before you regret it. You've got bad juju. You know Loony kicked it and he was hanging out with your woman."

"Who?"

"Gus, the head case. He could talk more languages and more bullshit. Fuck, that man had a brain when he wasn't fried."

"Gustavo died? My wife gave him meals and they talked. What happened?"

"How do I know? Campers found him curled up in the

woods like he went to sleep. They said he was dried out like a gourd, no smell."

"I'm sorry. My wife will take it hard."

'Maybe it's that sign you've been waiting for to clear out. We won't forget what you've done, believe me, fucker, we won't forget."

Bort spat and stomped toward his truck that he couldn't start until the third try. Alex could have told him what he needed but he didn't say a word.

"Poor soul," Masha said when Alex told her about Gus. "He meant no harm."

Alex wasn't surprised she took the news with calmness. He'd been seeing how the medications were slowing her down, putting smiles on her lips, even making her voice seem lower. Less tears. For now, this was a relief though he missed Masha's passion. He understood that the meds did all sorts of things to the body while they helped the mind.

Maybe he shouldn't bring up the conversation with Carlos now, but it seemed a natural way to solve everything that losing Ray and Bort's threat lead up to.

Masha listened to Alex. She looked relieved they weren't talking about her but she didn't agree to move on the basis of a phone call.

"We'll be trading our freedom for security. Backing off all the work we've done here."

"We won't lose our freedom, Masha. We'll have our own home."

"You'll always answer to them."

Alex nodded. "It's family. I understand you're not as close to them."

"I like everyone but not necessarily to see them every day."

"I told Carlos that soon it will be one year we're here and we've made so many good changes, not the least with Tomas. But Malvina Falls, nothing around here is our place."

"We're living our lives despite people who don't want us. Where will the money come from to build our home on this magical property?"

"I bring my skills which they need. Machinery is always breaking down. Another hand, maybe a little money if we sell or maybe rent."

Masha shook her head. "You ever see anyone who might rent here?"

Alex had foreseen Masha's objections but her haughty words irritated him. He didn't want to upset this calm they'd established.

"No rush, *amor.*"

"Your mother is always invited here."

At night Alex held her close but her own desire, usually so quick to rise and so necessary to fulfill, didn't meet his though he felt she tried. Her therapist, Dr. Shira, assured her desire would return with time, that it was the medication she'd get adjusted to. The best days were when Alex was working in the garage and she came to sit quietly and watch the sparks fly, watch his hands skillfully shape the metals with his blue flame. But when she had the day off and he was gone, she walked around the house unfocused. She cleaned everything she could see, worked a little in the garden that needed her attention. She never went all the way to the creek which had settled back down like a deflated paper dragon. She didn't like looking at herself in the mirror where she saw a woman with vacant eyes. And my chin, it's bigger than ever, she said to herself. Where are my eyes that Alex says sparkle with light? I don't have any light now.

She thought of Shira's eyes on the screen. She no longer saw the therapist as some sort of silly person with a sculpted pile of dyed hair. Shira listened attentively as Masha poured out her heart.

"Alex needed me so much. Maybe he won't need me any more, and find another woman," Masha tried to say off-handedly but nothing slipped past Shira.

"You speak of losing your husband but you say he's a good loyal man."

"He is."

"You told him effects of medication will go away. He has understood."

"Yes, but I've never withheld from him."

"Be patient. New meds will be better."

"I'm a plant without sun."

"Sun will come out."

"Love is breathing for me, it's my life."

"I understand. Love…love is our life force."

"I wish I had a mother like you who understands me."

"Your mother doesn't understand?"

"I never tell her any of this. I never tell anyone. I don't deserve to complain."

"Maria Sergeivna, a therapist is different from mother. Therapists don't judge."

Masha hadn't been cooking much but when Alex opened the door, he inhaled the rich smell of chicken roasting in the oven. A bottle of Argentine merlot stood uncorked. Masha hadn't been drinking with the medication so he limited himself to beers before a meal. Now he smelled wine on her breath and he saw a glass beside the stove. She had washed her hair and let it hang halfway down her back which he loved. He would never lose the happiness of breathing in her thick hair, the clean smell of her scalp. She wore a new pair of black jeans that fit snugly over her hips as if she were a twenty-year old.

"What a lovely surprise and you look good enough to eat." He nuzzled her ear.

"I'm starved. Let's have a glass and celebrate."

"What are we celebrating, *mi vida?*"

"I put away the meds. My second day, no meds." She twirled and kissed him.

He held her but made enough distance to look into her eyes. "Masha, you are beautiful and the chicken smells wonderful, but you aren't supposed to go off suddenly."

"I feel so good. I got along with everyone at work no matter what they were saying. Please, drink a glass with me and then call Tomas for supper."

Alex raised his glass to her toast.

"We'll go to Hawaii one day, lie in the sun, make love day and night to make up for these days."

At the table, Tomas said how juicy the chicken was. "You cook good, Mom."

"Thank you, son, but I don't think we'll be able to eat our own chickens, even when they're old," she said.

Tomas, a drumstick in his mouth, nodded. "Would be gross."

"No, never, we'll never eat our chickens." Masha began to cry. "No, no. That would be murder." She put down her fork, took a swallow of her wine and went into the bedroom where they could hear her sobbing.

"What's going on with mom?" Tomas asked.

"She'll be back. She's worried about the chickens."

"Chickens?"

"Ones we have."

"Oh. She always worries about something."

When Masha came out, her face was wet, her eyes red. "I'm thinking of our chickens. We are never going to eat them, are we?"

Alex and Tomas shook their heads and said together, "Never," but Masha couldn't stop crying.

Masha spent an entire morning pruning fruit trees. The pomegranate tree glowed almost red with buds ready to pop. For some reason, thinking of the red pomegranate flowers and the thousands of seeds within made her start crying. She sat on a welded bench Alex had made but she couldn't stop crying, tears just kept coming. Alex was so talented. What did she do to deserve him? She cried harder. When her tears finally stopped, she dried her eyes and tried to begin pruning the apple tree but time had run out and she had to get ready for work. At that moment, she heard a car stop in front.

Mrs. Robinson surprised Masha in the garden. She had a cigarette in her fingers and her realtor's notepad under her arm. Before Masha could stop her, she stubbed out a smoking butt in the groundcover just beginning to blossom with little yellow flowers.

"Mrs. del Calvo, I'm here to bring good news. The Mister isn't home?"

The way the woman asked this seemed to imply delinquency. Masha shook her head. "He's at work and I've got to get going myself."

"No problem. I can't linger. Leave you these." She handed over a color brochure.

"What's it about?"

"Look at the pictures of Malvina Falls featured in the Tri-County Realtor just out. See, our rivers, mountains, Trinity Lake, Mt. Shasta. Makes me proud."

"Always beautiful."

"Yes it is. When will Mr. del Calvo be home? I always say it's better to have all the parties present when we're talking a major life decision. I'll leave this with you to share with your husband. Any time I'll catch you both here?"

Masha held the glossy paper at a distance. "Day after tomorrow but we've got other things on our mind right now."

"Missus, long as I'm here, let me give you a heads-up. There's new prices in property, prices we haven't seen in ages, ever actually. You're about to be offered 30% maybe 50% over what you paid because these buyers are big time and don't count the money. With all the work you've done dolling up your place, you can take the profit and go somewhere you'll like more."

"What makes you think I don't like it here?"

"Like I said, let's discuss this when the Mister is home."

"You're talking about us selling our home?"

"You betcha. There's a new player called Renaissance buying up homes and offering them as second, even third residences for folks that don't count the change, like I said. They want peace and quiet for a week or a month or forever. You take your pot of gold, bingo, hit the jackpot."

"I don't know about peace and quiet around here," Masha said.

Mrs. Robinson laughed and squashed out her second cigarette under her shoe on the groundcover. Masha thought that if wealthy people came here with nice cars, they'd have to hire guards like the oligarchs did. She supposed this bit of information was exactly what would not be included in 'full disclosure.'

"Mrs. Robinson, why you don't like us?" Masha looked their realtor in the eye.

"Mrs. del Calvo, what gives you that idea?" Mrs. Robinson looked genuinely surprised by the question. "I like you and the Mister fine. I like what you've have done to this place. Maybe you made me the fool. I didn't see the potential but it's all good."

"But you never *liked* us."

"Ever considered that you didn't like me, young lady? That you thought I was just a dumb country realty lady with a nothing business?"

"No, we never thought that. To tell you the truth, I felt from the first that you wanted to hold your nose when you saw us."

"Not true, Mrs. del Calvo. We did have a certain life style here, my folks, my hubby's folks, theirs before them, and it's changed. I know you work hard in that hospital, have heard good things even if I personally think the virus is fake news. Folks are sick and you are a good nurse. You're just different from us, you think different."

"That's true. I didn't stop to see anything from your point of view. I appreciate your words. We only wanted a place of our own here but lots of people seemed enemies."

"Call me neutral, Missus. As long as we're having a heart-to-heart." Mrs. Robinson lit another cigarette and inhaled. "I've been feeling down, I guess you could say depressed, by how things were changing before you came. With the growing, the nastiness…plenty of reasons we won't go into but we've been down for a while. My husband and me, we're an old family who always did the real work with cattle and farming. We go to church on Sunday. Too many folks have lost the faith."

"I'd go to church regularly if it weren't so far. I'm sorry you feel depressed. I've always had a problem with depression. Up and down, worse lately."

Mrs. Robinson didn't look at Masha when she extended

her hand. "Then let's shake on some good news coming up. Give my best to the Mister."

After Mrs. Robinson left, Masha became aware her heart was pounding. She felt light-headed and hot. Was she safe to drive? She had time to drive slowly if she started now. She was so unnerved she couldn't remember what the realtor came for.

Masha arrived in the parking lot at Mercy in a full body sweat. She parked as close to the ER entrance as she could with her hospital employee tag.

Jane was in charge of the ER. "Hi Masha, what are you doing down here? Haven't seen you since the fires. You were amazing."

"Thank you, Jane. I can hardly remember those days. Even recent visits, a woman this afternoon, I can't remember what she came for."

"Maybe that's good," Jane replied.

"I probably do remember but can't think about it. I'm here because I have a shift coming up and my heart is racing and thumping all over. Would you check vitals?"

Jane, crisp in her scrubs, wrapped the cuff around Masha's arm. "Sit."

Jane pointed to a chair.

"Deep breath. High. Is that usual, Masha?'

"No. I'm usually fine. Stress at home. There's awful stuff going on."

"Sit for a minute and we'll take BP and do an EKG, OK? Take no chances." Jane took her pressure again. "Good, going down but still high. Sit over there and we'll see about your heart. Do you have panic attacks?"

"Nothing like this. I've changed some meds."

"For BP?"

"No, anxiety. I got off them a few days ago. Didn't taper off, went cold turkey. I have a prescription for a med that's got fewer side effects but I haven't started."

"Masha, not smart. Better talk to someone. Want me to call mental health?"

"I have a therapist, thanks. I'd prefer you report just about my pressure."

"I can do that. Let's take one more reading."

Masha sat with the cuff watching the numbers go almost down to normal.

"You just had an attack of nerves of some kind. If you're upstairs and need to come down again, I'll do the EKG but I think it's nerves."

"Thanks, Jane. I'll be OK as long as I'm on the floor. I'll rethink the med thing."

"You do. Good luck, Masha."

"Thanks again, much appreciated."

As Masha climbed the stairs to her floor she still couldn't remember why Mrs. Robinson had showed up all smiles and congratulations.

THIRTY ONE

Masha confessed to Shira, "I didn't wait until I finished the meds and started the new ones. I just stopped. They were making me feel I was barely alive."

"You went off?"

"I made a mistake. I had a scare and checked myself out in the ER."

"How are you now, Masha?"

"I'm OK. I started the new meds you prescribed."

"You have side-effects?"

"Not so much but I'm very tired."

"You can drive your body crazy, Masha. Not helping yourself. Please, now, continue new medication. Yes?"

Masha nodded on the screen. "Shira?"

Shira raised the thickly painted brows that meant she was listening.

"I had a dream my mother was calling from *Simferopol* to wake me up because I was in danger. I saw explosions and fires. I couldn't move, I couldn't wake up."

"What happens then in dream?"

"Buzzer went off. I woke up shaking." She paused. "I saw the Indian woman in the shadows, the woman who likes Alex too much and I'm afraid he likes her also, especially since I was unreliable. She was connected with the disaster but she isn't."

"From what you say to me, there is no reason to doubt husband. We speak how we have no control over what others feel, only you manage your own feelings. Always there will be younger women. Women can be most beautiful but nothing lasts. Remember the Queen in Snow White's story? Even if you are most beautiful, Elizabeth Taylor, there are always others younger coming along."

"I've always been afraid of losing love and everything that makes me safe."

"Dear Masha, I know *Chernobyl* was horrible, fires were horrible, friend's death, husband and son in real danger. We are all exhausted. I helped people in Russia to stay out of hospitals where they lose minds. Medications they use destroy. Here, medications can help for some time while we work on our divided cells."

"Cells?"

"Sorry, divided selves but cells also, maybe each person has many ancestors, many shadows of memory that are deep, deep inside."

"My little devil of memory starts out small but once I give it oxygen, it becomes a green monster, taking over my mind."

"Shine light, watch mind de-construct demon. You imagine, you can send away."

"But maybe Alex feels something for her."

"You send demon away, Masha. Put on fast plane away."

"I don't want to make Luisa disappear. I know she wasn't luring Alex from me."

"Good, you now see Luisa as person. You do well, Masha, very well."

"I feel ashamed. She never meant anyone harm." Masha felt that if Shira had been close, not separated by a screen, the woman would have reached out and hugged her, drenched her in the floral, insecticidal perfume she remembered the Russians sprayed in the plane they flew her in to America. That was a bad memory turned good.

THIRTY TWO

"Sorry to wake you. It's your mother." Alex placed a blanket over Masha's shoulders and handed her the phone.

Masha didn't say anything as she saw the image on her phone, a figure lying in what looked like a hospital bed with bars. His head lay flat with his Adam's apple jutting up, a cross held between his long fingers laced over his chest. An elongated Christ on the Cross over her father's bed seemed a mirror image.

Nadya moved the phone closer so Masha saw her father had his eyes closed with coins on them. His mouth, partly opened, hadn't been tied securely. Sergiey had lost his teeth years ago to radiation poisoning and been given a badly fitting false set that he removed at night into a glass. Without them she saw how sunken his mouth was, like a long-dead person, not her father.

Alex could hear the two women crying, one far, one beside him. A few words he didn't understand were spoken and then the phone went dark.

"Masha?" Alex waited until she had clicked off the phone.

"Father has passed. He is at peace, my father Sergiey Semyinovich Kochonok." Masha crossed herself and kissed the blank phone screen. "I suppose I expected this but not now, not so soon."

"Many difficulties at once, Masha. I am with you."

"I know." She held him and began crying but quietly, not the uncontrollable sobs of weeks before.

"I will never see him now. I could have gone to see him."

Alex pressed her more tightly. "You couldn't have known. What happened?"

"He hadn't left his bed for weeks but my mother never wrote or told me that. Only two days he was in the hospital."

"How are you feeling, my love?"

"Numb, I guess. Thinking I should I go to my mother. Thinking about Father."

Alex spoke almost in a whisper. "Your brother is close by your mother. He can go to her, not you going into a danger zone in your condition."

"Because I'm not right in the head?"

"I didn't say that. You're recovering from extreme stress. The dangers there won't help. Maksym will be with your mother. You can talk every day."

Masha shook her head. "Mama says he's in Istanbul, Turkey. He can't come back. She didn't say why he'd gone. I think he's running from Russians and gangsters."

"How does your brother make a living?"

"I've asked Mother in the past and she's always evasive. He's good with computers and he makes phone calls, she's told me. Phone calls! He's probably a hacker and an extortionist. A troll."

"That's awful if true."

"What is awful for them? They have to survive. I wonder if my mother is safe?"

"Masha, travel is too dangerous. You've seen the news. Russians are on the border with tanks. I don't think Maksym would just abandon his mother, your mother."

Masha shook her head. "I just don't know. No laws there."

They said together, "Like here," and smiled.

Masha laughed. "Here it's not really really serious. I don't like the guns but I don't feel threatened, not like in Russia or Ukraine. It's more like fake drama here, pretending to be tough. And like Ray and the men you work for, they're not bad people."

"No, they're not. Everyone wants some respect, even Bort stupid as he is."

"I still see that man with a scar who came once. He looked evil," she said.

"We've kept our distance. Maybe now they won't let us."

Masha asked for a special zoom session with Shira who appeared on her screen with hair in huge rollers, without her usual eye make-up, powder, rouge, lipstick or projecting eyelashes. Even with her nightgown up to her neck she looked naked.

"Forgive my appearance. I look like a scary old lady, a *baba yaga*."

"No, you look softer without the make-up. Thank you for seeing me."

"What's on mind your, *Mashinka*? How can I help?"

Masha liked the diminutive Shira was using for the first time. "My father has died. My mother showed me a picture of him on his death bed. I should have gone to see them sooner and I feel guilty."

"Very sorry, my condolences, my dear. Have you been to Ukraine since coming to America?"

Masha shook her head. "Too expensive, and Mother discouraged me. I don't know my country. I never did. We were internally exiled for so many years."

"Very beautiful country, *Mashinka*, mountains and sea, many times husband and me go to Black Sea. I was ashamed when Russia took Crimea from Ukraine. Now what is to happen with your country? Tell me about Father."

"His normal life ended the day of the explosion. He was always sick but he just kept living. What if my mother needs me?"

"Of course your mother needs you but she is far. You can talk easily?"

"Within limits, yes. That's what Alex says—talk to her. He's almost always right. He's more formed than I am."

"Formed, like what?" Shira's eyes reflected in a light she turned on beside her.

"Alex, he's the whole person but he's also my missing half and that's a burden for him, to be both himself and fill in half of me. I don't know if this makes sense, Shira."

"It makes important sense."

"It's not a secret. I've known this a long time and he must also but he thinks I'm the better half because I have more education and I earn more."

"He feels resentment for this, do you think?"

"No, he's proud of me and he's such a generous, forgiving person that he doesn't know how to be envious of others the way I am. He's secure, he's strong."

"Go on," Shira said. "You feel resentment about his strength?"

"No, yes, maybe sometimes. He can be contented and I never am. I earned a degree but I never worked to make myself a better person because I rely on him."

"Give me small example, Masha."

"Well…the new car, it's used but he loves it. He forgets about me when he talks of it and I'm thinking, he loves the car more than me. Stupid, I know. He'd never think that way. Also, but not exactly related, my mother thinks we roll in gold here and sometimes I feel like a piggybank for them. For her, now. I won't go there. You and Alex are right. I'll send more money."

Shira paused. "*Mashinka*, I shouldn't have to say what you understand. In Russia, in Ukraine, Moldava, everywhere in former Empire, few are rich and many are poor, so poor. If you can help Mother, do that and don't regret."

Shira's alarm went off. "Masha, I wish time weren't running out but I must put on face and go to clinic. Let me quote something about two people. When they meet soul mate, they meet actual halves of self."

"That's me and Alex, that's us. How did you know? Did you think that up now?"

Shira laughed. "Oh no, written thousands of years ago, Plato, how we always seek our other half. Something else from Plato, image of two parts of whole, like egg yellow and white, needing to find the lost half to be whole. It's the same idea."

Masha stared into the screen and sighed.

"One important thing, Mashinka. I see your daughter Adrianna today."

"You can tell her we talk but don't say anything personal."

"You and I talk in confidence. I am paid by insurance, you know."

"I will talk to her also. Maybe we—you and I—were meant to be a pair also. I feel a great relief talking to you. I never anticipated it. You truly help me."

"Always I try, my dear. You won't forget meds and we talk next week or if you need, sooner. Then I will have face on and be beautiful."

That afternoon, Shira drew Adrianna into her office and shut the door.

"You know the HIPPA rules?" Shira asked.

"HIPPA, all that paperwork, but I understand privacy is important."

"I am professionally talking with Mother, Maria Sergeievna, on zoom. I don't like secrecy, no spy in this heart, so I tell you today." Shira tapped her heart.

"I guess you have to tell me sometime. She knows nothing I say to you?"

"HIPPA both ways. No, I won't tell her you're pregnant."

"I'm not pregnant!" Adrianna looked shocked. "What are you saying?"

"I make a joke." Shira laughed but Adrianna was stone-faced.

"I'm a virgin, Shira, if you must know."

A look of surprise, then near laughter overcame Shira's

usual composure. Her crystal earrings jangled. "In Russia, we light icons to you. Few pregnant virgins are left."

"You're ridiculous."

"No, I meet women who have never known man and they are having wished-for child from sperm banks."

"You know about sperm donation? It's not exactly virgin birth, Shira."

"Life is still mystery, my dear, deep mystery."

THIRTY THREE

Maksym's call scared Masha but saved her searching to find her brother. "Sister, good morning," the man with no image and a familiar voice greeted her at 6am.

"It's still dark here, Brother, we're ten hours behind Ukraine. Why don't you use Facetime so I can see you."

"I'm not in Ukraine but difference is the same, Sister. I didn't wake you?"

"You're in Turkey, Maksym? I want to hear how our mother is doing."

"*Mashinka*, our mother needs your help."

"I know. I'd like to go to her but it's difficult right now."

"You don't want to come. You want to send her money. She is coping but her life is so difficult, new taxes on us by Russians every day."

Masha hadn't heard of the Ukrainians being taxed but the occupiers never stopped suspecting disloyalty and if they could drive Ukrainians out of their own land, they'd do it by whatever means.

"I will send an extra amount from my bank account to hers, the way we do it."

"No no, Sister," Maksym said adamantly. "Send directly through *hawala*."

"*Hawala?*"

"The Mohammedans have personal couriers all over the world. Very fast. You go with the dollars and within twenty-four hours, Mother will have local currency in hand."

"I've never heard of this," Masha said. "My husband and I

use Western Union for remittances and our mothers always received them."

"Russians will take the money. Go to the *hawala*. Mother needs money for our father's burial with no delay. His body lies waiting for the earth."

Masha stared at her phone. How could he speak such dry words, as if she had no feelings for her father lying somewhere on a cold slab. "I'll call our mother and make arrangements with her. How are you, Brother?"

The phone went dead.

The closest *hawala* Masha found was in Hayward, south of Oakland. Luisa lived in Oakland. Masha found an address, called to verify that money would be transferred quickly and was promised it would be. The fee sounded reasonable.

Alex questioned her decision. "We've never done this, Masha. Western Union was never a problem. I don't understand why you can't do that with Nadya."

"Maksym insisted that the Russians don't trace *hawala* transfers but they trace Western Union and the money can be taken or taxed. Let me try this once. Sending money is easier than making foreign travel plans, having to get a passport."

"True and I don't want you going there. Don't send too much. Maybe $100."

"I know, especially since Maksym told me to do this but $200 is better."

"$200 is a lot to lose," Alex said.

"The amount is not too much if it helps Mother."

"I'll go with you, Masha. That way I know you're safe. We can see my mother and Adrianna. I'd like to bring the angel for the gate to Carlos and Ditto."

"We can combine all that and spend the night. The angel is beautiful, Alex. You are a true artist with metals."

"Thank you, *amor*. We can visit our cousin's property. Now that they are becoming owners they are making many changes I'd like to see."

"If we start really early. I might visit a few of nurses I liked at Sutter. I don't know who's still there or even who survived the virus. I might call Luisa. She knows the East Bay. I've been putting that off and it's time."

"Masha, I hoped you'd call Luisa when you wanted to. How are you feeling?"

"More like my old self, Alex. I look forward to seeing your family."

"You think Tomas will be OK? Or maybe he'd like to go with?"

"I think he's OK here for one night if he knows we're not coming home."

"I'm very sorry, Luisa, you did no wrong."

"Masha, dear, I hoped you'd call. We've been so busy or I'd have called you."

"I really am sorry."

"Don't be hard on yourself. So much going on. I was

worried about you. How are you doing? How are you feeling?"

"Better, thank you. I've been talking with a therapist. I'm on meds. I was way out of line. How are you and Jorge in your new home?"

Masha heard the sigh, the long silence. "An apartment. You get a lot more for your money in Redding. It's so noisy with people overhead and alongside. You hear gunshots, too close to what we remember in Manila."

"I don't know how I'd adapt to a city," Masha said.

"I came down with shingles right after we moved in. Shingles are no joke. Incredibly painful. I had to postpone starting a new job at Kaiser in Oakland and we were short on cash."

"Can I help?"

"Cousins helped, and thanks, I got my first paycheck so we're OK. We have people here. Jorge's in NA. I go to support meetings. He's met other Filipino men so he feels better about the group. Addiction is life long, marriage to an addict is life long."

"My mother has had to live with my brother."

"You just learn ways to cope, at least you hope you do. Jorge is thinking of going to community college to get EMT certified. They'll do lots of background checks so we'll see. One step at a time. What news from up north?"

"Tomas has made a real turn-around, finding his passion in trees and forests."

"In Oakland there's encampments under bridges and alongside off-ramps by freeways. Hard to believe sometimes we're in the richest country in the world. These people would be better off where you live. They could shelter under the trees."

"They wouldn't be welcome here. Squatters come to a bad end. We saw it happen. Our Citizens drove them off." Masha paused. "Two weeks ago, my father died."

"I'm so sorry to hear. *Lo siento*. He wasn't well as I recall. How is your mother?"

"That's one of the reasons I called. Alex and I are coming to Hayward to send her money by way of *hawala*. Ever heard of that?"

"It's mostly a Muslim service. I know an Afghan who's trustworthy and quick."

"There are Tatars in the Crimea, Muslims, so maybe that's why Maksym chose *hawala*. He's not there though. He's in Istanbul. We'll send enough to help, not too much if it doesn't get to my mother."

"We've found them reliable and fast, never had problems. How is your brother? You seemed to have doubts about him when we talked."

"I don't know. I suspect he does scams on the phone."

"You mean like 'It's your grandson calling from Africa, robbed, lost passport?'"

"I'm afraid so. My mother is kind of his captive, especially now she's alone."

"We call it co-dependent," Luisa said. "Like me and Jorge."

"I guess like me and Alex. My brother is all she has left."

"When are you planning on coming to the East Bay?"

"This weekend. Does that give you enough time to see if you're free?"

"Depends on the time. Let me look at my schedule."

After moments, Luisa came back on the line. "Lunch time Saturday will work. I have a shift at 4pm to midnight."

"I can be wherever you want to meet by noon or a little after."

"Lunch for sure. Hayward has a big Afghan population and some great restaurants. I love Khyber Pass Kabob. We'll go to the *hawala* after lunch."

Masha decided she'd go by herself to meet Luisa while Alex stayed longer in Santa Rosa. She longed to talk with Luisa.

"So glad you called, looking forward to seeing you, Masha."

"Love you, Luisa."

"Love you back, Masha. See you at the Khyber Pass."

THIRTY FOUR

Masha looked out the window at the onion dome of the Perpetual Redeemer. She waved with a grimace. "Good bye forever you misers of little faith." She wondered if the priest and his wife were still depriving children of food and pleasure in life. "I got away because of you, but really forgiving them has taken a long time." She squeezed Alex' shoulder and he leaned over to give her a quick kiss on the cheek, then turned onto Ludvig Avenue where Carlos and Ditto's miracle acquisition of land exceeded any expectations of getting rich in America.

"The Portuguese really own all this land!" Masha exclaimed as they passed open fields with a small herd of cows, goats and horses sheltering together under oaks from the heat. Grasses had already dried. A small pond for the animals sparkled.

"Twenty five or thirty acres. The property is outside Santa Rosa city limits but Ditto told me it's sure to become incorporated so they could sell for a fortune but they promised the couple they'd stay on the land. Carlos and Ditto want to farm. Farming is in our DNA."

The bottom half of Alex' gate swung open beside a new sign, *Del Calvo Farm*. The angel on top would be a perfect welcome.

"Do you regret we didn't move here and have a share?"

"It would have been easier to see *Mami* and Adri."

"So you have regrets?"

He took his hand from the wheel and squeezed hers. "No,

I don't regret our adventure. We needed that time together, you were right about that."

"It's as if we moved to a foreign country where we didn't belong."

"I never felt that way even when I was new here."

"I didn't feel at home until I met you," she said.

"You sure you'll be OK getting to Hayward? You haven't driven on freeways."

"I've got GPS and once Luisa and I meet, she'll be with me."

"I'm glad you're meeting her but the family will want to see you."

"I'll be back for supper."

"Stay for a moment."

"I'll be late. Just say I'll be back soon."

Before Masha could get behind the wheel, Carlos's wife Dolores came out in her apron over skinny jeans. "Masha, *guapa*, how pretty you look!"

"It's beautiful here and I'm so happy for you and everyone." Masha let Dolores hug her for as long and closely as she liked to do.

Behind Dolores came her daughter Kim with a baby in her arms. In an instant, Masha saw that the bikini-body girl looked like a mother and not a tempting morsel. Gone were the long fake eyelashes, make up and skimpy tops; she was wearing a blue tunic with dark circles where her breasts leaked. She saw how proudly Kim was showing off her little girl dressed in pink with party bows in the wisps of black hair. Masha leaned in to look more closely at the dark-eyed baby and told Kim how beautiful she was.

So Kim had married Diego, the bartender and manager of the Lizard Bar. Everyone was employed in part of the family businesses. If they moved here, what would they expect of her?

"Hard work paid off. I'm proud and happy for you." Alex gave Dolores a big hug and praised Kim's baby without getting closer.

"We were lucky, we had good *suerte*. The *patron* was good to us."

"It's only been a year and so much changed," Alex said.

"Only a year but it seems a lifetime," Masha said. "Please forgive me, Dolores, I won't be here for lunch but I'll be back in time for supper. I'll see Adri and Mama then."

Dolores looked hurt. "You take something with, for now."

Masha didn't argue. She was hungry and needed a bite to quiet her nerves.

"They all want you here. And give my respects to Luisa and Jorge," Alex said.

He stood by their car waiting for Dolores' return, feeling a little embarrassed that Masha's independence looked like lack of respect for his family. What would it be like if they all lived close together?

"I think our move was hard but it was good. We've been lucky. I'm ready for a change." Masha kissed him, as if this were a reply to his unasked question.

"Still the love birds," Dolores said, bringing something wrapped in foil smelling of warm corn. "Not much but we'll see you for barbeque."

Khyber Pass served them a shared plate of savory lamb and vegetables.

"So delicious. The seasoning is perfect and I love the bread," Masha cleaned the sauce on her plate with the flat baked Afghan bread. "Even if we're too full, it's so good. One bite each."

Luisa also finished her full plate and ordered tea and Baklava.

"What a wonderful meal and it's like we never had bad feelings."

"I never did. I was puzzled but I know what being stressed can do."

Masha reached over to hold Luisa's hand. "We've had a lot happen. The kids are doing well and we could make money if we decide to sell and move back to Santa Rosa. I can tell I'm better because I want to make love more."

"You always did," Luisa giggled. 'You're such a sexy girl."

"Maybe too much, I don't know. Fills in the blanks, makes me whole."

"I've been on Zanax forever. Temptation is always there to pilfer a few more which we can do in hospitals. You saw the show *Nurse Jackie?*" Luisa asked.

"I don't want more drugs. *Jackie* was the saddest show." Masha could feel herself choking up. "I told you my father died. That's why I'm sending money to my mother so she can bury him properly."

"You did tell me and I'm sorry."

Masha told Luisa about finding her therapist. "She's Russian but I really like her. She really helps my stability."

She was about to say more but Luisa looked at her watch and signaled the waiter.

"It's almost three. It's quick at the *hawala*. We should go now. You don't want to be stuck in the commute traffic and I've got a shift at four."

When the turbaned young man came with the bill, Masha handed him her card.

"You don't have anything to make up to me, Masha. It's great to see you."

"You're holding my hand going into the *hawala*," Masha said.

"They aren't Taliban. They're the ones who got away from Taliban. No worries, the people are nice."

"How do you know all this, Luisa?"

"I told you, I've been using this *hawala* to send money to my children. When we couldn't find one in Redding, I wrote a check to Jorge's cousin here and he came to Hayward. I trust the guy and his wife, dignified people, teachers until they fled."

At a small counter in a room with light streaming in, Masha paid the $200 cash to a robust woman in a *kameez*, and trousers, a loosely-tied embroidered scarf pulled back over the part in her graying hair. When she came from behind the counter to embrace Luisa, her wrists jingled with many bangles "My daughter, how are you? You will have a cup of tea?"

Luisa apologized. "I must be at work and my friend

has a long drive." To Masha, she whispered, "This is a good woman, you can see that."

"I can, thanks Luisa."

"Delivery," the Afghan woman said as she shook hands with Masha, "delivery should be within the week. Be sure to tell your mother to bring identification."

THIRTY FIVE

Carlos took Alex around to his back porch which gave onto fields and oaks. How did the brothers decide who got the *patron's* house? Alex asked. Ditto showed him the new home he was building so the elder cousin got the big house and the younger would have a new more modern one. All along their way, Alex saw a dozen places he could help. His fingers almost itched for a tool to repair gates.

Carlos went to get them cold Coronas while they waited for Dolores to call for lunch. "Life of a farmer is good hard work, *Primo*. I feel it in my bones, that kind of tiredness of much done. I love the cows and they're good milkers. It smells good to be with the animals."

"We're getting old for nights in the club, the racket. I like my warm bed with Dolores. We're thinking of selling the bar to Diego and Kim. My son-in-law isn't too bright but he'll do fine and they still like hanging out with their crowd there."

"One year since we left and so much changed." Alex reached over and gave his cousin a hi-five.

"You had the fires, again. Both times you had it hard. We're on the other side of the city, thanks to God and our *patrons*." Carlos crossed himself.

"We never forget where we came from and how they suffer at home," said Ditto, who came out on the porch.

"Everything is *suerte*, destiny, good or bad. We say come, young *primo* Alejandro. Come fix this broken gate, make a harness right. We want the family together. We miss you and so does Ana Jesus." Carlos sipped his beer.

"I miss you guys and I'm happy you invite *Mamacita* to have supper with you. I miss her, leaving so soon after she arrived wasn't good. It's a long drive here."

"How is it up there?" Ditto asked.

"Up there I never relax."

"Why not, *Primo?*" Ditto asked.

"It's the folks there."

"What about the house you got for such a great price?"

"Our house is coming along great and Masha had her first garden. Tomas turned a corner, doing good in school and with plans. He's gotten into forestry, learning about trees, about fires. We've had some things with locals. It's not like a peaceful place we imagined beforehand."

"Lot's of trees and lakes," Carlos said. "Wish we'd had time to come and fish."

"Lots of trees and rivers," Alex agreed. "You can still come."

"What about *hombres* in the north. You don't get along with them?" Ditto asked.

Alex shook his head. "We've had *problemas* like I said. They don't beat us up like they did squatters but a few of them would like to. Ever hear of 'The Sovereign State of Jefferson?'"

The two men shook their heads. "Your kid growing up, time to come back here," Ditto said.

"He'd do better with the family close by, extra uncles," Carlos said.

"True. What's that wonderful smell?" Alex asked.

Dolores brought steaming homemade tortillas, and black

beans covered with crema, a heaping bowl of her *pico de gallo*. "Only a snack before we barbeque," she said. "Adri said she'd be bringing Ana Jesus at five o'clock but Masha didn't give a time."

"She doesn't want us to wait for her," Alex answered.

After finishing the last tortilla, both older men with their arms around Alex' shoulders, they walked toward the stalls for the cattle and horses. It wasn't exactly like twisting his arm, but Alex could feel the pressure in their muscles and minds.

"We'll make you an owner with us, one third owner. We're going to show you where you can enlarge one of the outbuildings or tear it down for a good modern house. If we had the *dinero* we'd do it for you now but we've already borrowed what we can to buy more cattle and interest rates are going up," Ditto said.

"We get top prices for beef, all organic, and we're selling the hay," Carlos added.

"Ana Jesus…she'd be so happy. You'd own your land again," Ditto said. 'She'll feel she's given your father what he deserved."

"*Hermanos*, you honor me. I can't say more now. Masha has to decide what she wants, too. We're getting offers on our house, cash to put in so it wouldn't be charity."

"Charity! You've been away so long that you are forgetting how we brought you up and we love you like our son."

"And I love you guys. You know, we have a dog, chickens."

"The animals will love it here," said Ditto. "*Primo*, you want to live close to your mother and daughter, your family and *gente* who want you with them," Ditto said.

"You'll fit right in with our association," said Carlos.

"Association?" Alex stepped back from the fence they were leaning on watching a cow and her calf. "I never want to join another association with guns."

The brothers laughed. "These are neighbors and old time farm people. We talk prices for the beef. We help each other. There's a grange where we meet, it's simpatico, mostly *gringos*, they like us fine. We all have families. We make barbeques together. We had a fiesta last week."

"Sounds a lot better than the association we've been kicked out of." Alex paused and looked around at flatland on all sides. "I've been welding stuff. I'd love a real shop to work in."

"That's a bitchin' angel you made. You'll have your own time," Carlos answered. "Not all work."

"I want to cherry up a Mercury in my garage, old style, you can help," Ditto said.

"Yeah, I dig that." Alex slapped both brothers' hands.

"Can be yours," Ditto said as they walked toward the hay fields high in grasses.

"What about the poor soil, I remember it was heavy clay, and the flooding?"

"Still a problem. We dig more drainage ditches, keep the water below the house. There was a reason rich people didn't settle here but now they'd pay a fortune."

"You talk with your wife. Wait as long as it takes to bring her around. You're the *hombre* of the family." Carlos said.

Ditto and Carlos continued to show Alex more he'd share

in, the cheese house, the milking barn, a pond for ducks, each brother with pride in all they'd manage.

"It will all work out for the best. What is ours is yours, *Primo*."

"*Todos juntos, la familia!*" Carlos slapped hands first with Ditto then Alex. "You come for the milking and feeding."

"Is Mother coming?" Adrianna was sitting beside Kim and letting the baby curl and uncurl tiny pink fingers around hers. "It's getting dark."

"She'll be here and just as surprised as I was by *Mamacita*." Alex squeezed Ana Jesus' hands and gave them a kiss. Ana Jesus had pink-painted fingernails and soft palms.

"She looks beautiful, don't you think?" Adrianna smiled.

"The photograph I always keep with me of *Mami* and *Papi* when they were young—she is like that again." Alex meant the words but he still wasn't entirely pleased to see his mother's whitened teeth, her shoulder-length black hair with reddish henna highlights. He'd barely gotten to know her again when she had long grey strands pulled into a bun and yellow teeth.

"*Abuela* used the money she earns baby-sitting and embroidering. She wouldn't accept anything from me. She asked me, 'Should I ask Alejandro before I do this?' I told her she didn't need permission. A neighbor colored and cut her hair and *Abuela* went to the dental training school my clinic recommended," Adrianna said.

"Maybe because there's an older neighbor who's paying special attention," Dolores said in Spanish and winked at Ana Jesus.

"We are friends," Ana Jesus protested with her hands up and cheeks blushing.

"David lost his wife. He's an accountant, a good man, very proper. He brings her plants with flowers already blooming."

"*Gringo?*" Alex asked.

Adrianna nodded, "Very *gringo.*"

"Stop discussing me, all of you," Ana Jesus protested. "David is a friend."

Adrianna saw how her father wasn't enjoying the conversation either. She even thought his eyes glistened with the beginning of tears.

Car headlights pulled into the drive. Minutes later, Masha stood under the lights. Alex felt relieved they could change the subject from the possible suitor of Ana Jesus.

"My love, you're here in time for supper. Everyone's here."

"Is that Ana with dark hair?"

"I can't get over it. I barely recognized my own mother."

"She's like a girl!" Masha ran forward to kiss Ana. "You look beautiful. Don't you think so, Alex?"

"*Si,*" Alex answered.

"I told her to go all the way, lipstick, earrings, dress," Adrianna said.

Masha backed out of the lights. "What's wrong, sweets?"

"Surprised me, just have to get used to it. I'm afraid I'm going to lose her again. She'll have a new life with someone named David, a *gringo* I've never met."

"Oh, that's news. I hope he's a good man."

Alex just shook his head. "We left her, I know that."

"Well, this happened and it's probably good. You want her to find happiness."

"Of course I do."

"Nothing and no one will be lost. I look forward to meeting David."

"When did you get so smart?"

"A smarter woman helped me. Oh, I love your hair." Masha hugged her mother-in-law. She smelled a gardenia fragrance and saw the crisp cream petal behind her ear.

"David grows gardenias." Adrianna sat beside Masha and hugged her.

"Romantic, I love it," Masha said.

"How was the drive and everything? You look good, Mom."

"Easy, no problems. Do you think David is serious?"

"I would say so. He's lonely and they don't have time to waste."

"You? You don't seem lonely without a boyfriend," Masha said.

"When I get my RN and maybe a scholarship to med school, I might think about dating but not now. I'm too busy."

"A doctor, you'll marry a doctor," Masha said.

"I'll be a doctor, Mom."

"Of course. Two doctors. Shira's taught me a lot about acknowledging."

"She's taught me, too,"

"I'm not out of the woods, yet, Adri. I have to do a lot

before I'm able to deal with stress. I'd like to be able to see Shira in person."

"She's larger-than-life in person, and she's very short."

They both laughed.

"I've even been thinking of going back to school and getting that degree in nursing beyond the RN."

"You mean a bachelor's degree in nursing?"Adrianna asked. "Would you be in classes with me?"

"Don't worry. I wouldn't start right away. The girls at Sutter were talking about being able to take a class at a time toward the degree while you work. I'll be on a slow track, way you behind you."

"Is this a way of announcing you're leaving that miserable county, Mom?"

"We may surprise you, coming with all our goods like gypsies to camp."

"You're not camping anywhere except home."

"You mean that, Adri? Only for a little while. We'll see, nothing's decided."

THIRTY SIX

Maksym's Facetime image came in shaky from the start. "You promised our mother money but you didn't send. Father will lie in unmarked pauper grave."

His voice sounded so rushed she wanted to tell him to slow down when the picture came into focus and she was looking at her brother's beautiful blue eyes that nearly broke her heart.

"No money?"

"No," he answered.

"I sent money via *hawala* a week ago. She has to go to the address to pick up."

His face darkened. "I don't know what you're talking about, Sister. No money."

"It must be there, in Simferopol. How are you?' she asked.

"I'm in fine health. You changed the subject, Sister."

"I'm glad you're well, Maksym. I sent the money. Maybe transfer is slower than they promised."

Maksym shook his head, then ignited a match that flamed from his shaking hands to his cigarette.

"No money has arrived. They cheated you. Go and send again."

Luisa had warned her and she knew from years of treating them that addicts stuck to their lies like the virus deniers. She repeated that she'd sent the money exactly as he'd requested. She didn't question her brother's truthfulness. "It will be there."

Maksym's phone went dark and she was left feeling she

preferred seeing the minarets and swallows floating in a blue sky behind her brother who was lying.

Luisa checked with the *hawala* when she went to send remittances home for her children. She asked about Masha's $200 to Simferopol because the recipients claimed they'd never received the money. The woman, wearing another bright head scarf lifted her penciled eyebrow and asked Luisa to wait. When she came back she had a receipt.

"A woman collected the amount. I can even describe her. Young, maybe Tatar."

"My friend's mother is an older woman, Russian-speaker, Nadezda Sergeievna."

"That's odd. You're sure?" Luisa asked.

"I'm sure, it's here on the screen if you want to see. Come around. There's probably a video because they record everything."

Luisa came behind the counter and saw the report on the screen. "Is it possible another woman came for the money and they gave it to her?"

"If she had some identification, or even none, anything is possible over there.

Maksym's next call began with views of a pink sky, wheeling birds silhouetted against minarets like paper cut-outs in a beautiful dawn over Istanbul that Masha could only imagine. She heard muezzin calls to worship, the first morning prayers.

"I'm leaving for Antalya in a few hours. Money has not been sent."

"What will you do in Antalya, Maksym?"

"No foreseeing the future but it will be warmer. I'm always cold. Wherever there are Russians and computers, I have plenty of work."

"Dark work?" Masha asked.

"You make a living, so do I."

"I'm a nurse. I've always done honest work."

"You live where streets are paved with gold, Sister. I'd be honest there, too."

Maksym seemed anxious, twitchy. Masha wondered how long his drugs lasted. The body wanted more and more. She wished he'd pan to the background again.

"Let's cut this short, Sister. I need cash to get to Antalya."

"I know a younger woman picked up my remittance to mother. I have proof. I'll send you $50 by Western Union. I won't go to the *hawala* again."

"Have pity, in our father's blessed name."

"Ask yourself that. You text me an address and you'll get $50, no more."

That night, Masha cried on and off for Maksym. What was she to tell her mother who refused to acknowledge that her son as well as the money were lost? They'd endured so much. She got up and took a long shower. She'd send the money again to her mother, this time Western Union. If Maksym gave her an address wherever he was, she'd send him a small amount.

A week later, Nadya thanked her daughter for the money. "A beautiful grave, Masha. Your dear brother sent yellow roses, father's favorite." Masha didn't confess she'd sent the flowers because it made her mother happy thinking her son cared.

"God bless," Masha answered with the sign of the cross.

THIRTY SEVEN

A battered blue fish of a car sputtered to a stop in front of Ray and Susan's deserted house. Alex stopped scraping paint he'd been working on to gaze at the vintage Bonneville with its silver sides clean of color but looking proud as a prize nonetheless. Incredibly made cars, he thought, well worth saving. He could have turned this one into a shining blue shark. But who was driving? Gas must cost a fortune. Should he duck back inside and be ready to defend himself?

The door swung open and a young man stepped out. Before Alex could see his face, the kid in baggy pants turned his back and reached for something in the back seat and Alex reflexively stepped inside.

The thin young person emerged with a duffle bag and Alex stepped back out.

"Hi, you lost?" Alex asked.

The kid laughed and squinted in the sun. "Not me, how about you?"

"I'm doing a little work on a friend's house. You don't know who I am?"

"Hell, yes I do. I thought I'd look around the folks' place first and then go to see you, Alejandro."

"Reno? How would you find us?"

"My dad sent your address. The creeps with the birds."

The boy was clean-shaven with short black hair and Alex suddenly felt weak with the recognition. "Reno, my god, you look like your dad must have."

"So I'm told. Don't be a stranger." Reno hi-fived and then

Alex was hugging him with a rush of family feeling as if his own prodigal son had come home.

"Hey don't break my ribs, Alex. I'm undernourished." Reno coughed.

"Oh no, we can't have you cough, please, no coughs."

"My throat's dry."

"We can solve that. I've got cold ones," Alex said.

"I don't have my dad's bad lungs, no worries."

They stepped back, kept their eyes on each other. "I miss your father more every day and I was just thinking about him like I always do."

"I never got to say good bye or tell him I loved him."

"I didn't see your father after he was sick but my wife did."

"The Russian?"

"Ukraine. Reno, how's Susan?"

"She took off for Colorado after Pop died."

"We've been hoping she comes back."

"Not anytime soon, that's what she said on the phone before I was out."

"Not a great homecoming, Reno, but I've kept your fridge going and there's cold ones." Alex walked into the dark kitchen and came back with two bottles.

"Pops always said you were a good guy except for a few things."

"Never bothered us. Your brother?"

"He's doing serious time. Lompoc was wake-up or I might be where he is."

"Glad you're out, man."

"I'm awake now. Read a lot, thought a lot."

"Like your father. Ray was quite a reader." Alex didn't like "Pops" as a way to talk about Ray but Reno had a big grin. Ray must have grinned like that once, Alex thought. He remembered Masha asking if he thought Ray had died angry. Alex hadn't tried to answer. "It would be awful for his soul," Masha had said.

"Did Pops ever talk about a guy named Jonathon?"

Alex couldn't remember a Jonathon until Reno said, "He's the guy taught Pops welding in juvey. Pops read to the guy. I kind of connect you and Jonathan as good men in his life."

"How about you come home for dinner so my boy Tomas can meet you? We're guys tonight, Masha has a shift, but I make a mean burrito."

Reno shook his head. "I think I'll settle in, just chill here, but thanks, man."

"I'll bring over more beers and a burrito tomorrow. You're family, son. Masha will want to put weight on you. She cared a lot for your dad. What's your plan here?"

"I'm going to settle in here, keep the wolves out."

"Good to hear. If the house is just left for kids to come and hang out, there will be a fire. We haven't done as much as we wanted to because there's been interruptions and Tomas still has a few weeks of school to finish up."

"Pops said you had run-ins with some of the badasses around here."

"It hasn't gone great since your father died. They don't make me feel welcome, to say the least. They want us gone."

"Bort's a true pig but you can get around him."

Alex laughed. "I haven't tried. So, Reno, how about Tomas

and I come over tomorrow, get a little work done, maybe some shopping for materials in Redding?"

"I've a few bucks. I don't need charity, man."

"I know that, Reno. Where did you pick up that tuna fish out there? Pontiacs last if you keep them up. I can do a little work."

"That's kind, man."

"I'm really happy you're here. Your father and I were working on a bench for your mother to sit on in the evening. He passed before we could get it done. I'd like to finish it with you."

Two days later, hot already for May, Alex was inside measuring the window frames. Reno and Tomas were outside scraping mold.

"What are you doing, kid, hanging out with these shitheads?" Bort yelled at Reno from the street.

Reno stepped down from the short ladder. "Bort, how's it hanging, man?"

"Why are you here? They're not one of us. We want the foreign fucks gone."

"You want to help fix up the place for my mom? We could use you."

"Anything that Mexican touches turns to shit. Your dad…"

"Respect, please." Reno turned to Tomas. "He's my pal. His name is Tommy."

"Fucking traitors." Bort moved as if he'd pull the ladder out from Tomas.

"You're a bully, Bort. I've met guys tougher ten times over.

But you and me go back and I don't want trouble. I'm done with that crap. You want to help us for my mother's sake or clear out?"

Alex had been listening inside to Reno handling Bort. A few moments later, he heard tires screeching on the gravel. Alex came out and said, "That was quick."

"Makes me think of my fucking brother," Reno said. "Bort treated me fine before. I was just a kid but he's gotten real mean."

"He wants us gone, and you might, too, for the sake of peace around here."

"We're chill aren't we?" Tomas asked in an almost tender voice.

Reno took hold of Tomas' shoulder. "Bort's just stupid. My dad wasn't stupid but he didn't break off with these dumb shits. He didn't like the Bible thumpers either."

"I honor your father," Alex said. "I've got measurements so whenever you want to take a break, let's head to Redding for the real burrito at the place where we stayed together during the fires."

"We didn't want to go back, but with you here, Reno, it's OK," Tomas said.

On the drive, Alex at the wheel, Tomas and Reno crowded together sharing a seat belt because they were both so thin. Tomas talked about Ray, how he'd become their only friend and saved them more than once during the fires, and how bad the nights had been with his coughing.

"Should have gotten him to the hospital then," Alex said.

"He wouldn't have gone," Reno said. "Don't beat yourself

up. Like I said, he loved you guys. You gave him respect."

They walked around the Star Motel, found their room, paused minutes without saying their thoughts out loud. When they settled into the taqueria, Alex listened to the boys talking about school. They both seemed to want to learn forestry of some kind. Reno had passed his GED at Lompoc and Tomas was finishing his junior year.

"Butte Community College has a bitching two-year program in fire," Reno said. "I did research and Butte is the best around here."

"Yeah? I want to study more but not just school stuff," Tomas said.

"Fire science academy, you learn everything. We could go as buddies, partners on the line." Reno made a fist. "We'll put out the fires."

"I've a year to finish high school."

"You study to pass a test, like I did inside and you have your degree in time to start fall semester. Test is easy."

"My sister aced it."

"OK. Let's pull it off. You start studying now and finish this summer." Reno slapped Tomas' hand. Tomas slapped back. Tomas had always wanted an older brother to tell him what to do.

THIRTY EIGHT

Mrs. Robinson arrived with a woman in a black pant suit who turned her expressionless face to Masha and introduced herself as a Renaissance Properties associate. Mrs. Robinson, in her jeans and graying braid, looked like a real person compared to this mannequin, and Masha felt a certain fondness for their realtor announcing her visit.

"Renaissance?" Masha asked.

"I spoke of her company. World wide, isn't that right?"

The woman nodded. "We are not bound by borders."

"That would be good news for everyone about everything," Masha said.

Mrs. Robinson cleared her throat. "They make properties shine. You've been chosen, first in line. lucky you. Little old Malvina proud again. Ms. Laufer here has written up an offer for you." She handed Masha papers.

Masha took the sheaf and looked at the first page. All she saw was a number representing so much money she felt her head spin.

"Really?" she asked.

"Mister gone again?" Mrs. Robinson questioned.

"When he comes home we'll go over this together. We need to give it thought," Masha said as if she were used to being offered a golden pot at the end of the rainbow.

Masha and Mrs. Robinson had exchanged looks of being allies but now their realtor changed sides. "We need to know quite soon, Mrs. del Calvo. Renaissance is looking at other properties so I wouldn't dally missing out on this windfall."

"Of course."

"Tell me please does the stream go year-round?" Ms. Laufer asked.

"Yes, though right now it's gone back to running low. You wish to see it?"

Ms. Laufer looked down at her high heels and shook her head. The swelling around the stockings that encased nylons squeezed into high, pointed black heels must be hurting, Masha thought.

"I understand you've planted a garden."

Masha felt Ms. Laufer wasn't the least interested in her garden but she wasn't going to let the woman's question go at that.

"With time, I'll plant miles and miles of sunflowers like in my country."

"And where is that?" Ms Laufer asked.

"Ukraine."

"Her husband is the darker one," Mrs. Robinson turned to Ms. Laufer.

"Alejandro is from El Salvador and I am from Ukraine. We're both citizens, the real kind, not the ones who just call themselves that and don't vote."

"No politics, remember our agreement for good neighbors," Mrs. Robinson said.

Again, Masha wasn't going to leave it. Good neighbors! She could tell this mannequin-lady about the neighbors but she spread her arms wide and came close enough to smell a floral perfume. "Miles and miles of sunflowers make you happy. We've been happy here. We love the trees, we love our garden more than our neighbors."

Mrs. Robinson cleared her throat but Masha was feeling the power to shock.

"No amount of money will make us leave if we don't choose to, you understand?"

"Of course. We never force decisions." Ms Laufer's waxy skin was reddening.

Masha knew it was time to stop acting up. She walked in front of both of them and opened the back door, leading them through the hallway.

"You want to see inside. You're busy women," she said.

Ms Laufer took in the living room, the kitchen with its old counter. "We'll have to stage, get rid of that sofa, replace it and the chairs with something sleek. The kitchen I'm going leave but of course it will be a total do-over."

"We won't change anything while we're living here. We already replaced the older appliances and everything here works. It's a good wood stove. Mrs. Robinson said it was an antique, maybe valuable."

"I'm sure it is. You have to give us permission to stage because it's part of the contract." Mrs. Laufer pointed to small print on pages Masha was holding. "You know where to reach me when your husband has read everything. You'll be pleased with the additional sweetener—no waiting for bank approval. We'd like you to commit by the end of the week so we can get started with our campaign."

"I can't promise you anything."

"You might want to be looking for somewhere temporary to live. Many people find the staging disruptive. We provide motel vouchers wherever you choose."

Masha, who was taller than either of the two women, drew herself up to as high as she could. "I don't like being pressured. Money isn't everything to us."

"It's business, Missus," said Mrs. Robinson.

"I don't like being pressured either." Alex held the papers. "It's so much money it doesn't seem possible. When it's too good to be true it's too good to be true."

"I agree. The amount is so much that when I saw the number, I started shaking."

"Why, Masha?"

"It's a shock to think of so much money. I didn't show my surprise."

"We'd be giving up so much of our hard work, moving again, but we'd have more money than we've ever had."

"Your cousins will be happy. We can be closer to your family."

"But you wouldn't, would you? Leaving your trees, your garden?"

"We've harvested the garden. I collected sunflower seeds. I think I'm ready to leave my hospital where I never felt right. When I visited Sutter, the girls were happy to see me, really happy I'd stopped by. They remember how hard it was during the worst of last year. They want me back. I'd have opportunities to study more, too."

"Think how the Citizens will celebrate that they forced us out. Bort will roar. What about Tomas? He doesn't want to see his father giving in and he doesn't want to move now. He and Reno are planning to study forestry at Butte College."

"I don't care about the Citizens. I'm thinking of Tomas, too, and how the men could take it out on him. How will he live peacefully if he stays?"

"If Tomas is with Reno, I think they'll leave him alone, and if he passes his GED at the end of the summer, he and Reno might room in Oroville.

"Oroville? That was the city where people voted against being vaccinated or wearing masks,"

"More of the same but the Fire Academy is somewhere outside Oroville. Masha, whatever these real estate sharks say is a deadline, they'll wait and we can stay until Tomas passes the GED. We're not going to any motel."

"If they don't like it, they can go right back where they came from," she said.

"Tomas will be in the fires again but Reno has a good head on his shoulders." Alex picked up the papers again. "This money dangling in our faces. They're offering to make us almost rich."

Tomas and Reno came in blowing on their arms as they hung up coats.

"It was friggin' beautiful at Butte," Tomas said.

"Language, Tomas," Alex said.

"Sorry. The Academy is cool, *Papi.*"

"We saw awesome training. You can take some classes online, too," Reno said.

"You're in time for soup, guys. How about a cold one?" Alex asked.

"Never!" the young men said, slapping Alex' hands.

"What are these, Tomas?" Alex stepped closer and pulled back bandages. Underneath gauze, the tattoos on both his son's forearms were oozing dark stains. On his right forearm was an inflamed dragon; a burst of flower under the reddened, bruised skin of his left arm went all the way up past his elbow.

"What's happening?" Masha came in, apron strings untied and dangling.

"For *Papi*," Tomas extended his right arm. "For you, Mom." Tomas showed her the left arm sunflower. "We wanted to wait a week to show you. They'll look better."

Masha fell onto the couch in tears. "Such beautiful skin you've destroyed."

"Mom, don't cry, please." Tomas touched the part in his mother's golden hair.

"Are they infected? Let me see." She leaned over and touched the flower. Tommy winced.

"It's so raw, son." She held out his arm and blew on the inked skin.

"They're healing, they're good. Mom, it's a sunflower, the Ukrainian flower you love. And *Papi*, the dragon is for you and Ray. I love you guys but I won't give you hugs because that hurts."

Reno had some darker vines that must have been older tattoos, and a swooping eagle that was new and looked defiantly inflamed.

"Oh *hijo*. You know what I remember about tattoos is that the bad guys have them. The cartel men. Why do you do this with your body, with your life?"

Masha, crumpled on the couch, kept her head in her hands. "Hoodlums, gangsters in Russia, Ukraine." She broke into tears. "Stalin on their shoulders. I hated them."

"Mom, *Papi*, it's not like that anymore. We honor you and we express our love."

"Masha, it's OK. What's done is done." Alex sat beside Masha and held her. "I know tattoos have a different meaning now than when we were young. I've seen plenty and I've gotten used to them."

"But not on our boy. I hate them." She lifted her face, her eyes streaming. "You're not respecting your bodies as you were given them."

"I thought you'd be pleased. They show our love," said Tomas. "I feel lots of respect, don't you, Reno?"

She stood up and went into the kitchen. Reno followed.

"Why did you make him do this, Reno?"

"I didn't make him do anything. Tommy wanted to show he honors your family."

"Thank God my father will never see this. It feels like shame."

"Just wait, they'll heal, Mrs. del Calvo. The girl was clean. She asked if we'd been drinking the night before and we said no. She'd said no aspirin or anything and we did what she told us."

Tomas came into the kitchen. "We did everything she said, washed with special soap, Mom. If you have any antibiotic creams, that will be cool."

Masha smiled. "I have creams. Was it really sanitary?"

"State of the art," Reno said. "I know because I had one gnarly infection when I did these inside." He showed her the vines. "This girl, she was cool, way cool."

"Getting inked makes you stronger," Tomas said.

Masha rolled her eyes. "How is that?"

"You take the pain and you don't say anything," Tomas answered.

"Thank you for the sunflower," Masha carefully gave her son a kiss. "I can't look at any of it now. I wasn't ready for this. I won't recognize my baby son."

"You think mom will be OK, that she'll get it?" Tomas asked his father.

"She's worried about you leaving us and being in danger. This doesn't help."

"You're the dudes talking about leaving us and going back to Santa Rosa."

"Just talking, nothing settled," Alex said.

"Where would you live if we're not here?" Masha sat down on the couch.

Without a moment's hesitation, Tomas answered, "At Reno's folks house. We're going to be fixing it up. *Papi*, we can look after ourselves. We're really stoked."

"Will we get him back?" Masha sipped a glass of wine and dabbed tears from her eyes. Tomas was listening to music in his room. Reno had gone back to Ray and Susan's.

"Not the way he was when we brought him here a year ago."

"Is that a good thing?" she asked. "The tattoos scare me."

"I don't understand that either but I know it's not gangs or criminals. It's just what they're doing."

"Did you see how inflamed they were?"

"They'll heal. He's not getting into trouble, he's found a purpose."

"So different from us, Alex. Just going from one thing into another not knowing if it will be good."

"Think of how different we are from our parents, and each other."

"Us different?" Masha's heart fluttered. "We have the same eyes."

"I know."

"We found each other because we match perfectly."

"I know, *amor*."

"You could have gone to college if it wasn't for me."

"I'd speak pidgin English if it wasn't for you. I learned the rest on my own. If Tomas gets a serious education in fires and forestry, he'll have a degree and a profession like you have. He'll be able to work anywhere."

"I hoped he'd go to a real college."

"That's Adri. She was always wanting education, like you. Tomas likes to work with his hands. I think he and Reno will make a good pair."

"I remember those days with you at the college. We couldn't not be together. Will we have date nights back in Santa Rosa?" She undid the band keeping her hair back.

"Your beautiful hair." He pulled her close with his hands cupping her cheeks.

"Of course we will. If we do decide to move, let's take a vacation, something special, go somewhere we've never been."

"Not with family, just us?"

"Just us, my love."

"Two date nights a week, Alex?" she pushed him back on the couch.

Acknowledgements

Thank you to my writing friends who read and listened to *Masha and Alejandro*, Liza Prunuske, Andrea Granahan, Mary Gaffney, Marylu Downing, Robin Beeman, Christine Walker. The spirit and wit of Susan Swartz was always with us. Thank you Anne Marie Ruff Grewal for early readings. Thank you Michael Morey and Michael Levitin for the eagle eyes you brought to the pages later on. I owe many thanks to welder/artists, James Selby and John Pashilk, who showed me they can be witty and skillful with incredibly different materials. Thank you, James, for holding my hand to weld my own piece. My reading in print and online was too various to cite particular sources as I tried to inform myself on immigration; conditions in the Ukraine leading up to the Russian invasion; welding; our years of wildfires; the inland counties in California and Oregon where taxes are low and law enforcement rare; the pandemic with its divisive vaccinating and masking policies, and the toll Covid took on medical resources, nurses especially. Special thanks to the Jewish Community Free Clinic in Santa Rosa where people from all over the world are treated to care without charge. Heartfelt thanks to Pam Carpenter of PlanA Design who read and designed the book. I am fortunate Spuyten Duyvil, Tod and Aurelia, chose to publish *Masha and Alejandro*. Thank you.

Barbara L. Baer
Forestville, CA 2024